Where We Go From Here

SAPPHIRE HALE

CONTENTS

PLAYLIST

Guys My Age – Hey Violet

Big Energy – Latto

Boss – Doja Cat

Soap – Melanie Martinez

Novocaine – Maggie Lindemann

Crushcrushcrush – Paramore

Last Night – Morgan Wallen

Round Here – Florida Georgia Line

Country Boy's Dream Girl – Ella Langley

Unlock It – Charli XCX

Topless – Breaking Benjamin

The Kind Of Love We Make – Luke Combs

Leave The Night On – Sam Hunt

She Likes It – Russell Dickerson ft. Jake Scott

To access the official Spotify playlist visit www.sapphireauthor.com

CHAPTER 1

Harper

I'm about three-thousand-dollars deep in Uber bills when I realise that this was probably not my best idea.

"Actually, maybe we should turn around," I say, my eyes sliding over to my hastily crammed hand-luggage on the seat beside me. The fact that I brought my wrinkly childhood growly bear is confirmation enough that I'm not exactly treating this impromptu getaway as a short-term solution.

And the word 'growly' is literal. It's one of those stiff-limbed vintage teddies that growls when you tip it upside down. When we hit a dip in the road a few miles back it made a sort of *harrumph* sound that had the driver warily glancing back at me.

But I digress.

Did I really think that running away would make me feel better? The delay in my flight from LA to

Montana made the plane journey last more than three hours, and then I ended up getting five different taxis to take me up the twists and valleys that lead from there to Phoenix Falls. I glance distressed out of the window at the side of the vehicle and I try to think of something positive.

A change is as good as a rest after all, especially when it comes to getting the creative juices flowing. And I'm literally a screenwriter. I'm sure that there's a story somewhere amidst all of this chaos.

I clear my throat to try and capture the driver's attention but he just shoots me a disbelieving look and remains silent as he puts the car in park. Yes I did just suggest turning around one second before we reached our destination. The driver can't believe his luck and is consequently unwilling to jeopardise this eight-hundred dollar relationship that we just formed with anything as risky as "talking" or "stating opinions". If only the rest of his sex were as considerate, maybe I wouldn't be in this mess to begin with.

I roll my lips into my mouth, tensely quaking with *what-the-hell-did-I-just-do* nervous spasms, and then I finally push open the door to the backseat, clutching my travel bag like a life jacket and shutting the cab up after myself. The driver is almost as much of a wreck as I am. He thinks that he's just been *Punk'd* and that I'm about to murder him in the middle of this deserted holiday village.

When he realises that this really is my destination – a semi-reconstructed cabin retreat up the mountains at the back of Phoenix Falls – he can't get to his notepad fast enough, scribbling down his digits like his life depends on it. He hands it over to me through the rolled-down passenger window and I pluck it between two fingers, glancing down.

Name. Number. Smiley face.

I offer him a small almost-smile in return and then he begins to slowly pull away, checking for me in his rear-view every few seconds. He's making sure that I'm not about to change my mind and have him take me back to the last drop-off point that I was at, which was approximately one billion miles away from this one and where I said goodbye to disbelieving taxi-driver number four.

The disappointment in his face when I don't wave him back would almost be an ego-boost if the past month that had just happened to me *hadn't* just happened to me. But it did. There's no denying it. And now I'm feeling in no way gratified by any male attention.

No more men, ever.

I re-hoist my luggage and raise my chin, feeling that end-of-summer clarity in the evergreen air. The warning clouds overhead are hovering dangerously dark and stormy, but even they hold off, sensing that I could snap at any moment. Mother Nature is on my side which only re-solidifies my stance.

No more men, no more men, no more men.

I round the corner and stop short.

Five male heads turn in my direction.

So admittedly my new standpoint would be easier to embark upon if I hadn't just pulled up to a building site mid-reno, where it's being redeveloped by an all-male team of lumberjack handymen. Obviously this is a test from God, showing me the way through a baptism by fire.

I pray for strength and then whisper *Amen*.

As I begin to walk their way I spare them a glance, quickly wishing that I hadn't. They're what I would describe as "dangerously tall". I readjust my trucker cap over my hair, blowing the soft baby-blonde tendrils out of my face, and I walk purposefully past the whole bunch of them, only shooting back a stare when I sense their eyes still burning into my own. Each one of them looks away with their eyebrows slightly raised. They're unfamiliar with my kind entering their territory and not one of them knows what to do about it.

Okay, so I'm a little gratified, especially by how well-behaved they seem to be reacting. Did they know that I was coming? I mean, *I* barely knew that I was coming, at least not until taxi driver number one, who I must admit took the brunt of the lot.

I pull up my phone and tap through to the Messages app, purposely making my eyes go blurry as I scroll past the *I'm sorry*'s and the *hear me out*'s. He's been texting me from other people's phones because he evidently assumes that I've blocked him. Which I have. And now I'm going to have to block everyone else too.

Finally I come across the messages from my mom, the no-nonsense tycoon behind Ray Corp's small town vacation retreats, and I tap on the rectangle to open up her instructions.

I scan through her text bubbles and then look up, scanning the cosy valley for my new hideaway.

Where are you little bungalow?

"Ma'am?"

A voice sounds out from the middle of the pack

and I twist slightly to catch its owner. Deep bass, confident and casual. He sounds like a heartbreaker.

Not my problem.

"Sir?"

His cheek ticks up and his gaze steamrolls down my torso. I narrow my eyes on him.

"Can I help you with something?" he asks.

Wouldn't you like to, I think to myself. I wait until his eyes are back on my face before I say anything. He likes what he sees and that riles me senseless.

"I'm good."

The words *I'll bet* are so obviously on the tip of his tongue that I can practically see them. I give him an *I dare you* expression and he shakes his head, smiling.

"You sure? You look a little lost."

So they weren't expecting me. I'm yet to decide if this is good or bad news.

"I'm not lost," I tell him, lifting my chin a little higher. "I've been here many times."

"Pine Hills is closed until the New Year. It's under construction." He taps the side of his large black truck, where the words *Coleson Construction Company* are printed on it in thick orange script.

I groan inwardly. This is the guy heading the reno? My mom spared me the fine print but I know the gist. Coleson Construction has already been here for the past two months, fixing up the plumbing, electrical, and external framework issues, and now the joinery team is going to be here for two more, kitting out each cabin with new flooring and bespoke furniture, handmade on-site here at Pine Hills.

I blink myself back to the here and now.

The laid-back smile on this guy's face makes my eye

twitch, but I'm a professional and I can handle this. I choose to shake off my irritation and outstretch my hand towards him.

"Mitchell Coleson? I'm Harper. Harper Ray."

He looks down at my outstretched hand and understanding suddenly dawns on his face. So he *was* expecting me. Now he realises that he just softcore-flirted with the keys to his pay packet, and for the second time in the space of two minutes I'm being regarded with the cautiousness of a ticking time-bomb.

He looks at me with newly hardened features. He's all business now.

"I'm not the man you're looking for."

My brow creases in confusion and I drop my hand. "Oh?"

"Mitch already left. He's been working with the crew and I all summer, but this is his baby now. He's the joiner, and it's pretty much interior stuff from here on out. My work here's done."

Thank God.

"And you are?" I ask.

He pushes his tongue in his cheek and flashes a look to one of his co-workers. "Jason, his brother. You can call me Jace."

I won't be calling you anything.

"So you're the eyes that they sent up here to keep us in check?" he asks, one big shoulder resting against the side of his truck.

Now that I know that this isn't the man that I'm looking for I turn away from him and start scanning for my bungalow again. It's been over a decade since I was last here so it's hardly a surprise that I can't quite remember its whereabouts. Pine Hills is heavenly, a series of small wooden cabins set up against a backdrop of lush encroaching forest. There's a Nature Trail running parallel to the land for visitors who want to explore the woods more deeply, plus a little town up the mountain, a small drive away.

Despite the rolling black clouds the sky behind them is a dusty blue, and the high-climbing trees are startlingly emerald. The temperature is mild and it gives me that early-autumn feeling. I inhale deeply as a wave of nostalgia washes over me.

After a few moments of taking in the landscape my eyes finally land on the bungalow up ahead. It's a little different to how my teenage brain remembered it. It's one-level and it's longer than I recalled, with two doors set near the centre. They are two attached living spaces, which means that technically I could spread my stuff across both of the halves, but I've travelled so light that it renders that option unnecessary.

My eyes flicker back to Jason, the construction head who has just finished his stint of demo-recon. That makes sense, considering the fact that the weather will be turning soon and the outdoors work is better executed in dry conditions. If he's about to leave then there's no need for him to know where I'm going to be sleeping.

But he seems to understand what's happening right now, my thoughts unspooling directly into his, and he nods his chin over to a nearby portacabin, saying, "Everything you'll need is up in the office – keys, blueprints." He ticks them off on thick tan fingers. "I can show you if you'd like, and you can have the keys for the cub."

I inconspicuously chew on my bottom lip,

disinclined to accept his assistance but also aware that there's no 'i' in 'team'. Even though my mom allowed me up here to secretly salve my soul after the break-up, on the official books it looks like I'm here to supervise the Pine Hills renovation. If it isn't me checking that Ray Corp's plans are being brought to life it'll be someone else, so I may as well get off on the right foot with the people who are involved.

So after a beat I manage to choke out, "That would be helpful, thank you."

Jason's mouth curls up at one corner as he begins leading me up to the cub, a secret look behind his eyes saying that he can read me like a book.

We walk up the wide entrance steps and he unlocks the door to the office. Then he pushes it open and steps back so that I can walk through.

I fold my arms across my chest and my luggage hits against the side of my hip. "I'm good here."

He watches me cautiously for one moment and then nods. He looks down at the metal o-ring in his hand and begins the slow key-extraction process, a sharp white canine biting into the bottom corner of his lip, brow creased as he removes the cubbie key from the bundle. When it's free he holds it out like a peace offering.

I extend my palm. He drops it gently inside.

He points to the back wall and I glance over to it. It's fitted with a series of small labelled hooks, each adorned with multiple keys.

"The keys are for each of the cabins, plus all of the out-buildings and electrical boxes. Reno plans and documentation are on the table. Duplicates are in the folders over there."

I scan the wall. I can't read the labels from this distance. "Is there a key for the bungalows?"

"The bungalows?" He looks surprised but he doesn't let it faze him. He walks inside the portacabin over to the back wall, unhooks two separate keys and then comes back to the doorway, leaning against the dark green frame. He dangles the keys in front of me and they jingle together.

"Two keys, one for either side." Then, wary, he adds, "You inspecting them or something? We gave them the same pipe-work and re-wiring that we did to the cabins."

"I'm not inspecting them. I'm staying in them," I tell him.

His eyebrows shoot skywards. "I beg your pardon?"

"I'm staying in them," I repeat, glancing up at him a little irritated.

"You're staying on-site?"

"Yes." I frown. "Is that a problem or something?"

I thought that he was leaving? What's it to him?

"Uh, not for me," he begins, scratching awkwardly at the back of his neck. The curl of his bicep catches my attention and I suddenly begin to wonder what his brother Mitch looks like. Is he younger? Older? Do they look the same? Are they... built the same?

A little shiver runs through me. I can't deny it: men do not look like this in Los Angeles. The men there are smooth, un-weathered, softened by years of privilege.

But here?

These men are hard lines and solid muscles, thickened and compacted by a lifetime of manual labour. Sandpaper grit raking up their throats and laugh lines creasing around their eyes. Sun-kissed jaws. Large calloused hands.

I do a little cough and divert my eyes.

I hear a series of engines rev to life and I turn to see that his crew are leaving for the day. Truck after truck after truck, they drive slow and safe off the site, their eyes sliding curiously our way as they depart.

Jason brings me back to the present.

"Ma'am, I'm sure that this is all legit and everything but, uh, I gotta admit that this sounds like a legal accident waiting to happen. Mitch could get in serious shit if you get injured on-site. Do you have clearance?"

"Of course I have clearance," I say, alarmed. I have literally no idea what that even means.

Jason gives me another wary look but then decides that, being one of the only heirs to the site he's just wrapped up on, I must have the documentation to be here mid-upheaval.

"Then you're all set," he says, the toe of his boot tapping an agitated little rhythm on the threshold of the portacabin. Something is bothering him. I decide not to ask.

Instead I back-step slowly down the two stairs and I point to the bungalows over my shoulder. "I'll be making myself at home then. Have a pleasant evening."

His brow is creasing in agony and he scrubs at it with his hand.

"Are you… are you sure that you want to stay on-site? Like, are you *sure*?"

Clearly he thinks that I should not be so sure. I hate how easily that triggers the anxious whir in my belly.

"Is the surveillance system back up?" I ask.

"Yeah, all the electric should be working," he replies.

"Then I'm sure."

He raises his hands in defeat. "Okay." He says it like *your funeral.*

He must gather how guarded he's making me feel because he half-laughs and says, "I'm sorry. The site is secure. It's just... that's not what I'm worried about."

My frown deepens. "What *are* you worried about?"

He looks over in the direction that all the trucks just drove in. Then he shakes his head as if he's trying to relieve himself of a thought.

"Nothing," he says finally. He gives me a tight smile when he looks back down at me and then gestures politely to the bungalows. "Want me to carry your bags?"

Yes please is what I'm thinking. "No thank you," is what I say instead.

"Alright then." He glances at me for one more moment and then breathes out a deep exhale. "Lock up the cub when you're done in there, and I... I hope you settle in nicely."

"Bye, then."

"Yeah, bye."

I watch him as he trudges over to the last truck in the dirt, mounting it with a surprisingly light foot and then slipping his phone out of his pocket the second that his door is closed. I watch him shoot off a text, toss the cell, and then he straps himself in and kicks the engine to life. His eyes are almost disbelieving when they land on me for a final time, as if he can't fathom that I'm really here, on this construction site.

You and me both, buddy. If you'd asked me one month ago where I would be right now I would have said something along the lines of *working on a new screenplay* or *looking at my diamond*. Not quitting the project before it's barely begun and fleeing Los Angeles like a runaway with a bare ring-finger.

A dull ache stirs in my chest. I'll rub it when he leaves.

Jason offers me a careful wave and I return it with equal levels of self-preserving wariness.

Just before he's out of sight I swear that I see another headshaking smile.

CHAPTER 2

Mitch

I wake up facedown, naked.

I know that it's 5:29 without checking the alarm next to me because my body operates like clockwork and I've been waking up at the same time for the past ten years straight. Hell, maybe longer. I lift up onto one elbow and take a hold of the alarm on the bedside table, turning it off from the bottom, knowing that when I get home from the site tonight I'll be switching it right back on. It's an unnecessary precaution to make sure that I'm never off-schedule, and I've had it since the first day that I started my company. Needless or not, I've kept it going.

I place the clock back onto the dresser and I roll heavily onto my back. I lift an arm to drag a hand down my face and the sheets fall and crumple halfway down my abs. I rest both of my forearms behind my head for a good minute, allowing my body to reacclimatise to the fact that there's no one in the bed next to me, no one is going to *appear* in the bed next to me, and therefore I need to cool it right down.

I give it two minutes.

It doesn't cooperate.

Fine, I think to myself, steeling my jaw and squeezing my eyes shut.

I'll just go about my morning hard as nails.

I pull on a pair of joggers and go downstairs to make a quick breakfast, glancing at my cell that I'd left out on the kitchen counter the second that I came in yesterday evening. There's a missed call from my kid's landline, but that's no worries because I already rang him on my landline last night, even though I hadn't known that he'd tried calling already. And then there's a text from my brother, Jason.

It reads: *It's all yours.*

Yesterday was the last day that I'd be working with Jace and his recon guys on the Pine Hills gig, and from here on out it's going to be just me and the joinery team. We've spent the whole summer doing the place up – there's not one piece of panelling on that site that hasn't been lifted, drilled, and polished by my own two hands, and I'm happy as hell that half the job is already done. Now we're down to the big interior pieces: cabinets, bed-frames, headboards. Heavy shit that has to be treated with care because the human eye is drawn to minute flaws. I could spend weeks making one piece picture perfect but if it's one millimetre out everyone's going to notice.

I pop up my toast, paste on the spread, and then I finish it off in a couple of bites. I'm on my way upstairs in under two minutes so that I can take a shower, pull on my uniform, and get back to work.

I slip the tongue of my belt through the metal buckle one-handed as I dismount the stairs, chucking on my boots and then grabbing a waterproof as I exit the front door. By the time that I'm in my truck I've already got my cell dialling my brother on speakerphone, and I'm off the driveway before it even connects.

"You know that today's my first day off all year, right?" His voice comes through the line deep and scratchy. Someone just woke up.

I almost snicker. "I'm heading to the site right now. Just ringing about that text you sent."

We aren't texters, so I know he's baiting me with something.

"Aw man," he groans, the line crackling as he moves the cell from one hand to the other. Jace lives even further away from Pine Hills than I do. In fact, his place is so distant from most of civilisation that our phone calls exclusively sound like they're coming from the bottom of the Atlantic.

I indicate at the junction, waiting for him to get to it.

"You won't believe me even if I tell you," he says. There's a tinge of disbelief in his voice that makes my eyes narrow.

"What is it?"

He blows out a breath and, after a few beats, a coffee machine whirs nearby. "You'll know it when you see it."

I grimace and ease my foot back down on the pedal. "You're spoiling me," I deadpan. "Is there something at the site? Don't tell me they sent twenty batches of the wrong wood polish again or I swear to God I will lose my fucking shit."

"I shouldn't have said anything," he mumbles, still half asleep. "But, like, you're fucking *welcome* in advance for the warning. I don't wanna pre-empt you too hard but, seriously, you're either gonna be livid or, like…" He searches for a word. "Euphoric."

"You call this a warning? You are one cryptic shit." Doesn't matter that he's in his thirties. Once a little brother, always a little brother.

I can sense that I'm not about to get more out of him and I don't like talking on my cell whilst I'm driving so I punch the end call button and then flip the phone over when I reach the next red light. If I catch a single glimpse of Jace texting me something cagey I'm going to shot-put the thing out of my goddamn window.

No more distractions.

The drive is smooth-sailing the whole way up to the foothills. It's overcast but it isn't raining yet and we should have at least a few weeks before it gets Phoenix-Falls-torrential. I catch glimpses of the newly spruced cabins before I take the final turn in and I can see from here that the wood is still good and dry. Ideal paint and polish conditions. I make a mental note to bump that up the agenda.

It's only when I'm finally pulling into the site that the curiosity piqued by Jace resurfaces to the forefront of my mind.

Euphoric? Big word for 5:45 in the morning.

There's only one thing that could get a guy feeling *euphoric* at the crack of dawn.

I put the car in park and sit back, folding my arms across my chest as I scan the site. There are no other cars here. Not gonna lie, that kind of puts my theory to bed.

I could've sworn that the only reason my brother would be acting scrambled would be due to a woman, but I can see clear as day that there isn't a single piece of timber out of place. No new vehicles in the dirt. I lean back to check if the cub's in use, but even those blinds are drawn.

Maybe someone *is* coming but they aren't here yet. Like the person who owns Pine Hills, something Ray. But that doesn't exactly align with Jace's attitude – the guy sounded stoked.

I re-grip the steering wheel, tapping at it with my thumbs, and I try to think over if I've forgotten something. My day-to-day schedule has been solely physical lately so I haven't had much time for mulling and contemplation. I wrack my brain and try to work it backwards but all that I want to think about is the task at hand. Working the Pine Hills gig is a huge deal for us – the contract is heavy and, if we pull it off, I know that the owners have at least five more locations like this one that I want my name all over. It's heavy lifting followed by a heavy payslip. Sign me the fuck up.

I click open my door and step down into the dirt, the gravel crunching under my boots as I work my way around to the back of the truck. I throw back the tarp on the bed and start unloading the equipment I don't keep on the site overnight, hauling my toolbox under one arm and gripping my fist around the larger gear. I use my free hand to get the key to the office from the front of my pants, shifting the toolbox a little higher against my side to stop it slipping as I unlock the door. Once it's open I head straight to the desk and put the pieces of kit down, ready to retrieve the rest, when my eyes suddenly catch on the board on the back wall and a frown forms on my brow.

Huh. That can't be right.

I move around to the back of the desk, leaning against the edge of it and folding my arms across my body as I look at the two empty key hooks. *Bungalow A* and *Bungalow B*. Not one key to spare. I scan my eyes across the rest of the pegs, wondering if they've gotten mixed in with one of the cabins, but it doesn't look like any of the other hooks have been touched. I look down at the silver o-ring that I'd wedged down my pointer finger, a series of too many keys dangling from it, and I let out a gruff sound whilst I appraise them. Good job I've got duplicates of my own otherwise that would be a pain in the ass. I'll have to get a couple spares made from the ones I've got but that's a job that can wait until the end of the day. It's not crucial at this second.

But what is crucial at this second is why the hell someone's taken the keys to those bungalows from my goddamn office.

I roll my neck and then stand straight, heading for the door with a new destination in mind.

I'll get the rest of my gear from the truck after I've checked out the bungalows. I can't think why any one of the guys would have taken them, especially seeing as half the crew just finished up on this gig. When Jace and I signed this project the owner originally suggested that we take up an on-site residence whilst leading the renovation, but we'd declined because we live close enough to drive back and forth each day. And no-one really wants to be living at their office twenty-four-seven, even if they're technically on site around eighteen-five.

Would Jason have taken the keys? Seems unlikely. The more plausible answer is that he did a last-minute check of the site before he left and forgot to bring the keys back to the cub.

Unless it wasn't a member of the crew.

My steps get a little heavier, a little faster, as I contemplate that we might have a squatter on the site. An offender. Teenagers messing around.

I shake my head. Not on my site.

I work my way down past the vacation cabins, eyeing them all briefly to check that everything is still the way I left it, and then I finally reach the clearing path that leads to the elongated double-bungalow, the stopover spot for the family that owns the place. There's a small garden at the front of each, with currently-bare flowerbed trims to make them homey. I neaten up the edge of one with the toe of my boot as I step up to the door that used to be labelled 'A'. I stop briefly just outside and I hold still, checking if I can hear anything. Maybe I would be able to if we hadn't just fitted the best double-glazing in the freaking country.

I lean back so that I can see all of the front windows. Curtains are still drawn. So far, so good.

Then I grip the door handle, pause for a moment, and tug.

No give. Jace must have locked up.

Unless it wasn't him.

The thought comes like an itch that I have to

scratch and there's no way now that I can't check, just to make sure. I flip through my keys until I come to the one with the words *Bungalow A* taped to it and I slot it straight through the lock with no hesitation. Twist, tug. I'm in.

The bungalows are laid out in mirrored floor-plans, so where Bungalow A opens straight into the small living-dining-kitchen space with a bathroom at the back and the bedroom to the left, Bungalow B is the reflecting opposite. They're technically one-story with the exception of the balconies. A stairwell at the back of the kitchen leads to a square door panel in the ceiling, opening up onto the roof that's bordered in to keep it safe.

Being separate entities from the holiday cabins we've left the bungalows in pretty much their original form, but we did clear out some of the old furnishings with the intentions of sprucing them up when we re-kit the vacation properties. Right now the dining space is without tables or chairs, although we made sure to keep those fridges on hand for the crew's food. My eyes flick across the empty space, feeling like something is wrong. There's nothing out of place but something feels a little... different. Warmer. Steamy? My frown deepens as I decide to breach the threshold.

Why the hell is it so warm? I'll check the bedroom and then I'm out of here. No point getting paranoid about some missing keys when they could have been taken for any number of reasons, justified or otherwise.

I've just about talked myself down from thinking that something's amiss when my body finally reaches the bedroom doorframe. My breathing halts when I see what's on the quilt. The *used* quilt. A quilt that's crumpled and fluffed up, like it's been tossing and turning all night.

But the quilt isn't the problem here.

If this is a joke from one of my men, someone's ass is getting fired *today*. I take a step closer to the slinky red lingerie set laid delicately on the bed and my neck gets hot, my jaw suddenly setting hard.

See-through lace cups supported by two slinky ribbon straps and – Jesus – a pair of red panties, with barely enough fabric to cover an inch of skin.

I roll my shoulders and try to settle my heaving chest.

This is the most unprofessional shit that I've seen in the past fucking decade. My hands are twitching by my sides as I try to work out which of my men would be stupid enough to do this.

They're solid guys, or so I'd thought. I can't imagine any of them pulling a prank like this.

Lingerie? Fucking *lingerie?*

I hear a soft gasp behind me.

Then all hell breaks loose.

21

CHAPTER 3

Harper

I tentatively lift a pinkie finger under the spray of the shower, bracing my body for the ice-cold nip, but instead I experience an all-body exhale, a golden sigh of relief as the water that I've been running for the past three minutes laps at my skin, warm and wonderful. I didn't shower last night because, after catching taxi number six to grab food in town, I was no longer walking amongst the living. I said a little prayer by the end of my bed, relieved myself of the last of the day's tears, and then I crawled under the covers, hoping for a speedy departure.

I got it. I fell asleep for the first time in four weeks without family betrayals or cheating fiancés sinking their teeth into my subconscious, and I woke up with the deep autumn mist peeping around the wooden frame of my window.

I step under the spray and try not to cry as I rub my ringless fingers up and down my body. What a marshmallow. *Get a grip, softie.* Bad stuff happens to people all the time – I should just be grateful that Evan and I broke up when we were only two years down the line.

Imagine if it had been longer.

Imagine if we had actually *gotten married.*

I shudder at the thought, scrubbing the heels of my hands under my eyes as the tears blur in with the stream from the faucet. I twist it off, letting the steam curl into my lungs and soothe me from the inside-out, and I distract myself by mentally itinerating.

I'll get dried and dressed in that cute as hell lingerie set, then I'll cover it up with something big and comfy, then I'll text my mom to thank her for this reprieve–

Suddenly my body goes still and my head snaps to the right, a muted clinking sound capturing my attention.

Did I just hear something? I stand stock-still in the glittery shower mist, eyes wide and unblinking, lips parted in surprise.

I wait it out. The clinking stops.

Did someone just… unlock the bungalow? I mean, this is a construction site, I know that it's in use, but I wasn't exactly expecting anyone to *enter my living room–*

Heavy footfalls sound in the direction of the bedroom. I grab my towel like it's a military jacket.

I'm about to be sledge-hammered, naked, in the middle of nowhere. I look up at the ceiling and think, *this is karma for what I was thinking about the Uber driver yesterday, isn't it?*

The biomes in my tummy go into a full-on meltdown.

I remain unmoving, my mind a sheet of panic, before wrapping the towel tighter around my body and stepping out onto the mat, my fingers clumsy with fear. My stomach is writhing. I wish I didn't have wet shower hair because it's only adding to the horror movie ambience.

As quietly as I can I twist down the door handle, pushing at it gently as soon as it's free. Is this stupid? Should I have stayed in the shower? Like, forever?

I tip-toe across the new flooring in the living area and then, after a pulse-steadying inhale, I peer around the doorframe, straight into the bedroom.

I let out a soft gasp and stumble backwards.

There's a man standing at the foot of my bed. He looks like he's around two-hundred-and-fifty pounds and six-foot-a-million, wearing navy cargo pants and a matching shirt. The soft dark fabric is stretched thin across his shoulders. My eyes trail down his exposed tan arms until they land on his behind, and my lashes flutter as I take in the shape of his strong hips. I've never seen a man look so capable.

My brain fits the pieces together. He's wearing a uniform – a *building site* uniform – which means that he's clearly part of the renovation team.

Except for the fact that he obviously didn't know that this bungalow was occupied. Because he's standing ramrod straight and his eyes are locked squarely on my lingerie set, strewn tauntingly across the ruffled quilt.

And then he hears me.

He turns, startled, and the second that he catches a look at me he stumbles backwards too. Straight onto the bed. He throws out a large hand to steady himself but he grips right into the crotch of my slinky red panties. His eyes fly down to the fabric in his fist, lace slipping eagerly up the lengths of his fingers, and he immediately whips his arm back into the air, cheeks turning crimson. My eyes drop to his splayed thighs and my toes almost slip in the mini puddle that I've created on the wood. The curtain-drawn sex ambience and his testosterone-laden body-heat have me gripping my towel tighter, my hair clinging to the back of my neck.

He looks like a sex demon from one of my erotic sleep paralysis nightmares. He's got deep caramel skin and roughed up hair. A hard-set jaw covered in stubble. And his eyes? They're sparkly ice-crystal blue. Post-summer-storm blue, and twinkling like diamonds.

Speaking of diamonds – my left hand is now void of one and I'm wondering if his is equally bare. My eyes travel down the muscles, cords, bones in his thickly-packed left arm, but they're disappointed to find that the adjoining hand is now buried deep in the front pocket of his cargos, a knee-jerk reaction to panty-gate. My gaze remains on the area until I realise what I'm actually staring at and I blink away like I've just experienced momentary blindness. Lucky for me that is not the case. I clench my fists a little tighter.

We stare at each other for three more seconds in complete silence, the only noise in the bungalow our ragged inhalations and the sound of his cargos scraping agitatedly against my sheets because his right leg will simply not stop bouncing. He looks like he's in his late-thirties, maybe early-forties, and he's so viscerally *male* that my knees literally shake.

Was it really yesterday that I was saying 'no more men'? Let me rephrase: no more men, with the exception of this guy. I've never previously considered an affair with a stranger but right now all that I can think about is carpet burn and bite marks. My body is pumping oestrogen like it's my fucking vocation.

I have never seen a man like this in my whole damn life. Maybe I wouldn't mind if he actually murdered me.

On that note he suddenly shoves himself to his feet and he swallows thickly, his Adam's apple working a full-time shift as he ambles out of the bedroom doorframe.

I step out of his way and the movement makes his eyes flash back to mine. He grunts, low and tight, and then he looks away with his brow creased in pain, his shoulders so rigid they could crack a boulder.

"I'm so—" He grimaces as he speaks and I take another step backwards. His voice is so deep I feel it under my towel.

He turns so that his back is to me and he walks to the front door which is still partially ajar. He opens it wide and then borderline keels over, his fists gripping into the panels on either side of his body. My eyes sweep the breadth of the doorframe and a pleasurable light-headedness sheaves my brain.

His shoulders are the exact same width as it.

The little screenwriter in me flips open her notepad and scribbles in a big glittery love heart.

This man is a romance story waiting to happen.

I pad silently closer and his spine snaps up straight, sensing me like an animal does.

"I'm so sorry," he rasps, his eyes diverted and

looking out at the expanse of the Pine Hills valley.

I'm not. He's blocking me into my own bungalow and I don't mind at all. I want to make myself a coffee, sit back and enjoy the view.

"I had no idea," he says gruffly, and then he twists his head slightly so that we can lock our eyes together again. He looks like he's in agony. Pleasure-pain agony.

"I, uh… I work here," he continues, and for a split second I swear that his eyes finally stray south of my face. They flash to the hem of my towel, the tops of my thighs, and then he's biting into his bottom lip and forcing his head back to face outside again.

He looks angry. At *himself.* And it's the hottest thing that I've ever seen.

I look down at my body, wondering how I can magic-spell some clothes onto myself. As much as I could enjoy this man taking in his fill of me, the extreme rise and fall of his chest as he rakes me with his gaze, I am aware of how inappropriate this is. I don't know who he is. He doesn't know who I am. *I am fantasising about having an affair with him.* For all I know he really could be married. I try to scope out his left hand again but it's now tucked safely under his bulging bicep.

Darn it.

He turns his head so that I can take in his profile, his eyes cast down, a promise that he isn't looking. He licks his bottom lip and then says in a deep voice, "We aren't supposed to have any residents on site until the New Year so I had no idea that anyone would be in here. I saw that some keys were missing and I needed to check it out. The room, I mean! I had to check out the room, not… I'm not checking out anything else."

He swallows again and shifts the waistband of his pants. I lean against the wall to my right for support.

"Christ, this is unexpected. I'm sorry about all of this." He sighs and wipes his wrist across his forehead. Is he sweating? That'd make two of us. "Could you please do me a favour and meet me in my office at some point this morning, so that we can discuss this? When you, uh…" He scratches at his jaw and his stubble makes rough scraping sounds. "When you're… clothed," he finishes, his skin dark and flushed.

Am I in heat or something? My throat has gone so rusty that I have to cough multiple times before I eventually manage to choke out a husky, "Okay."

Apparently one word in my dulcet tone is truly the final straw. He rolls his lips into his mouth, nodding curtly once, and then he's storming down the bungalow's path with more intent than an American sniper.

I give my limbs a few seconds to recalibrate, and then I toe the door closed.

Oh dear. It's been less than twenty-four hours since I arrived at my new "job" and I already seem to have lost my mind. A Viking just broke into my bungalow and somehow I am seriously considering taking up his invitation to meet him in his office.

Wait – his office?

Did I just meet the guy who's running the renovation? In my towel?

Did you not also just have your heart broken, your trust betrayed, and two years of your life pulled from underneath your feet?

It's too much stimulus for me to take in. I kneel

down on the foot of the bed, reach for the pillows so that I can clutch my bear, and then I hold it to my chest as I bow my head into the quilt. If I was to pray now I'm not sure what I would wish for.

I don't want to look backwards but I'm not sure that I'm ready to take the first steps forwards either. And a guy isn't going to fix that. Whether or not that man outside made my pulse pound like a jackhammer, he is simply another guy with no good intentions. I know what men think of me now: I'm a place-holder. A stop along the way.

I'm replaceable.

And it's not just the guys, my brain reminds me.

As if I'd forgotten. My own flesh and blood couldn't even find it in their hearts to respect me.

Just like that I'm back to my earlier sentiment. That man out there definitely needs to be kept at arm's length. No more cutesy courtships. No more guys.

I still on the quilt, willing myself to be uninterested.

My body has other plans.

I pad quickly over to the window and then peek out between the curtains. A thrill zaps through my belly.

He may be halfway across the site but he's still looking back at me.

CHAPTER 4

Mitch

Who the hell is that?

The second that I mount the steps to the portacabin I'm texting my brother, telling him to call me right now. He's gone radio silent so I know that he knows exactly what's up.

There's a chick on site.

When did she arrive? Did Jace see her last night?

Is she *meant* to be here?

Hell no. Her being here is way too dangerous. She could... hurt herself. The picture of her clutching a towel around her shower-flushed thighs, hot sparkling water droplets trickling down her arms, sucker-punches me square in the stomach. I rake a hand across my scalp as I kick out the chair behind my desk and I heave my body down onto it. I rest my elbows on the table, steepling my fingers into a fist and then knocking them in a gentle thud against my forehead.

There has clearly been some sort of mix-up. Maybe she had planned to vacation here for the fall and the admin team forgot to reschedule her stay for after New Year's. It doesn't matter – I'm going to fix this. Get this chick off base so that no-one gets hurt and this project gets finished ahead of schedule.

No distractions.

I stretch the muscles in my back. This is not what I needed for my first day as project lead. But she'll be coming to the office soon so we can get this situation sorted and then everything will go back to exactly the way that it was. It will.

I try to unclench my jaw.

It. Will.

I need to occupy myself with something that doesn't involve glancing every ten seconds through the open door, searching for pretty eyes and long legs at the base of the tree-line. I throw my file open with more forcefulness than I intend, attempting to make sense of the words on today's agenda.

Yeah, that's not happening. Something primal has just been flicked in my brain and suddenly all I can think about is that hot young distraction. Is she going to come and see me in the office? Is this the last time that I'll ever see her? Is she wearing any clothes yet?

Damn. I pinch the bridge of my nose with my fingers as I try to uncoil the tight flex in my abdomen. Then I remember that these fingers were just tucked into the gusset of some red lace panties and suddenly I'm looking at my hand like I need to hack it off.

I feel guilty as sin. Accident or not, that was not okay – and speaking of *not okay*, let's talk about how my body is responding right now. I'm getting hot under the collar and my palms are flexing like they need to be filled with something. Some*one*.

Growling, I throw myself upright and storm across the cub, yanking open the blinds on each of the windows. Maybe some morning light will help scorch the thoughts of wet womanly thighs from my brain. But when I reach the final pane I suddenly catch a glimpse of a woman's figure – lithe and golden, with her hips swaying from side to side – and I'm so ready to combust that I literally tear the entire valance off the wall. The slats unravel like a dam breaking free and I blink down at it, trying to think of what the hell I'm supposed to do now.

My eyes flash back up to her. She's closer than she was before, probably only about thirty feet away. She spots me at the window and tucks a soft tendril behind her ear. I toss the shutter to the corner of the room and then make my way straight over to the entrance.

On second thoughts, I glance down to the front of my cargo pants. Okay, so she's gotten to me. She's a beautiful woman and my body damn well wants to remind me of that fact.

Fine, I won't greet her at the door. I gesture to her from the frame, signalling that she can come inside, and then I make my way back to the desk, rubbing a hand down my jaw as I think of how I'm going to handle this situation. I sit and spread my thighs apart to give my lower body the expansion room that it needs but then, after a long groan of relief, I realise that I can't do that with this woman sat directly opposite me. I swallow down my ache and shift my legs a little closer together.

Fuck no, that ain't happening. I skirt the chair right under the desk and allow my legs to splay as wide as they want. I almost grunt with satisfaction. The perfect crime.

I try to quickly clear the work surface as she gently pads up the stairs, mainly so that I can compose myself before I have to meet her eyes again. Eyes that not more than fifteen minutes ago were looking down at me as I fell on her warm unmade quilt, panting like a motherfucker as I got a handful of sexy red lingerie. And I swear that, in that moment, there was something heated in her eyes too – like maybe she wanted me to stay on the bed so that she could climb aboard. Get those soft soaked thighs straddling my lap. Drop the little towel and give me a morning to remember.

Jesus Christ. I grab a pen from the holder as she breaches the entryway and I stab the lid straight into my quad. *Get it together, asshole. She's not for you.*

She points to the chair in front of me.

I nod and press the lid in a little harder.

She's wearing a cream zip-up jumper and a pair of jeans that make my temples throb. She turns slightly, her hand reaching for the doorknob, and I almost flip the table over to stop her from what she's about to do.

"No, please – leave the door open." The side-shot of her perky behind is enough to make me firmly reiterate myself, stating loud and clear, "Do not close the door."

It's just turned October but one step inside my office and the whole place smells like summer. Where did this girl come from? I need to get her a First Class flight back there as quickly as possible.

I'm about to take the lead with this conversation when she suddenly sits down, arches her spine and says, "I think that there's been a misunderstanding."

My brow dips in the middle. Technically, that was going to be my line. I try not to focus on her sweet raspy voice as I unclip the project itinerary from the front of my folder, instead honing in on the little flash of lightning flickering behind her eyes.

She crosses one knee over the other and I have to physically restrain myself from letting my eyes drop down to her lap. "I'm not here to holiday," she explains, her demeanour calm and composed. "I'm here to supervise."

I'm no longer interested in the paperwork. Did she just say what I think she said or am I having an auditory hallucination? When I scan her face she doesn't look like she's kidding. In fact, she looks like I'm annoying her.

Now I'm really frowning.

"To supervise," I repeat.

"That's right," she says, one delicate eyebrow beginning to rise in defiance.

Why am I getting the feeling that this chick is about to become a real piece of work? I narrow my eyes on her, thoughts of her shower-soaked body quickly swirling down the drain. "Am I supposed to know who you are?"

"Are you the boss?" she asks.

"Damn straight," I reply.

"Well then let's get another thing straight. I'm *your* boss. And you should have been told that I was coming."

I wrack my brain. What the hell is happening? I

definitely had no clue that anyone was coming to the site, let alone this perky blonde bombshell with her fuck-me jeans and tiny towels. Her eyes are molten as they bore into my own and a glint of something dark licks in my abdomen. We're staring like we hate each other. Fine by me.

I wipe my thumb across my bottom lip and flip to a clean page in my folder, lifting my flagellation pen over the ruled paper.

"Name?" I say gruffly.

"Harper Ray."

And there it fucking is. I toss the pen down, nodding my head as I meet her gaze again. Her lips are pinched, fighting a smile, and her eyes are glittering with relish. Yeah, I know that surname. She's one of the owners – or, at least, she's one of the owners' kids. The word 'entitlement' is practically printed across her forehead. Daddy's given her a job to fill a blank space in her journal and now she thinks that she can crack a whip on my site because she's a princess millionaire.

This is just what I needed.

I realise that Jason had probably been informed about this sudden check-on-the-inheritance family visit but forgot to share it with me on top of the million other things we've had going on before he handed me the reins. I roll my shoulders and decide to cut the guy some slack. Even if he had known that someone would be stopping by I don't think that anything he could have said would have prepared me for this.

For *her.*

"And you're Mitchell Coleson," she continues, fingers tapping agitatedly against her knees. Don't think that I didn't notice the little tremor in her voice this time. Like saying my name out loud... did something to her. My eyes fall for a split-second on her lips and she quickly wets them with the pink tip of her tongue.

"Yeah," I grunt. "Mitchell or Mitch."

She re-crosses her legs. I spread mine a little wider.

"Well Mr. Coleson, now that we've got introductions over and done with I wanted to let you know that Pine Hills is important to me. It's my family's business and I want to make sure that the team we've got over here is up for the task. I see that the exterior work has already been completed so I look forward to seeing the interior craftsmanship coming into play with the furnishings." She sounds like she's reading from an autocue. She pauses, her eyes scrape me up and down, and then she adds, "You know, if you'd like to think about continuing future endeavours with Ray Corp, that is."

Dangle that ultimatum in front of me why don't you. I can't help the exasperated half-laugh that I breathe out in sheer disbelief.

"Is that a threat?" I ask.

"It's just something to consider," she shrugs, eyes on her nails.

"Right. Fine. Let's get to the minutiae then." Namely: *what the fuck are you going to be doing whilst you're here?* "What tasks are on your agenda?" I ask.

She pauses for a beat, lips parted but with no words coming out.

Great. She doesn't even know why she's here.

"Listen ma'am—"

"It's Harper."

I swallow hard. "Harper, right. I appreciate the fact

that this is your family's business but you hired the right team. I've been doing jobs like this since–"

Now it's my turn to pause. How old is this chick? Have I been hammering nails and hauling wood since before she was born? Please God tell me that that is not the case.

I lean back in my seat and choose to rephrase. "I've been working this business for a long time. This ain't my first rodeo. Your property could not be in safer hands."

Her eyes momentarily stray to my hands, spread out flat on either side of my groin. Like I'm presenting myself to her. I quickly tuck the chair closer under the desk, stomach clenching when our knees accidently knock together.

I swear to God I'm one second away from getting a nail-gun and stapling my boot to the floor, to stop my damn leg from pounding up and down.

I clear my throat and jab the blunt tip of a finger onto the itinerary in front of me. "Everything's on track. We're under budget. If you need me to send you copies of the docs I'd be more than happy to–"

"Actually I'm... I'm relocating."

I blink at her. The word 'confused' would be an understatement.

"You're relocating," I repeat, not sure what she's getting at. *So you're here because...?*

"I was in the market for a... bungalow."

"A bungalow." She's fucking with me, I know that she is. She looks shifty as hell and if she bites her lip any harder she's going to make it bleed. *Why is she lying about this?* There's no need. She should just come clean and say that her papa wants her on the payroll any which way. But I give her the benefit of the doubt because I don't exactly hate having her here in my office.

"What for?" I ask.

"To live in," she bites out. The way that she says it sounds a lot like *you stupid asshole.*

That's not exactly what I meant. Why is this chick who probably lives in a mansion back home interested in relocating to the hills on the outskirts of a small town suburb? What's she running away from?

I scratch at my jaw. "So you're… staying on-site. Indefinitely." My eyes scan her one more time. "So that you can stay in the bungalow."

Her eyes are so big that for a moment I think that she's about to cry. She's lying to my face and I'm dying to know her true motive.

"Are you old enough to be on a site like this? You must be, what, twenty-two? Twenty-three?"

"Twenty-eight. Thanks though."

My heart halts in my chest. She's… twenty-eight? *Still not for you, man.*

"I've been on sites before so this is no biggie. I'm going to be residing in the bungalow and simultaneously checking up on the progress of things. You won't even know that I'm here."

Un-fucking-likely. One, I would *eat* this fucking pen lid if it turned out that she'd even stepped foot on a site like this before. And two, I would have to be stone-cold dead to not know that she was here.

I flatten my hands on the desk, palms down, trying to reason with her. "You haven't even been inducted."

Her eyebrow ticks higher. "Isn't that your job?"

I blow out a long breath. "Is this a test? Were you

sent here to see how we handle distractions?"

Wrong thing. I said the wrong damn thing.

Next thing I know her chair is making a loud scrape backwards, her fists are turning white-knuckled next to mine, and she's towering over me. Second time in one morning. It's my lucky day.

"If this was a test I'm not so sure that you'd like the results. A 'distraction'? That's what you're categorising me as? I have every right to watch over how you're manhandling the properties listed under my family's name so, congratulations, because you just hired yourself a hawk."

I rise to my feet and now she's the one being towered over. She scowls up at me like I'm a tree she wants to hack down. "This is protocol. I'm saving your ass from a legal nightmare. In fact, scratch that – I'm saving you from *potential physical harm*. I'm looking out for you. So whether or not this site is in your inheritance, you need to go back to daddy for a different toy to play with."

She leans a little closer. Goddamn, she smells good.

"Actually," she says slowly, dropping her voice to a smug whisper. "This site belongs to *mommy*."

I arch backwards and stretch the column of my throat before locking my eyes back in with hers. It looks like I can kiss goodbye to this project getting done on time because I've just hired myself a beautiful twenty-eight year old distraction with an entitlement issue *and* an attitude problem. If she wants to spend the next two months getting in the way then fine – be my guest. But I'm a grown-ass man with a job to do and I'm going to keep this professional, so help me

God.

"You need a site induction before you can stay here," I tell her levelly.

"Induct me then," she snaps back, furious.

She's flipped a switch on me and I'm struggling to keep up. Twenty minutes ago she was a pink-cheeked sweetheart. Now she's twenty lawsuits waiting to happen.

Is this because I accidentally grabbed a handful of her lingerie? I already got a prolonged look of disdain from the teddy snuggled between her sheets and I was kind of hoping that that was the end of the matter. That it could be pushed aside and forgotten. But that was before I knew that she was actually thinking of living on this construction site and that I'd actually have to make eye contact with her every damn day.

Get this under control, Coleson.

I try to placate her, praying that I'm not coming off as patronising. She's still glowering up at me in defiance, but there's a slight tremble in her chin that I'm going to pretend I didn't just see.

"I think we may have got off on the wrong foot, and it doesn't need to be this way. I work long, and hard, and fast. I want to see this project through with no accidents or delays, for the sake of your company and mine."

I look intently into her eyes, trying to show her how sincere I'm being. Maybe she really is concerned about her family's site but I wasn't lying when I told her that this project was in the most capable hands.

Something wavers behind her pretty irises and suddenly I'm getting a better read of her in this silence than any amount of talking would have uncovered. She looks vulnerable as hell, like she doesn't know what she's doing. She doesn't trust me because she doesn't know me, but for some reason she's *here* rather than in the safety net of wherever it is that she came from. Which means that wherever she came from is even less safe than *here*.

I frown at the realisation and she puts her shields back up.

"I'm staying in the bungalow and I'm overseeing the rest of this project." She states it like a cold hard fact. Somehow it still sounds honey-sweet in that sexy breathless rasp of hers.

Suddenly her hands are sliding across my desk and I watch as her graceful fingers climb onto my work folder, grip it and then snatch. She flips it open until she's found the project calendar and then she's snapping a photo of it on her cell, quick as lightning.

I jerk my chin at her. "What's that for?"

She squishes the phone into the front pocket of her jeans. "So I can get myself nicely acquainted with your very busy schedule." She thinks for a moment. "Maybe I ought to get myself an office, too."

I flip the binder shut and shove it back to my side of the desk. When her eyes meet mine they're crackling with heat.

I shake my head at her and her energy sizzles wilder.

Just act like she's not here. Keep this professional.

I give her a curt nod of my head – polite, civilised – and say tightly, "I look forward to having you around."

She dips her hands in the back of her jeans and says, "I look forward to my long thorough induction."

Hot damn. There's nothing polite or civilised that I

can say to that so I just nod again and swallow thickly. "See you around," I say conclusively, meaning: *get the hell out of my office.*

She looks at the stitches on the left side of my shirt and reads the text.

Coleson Joinery. Mitchell Coleson, Team Lead.

Then her eyes are back on mine and she gives me a casual shrug, like *yeah maybe.*

"See ya," she says at last, that raspy caramel voice settling low in my abs.

I wait for her to turn around and then I lower my body down onto the seat, wary and unsettled. There's another feeling too but I refuse to acknowledge it.

It's been a couple of years since I last got entangled with a woman and there's absolutely no need to break that pattern now.

I hear her shoes hit the top step and I let my eyes glance up at her, my body still crowding over the paperwork on the table.

The last thing that I see as she leaves my office are her delicate golden hands tucked in the back pockets of her jeans, involuntarily tugging the denim slightly down at the back.

And I swear that, for the briefest of moments, I see a lightning flash of red lacy underwear.

CHAPTER 5

Harper

I've taken residence on the roof-top of my bungalow
so that I can oversee the entire site, knowing that it's
what irritates Mitch the most. I've come out here every
day for the past week, stirring my coffee with evil
satisfaction as he glowers at me from his makeshift
joinery workshop in the centre of the hill that rolls
between the cabins.

The sound of Mitchell's scary truck revving into
Pine Hills each morning is the alarm clock that I never
knew I needed. The second that I hear it I hop out of
my sheets and I rip open the curtains, waiting for him
to spot me through his windshield, dismount his
vehicle, and then slam the door shut. His eyes don't
leave mine the entire time.

I make coffee number one of the day whilst we
have our standoff and then I take a nice prolonged sip.

Then I whip around and give him a full two hours of the cold shoulder. I wash and dress with more enthusiasm for a day on the dirt than I've had for the past five movies I've written. Then I get my notebook out, grab coffee number two, and head to my lookout point to "oversee".

Let's be real, I'm not actually here to supervise. I've seen the digital updates that Mitch and his brother have been submitting over the past two months and they are more than capable to see this project through. All I needed was a semi-plausible excuse to be here that didn't involve revealing the fact that I was recently not only romantically jilted but betrayed from the inner circle too.

I rub over the dull ache in my chest with my bare left hand and then I settle back in to what I've really been doing.

I've been hate-writing the beginnings of a revenge-fantasy manuscript that is so thoroughly unhinged that it will never see the light of day. Previously it could take me months to come up with a fleshed-out concept but, funnily enough, being treated like shit really does dose you up on *so-be-it* resignation crossed with *fuck-you* insanity. The only problem is that the script is supposed to be about my ex-fiancé, but the bronze muscle-machine that I've been watching every day has without question obliterated his physicality from my mind. I can barely remember what Evan looks like. Which means that, whether I like it or not, I have semi-subconsciously given the handyman in front of me a starring role in every line that tumbles onto the page.

I look down at my notebook and feel a pang of

something like guilt. I don't want to think about my ex-fiancé and I have a man who looks like he was cooked up in a romance novel less than forty feet away from me. I tap my pencil on the page and decide to turn a new leaf, literally. I scribble over the page until it's an undecipherable slate-gray mass, rip out the offending evidence of my unmistakable psychosis, and crumple it up into a compact little ball. Then I stand, lean over the balcony, and fling it straight across the site into the skip right beside Mitch's workshop.

His eyes zip to the ball of paper and then flash straight up to me. There's a heavy scowl on his brow. I watch his forearms flex, delighted.

Over the past seven days the man has not spared me a single word, communicating solely in prolonged glances and belly-flipping grunts. I take this opportunity to study the hard lines of his body and, without him knowing, I begin to trace the heavy angles of his frame delicately onto my notepad. Harsh cheekbones glowing with the exertion of his labour, thick shoulder muscles hulking beneath his navy shirt. It's an intriguing colour on him; its darkness only emphasises the depth of his stark tan, whilst simultaneously contrasting the crystal facets of his eyes. He looks away from me and my body does a little shiver of relief.

I look down at the paper and add in the finer details. Although my formal work in LA was strictly as a screenwriter I was clinically obsessed with the storyboard artists. Getting to know the unique flavours that each of them added to their character designs continuously ignited a curiosity-sizzle in my brain.

My fingers hover over my secret drawing of

Mitchell, wishing that I had some watercolour paints to add a splash of red to his cheekbones, an ice-cave blue to his eyes. Instead I shade in his irises, leaving a little white circle of light in each to mimic his inextinguishable sparkle.

My brain gives me a slap across the frontal lobe, scolding me.

Stop it, Harper. He's just a guy. He is not *your new muse. Remember how well the last one went?*

When I look back down at him he's got safety goggles drawn over his eyes and thick gloves pulled up his hands, one palm spreading up a large sheet of wood whilst the other clicks a power-tool to life. One of his crew members is set up at the next bench doing the exact same thing, head bowed low over his intensive task.

Okay, so he's skilled. Whatever. I decide to cancel out my lusting by turning my back to the valley, instead facing the pine forest that obscures my view of the mountains. I stop my incessant doodling and instead try to think of some possible cons to this man, dotting them around the sketch of his gruff handsome face. I only manage to come up with *'Dangerously strong'* and *'Hot dork?'* before I realise that it has all gone oddly quiet down there.

I turn around and glance back down at the site.

Oh dear.

It's late in the afternoon with yellow opal light trickling in through the trees, and from its current angle the sun is casting an otherworldly jasper glow on the hard-set face that is now frowning up at me. A member of his team is talking to him with an almost embarrassed look on his face, sparking my interest when he gestures vaguely in the direction of my bungalow.

I raise an eyebrow at Mitch, asking *Yes?* but he merely glowers on, sharpening the blade of a manual saw, casually like a serial killer would.

I almost smile. Then I begin cataloguing the thick muscles of his forearms.

When he turns to face away from me, his conversation still going strong, I shield my eyes with a hand and stare directly at the sun. One week in the woods and I have already taught myself how to tell the time from the solar positioning. I squint my eyes, thinking long and hard before I make a guess with myself: *six-fifteen.* I check my phone and see that it's four-thirty. Close enough.

In fact, this is very good news. It's prime irking time, which is my favourite time of the day. It allows me to both keep Mitchell at arm's length due to the fact that he will undoubtedly hate me, whilst simultaneously satiating my desire for male companionship by performing the actions which *make* him hate me. Namely: being myself.

Time to get hands-on.

I flip open the hatch to the bungalow's descending staircase, clip-clop to the ground floor, and then I pull open the front door.

I get the shock of my life.

Mitch is standing on my little step, meaty fist raised like he was just about to pound a hole straight through the wood. He drops the fist when his eyes lock in with mine and then he swipes his tongue over his bottom lip, so enraged that he can't keep still. I pretend not to notice how the haze of testosterone emanating from the broad planes of his chest is making my thighs shake. Luckily he's so infuriated that he doesn't notice. I blink innocently up at him, waiting for him to brighten my day.

"You're hilarious," he growls, eyes giving me a reluctant once-over before they flick back over to the front of my door.

Oh yes, I'd almost forgotten. I can't help the smug little smile that suddenly dimples my cheeks, arms folding across my chest so that I don't combust with satisfaction.

I may or may not have acquired a tiny metal plaque, engraved with the words HEAD OFFICE, and then stuck it squarely on the front door of my bungalow. You know whose office doesn't have a little professional plaque? Mitch's. So for all intents and purposes my bungalow really *does* look like it's the Head Office.

"I spent all summer making these doors, changing them from the old ones." A palm spanning a width larger than my waist hovers tentatively over the plaque, hesitant to touch it. "What'd you stick it on with anyway?" he asks gruffly, a deep crease between his brows.

I stuck it on with glitter-glue.

"Cement," I say instead.

His head whips back to mine, eyes wide with horror. I let myself snuggle down in his discomfort for a good ten seconds before I submit.

"Kidding. Oh come on, what's the problem? You really think that your guys can't tell the difference between my whimsical bungalow and your boring office? You're insulting them." I'm not being sarcastic.

I've seen the work that's been happening over the past week and I'm both amazed and annoyed by how talented these men are.

He takes a huge step backwards, shaking his head. "I thought you weren't going to be an issue. Stop messing around on my site."

I raise a finger. "Need I remind you? This is technically my site."

"And you hired *us* to fix it. Let me do my job."

He has a point and suddenly I'm embarrassed. I'm letting my personal issues interfere with a guy who doesn't deserve my shit, a guy who infuriatingly seems to be one of the most capable and level-headed men that I've ever witnessed. If this was LA, he would have already quit. Or demanded a raise. Or performed any number of other petulant childish stunts.

Stunts like the ones that *I've* been pulling. I swap my notebook from my left hand to my right and give my aching heart another rub.

He notices, and his frown deepens.

I lower my hand, twiddling with my vacant ring finger. "Fine. Sorry. You can take off the sign if you want."

I watch his eyes narrow on mine before flicking over to the plaque on the door. He's longing to tear that silver sign off so hard that I can palpably feel his agony when he takes another step backwards. My lips part in surprise. *He's going to let me keep it?*

He looks over his shoulder towards where he was just sawing and then he turns to give me a steady authoritative stare. "I'm going back to work now," he says, still tense. Then with a parting glance he trudges back down the path, the muddy prints of his boots leaving a trail straight to his workshop.

I watch after him, amazed and alarmed by how level-headed he's being. Is this how all men are outside of Hollywood? I seriously doubt it. In which case, I probably shouldn't take it for granted that I've just struck gold in the literal middle of nowhere.

I mull over his words as he gets back to his task, a bulky bag of wood cut-offs growing larger beside him.

I'm going back to work now.

Hm. "Work".

I look down at my notebook and think about my rekindling creative juices. I'm in no hurry to start writing another manuscript – in fact, a break away from the same task that I always do is probably healthy.

When I look up at the valley of cabins I'm suddenly seeing everything through new lenses, each separate task surrounded by a gold *pick me* shimmer.

I want this guy to respect me. I don't want him to think that I shouldn't be here even if, technically, he is correct. And I don't want to be a pain in the ass to a man who seems *good*. I can save that for the next time I see my ex-fiancé.

I look down at my outfit, checking to see that it's site-suitable. I'm wearing pale denim jeans and my favourite baby pink zip-up, but the flip-flops are a little amiss so I kick them off and tuck my feet into a pair of boots instead. They're sort of... faux hiking boots. They're the shoes that you don't mind getting a little muddy, khaki with a tall lip and rubber soles, and in a previous moment of whimsy I threaded a different pair of laces over the metal notches, in sugar-frosting pink.

My cheeks heat up but I try to override the ache in

my belly, telling myself that it's okay to be myself, it doesn't matter what anyone thinks of me, here or anywhere else. I like pretty things and other people shouldn't have a problem with that. I mean, would I judge a guy for having a killer six-pack?

Maybe it's the same for guys. Maybe they actually don't mind women embracing hyper-femininity. We aren't in high school anymore – live and let live, right?

Wrong. I lock up the bungalow and begin making my way across the lush slope of the valley when I hear a car door open and my head turns curiously over my shoulder. A guy steps down from the side of a white van and a small frown touches my brow because I don't recognise him or his vehicle. I guess that it's one of the crew on a break but I'm not entirely sure. I give him a cautious smile, my eyes riddled with *stay-back* wariness, but he heads over to me anyway. He's flashing me his teeth and his message couldn't be more clear.

I swallow and try to up my pace.

"Hey," he calls over to me, and a prickle rises on the back of my neck. I hope he can't scent my fear.

"Hi," I say back, my voice painfully light and sweet. *Stay away, stay away, stay away.*

"What're you running for? I just wanna talk." The smile in his voice makes my back muscles constrict.

I stop walking and turn to face him. He's obviously in his late thirties and he's not exactly unattractive but there's something about the way that his gaze slow-glides down my hair that makes me want to wrap it into a bun and then shove it under a trucker cap.

"What's a thing like you doin' here?" he asks, eyebrows raised, cocky, omnipotent.

My mind flickers back to when I met Mitchell's brother Jason and he asked me a similar question. Only in that instance I think he was going to offer me directions *away* from the area. This guy looks like he's revelling in my misfortune.

He reads into my silence. "What, you don't talk? I'm not gonna bite, Missy."

Another flash of his teeth makes me believe otherwise. I try to placate him.

"This is my project," I say, half-true, gesturing vaguely to the beautiful wooden cabins.

He laughs like I've just told a joke. "Good one. You one of their Missus or something?" he asks, picking up some rogue timber and chipping off the outer layer of mud and dirt.

It takes me a moment to even understand what he just said. *Does he mean am I with one of the crew? Romantically?* Surely Mitch would have told everyone who I am and why I'm here by now.

All I manage out is, "Uh…"

He nods like he gets me, his crooked grin making me slowly begin to start back-stepping again. He misreads me completely and says, "So it's a no-label arrangement. Sounds good to me."

I can't hold in my alarm. "What the hell? No. *No.* Who the hell are you?"

I'm so mortified that I fully turn around, set on walking as close to the centre of the base as possible, when I suddenly feel a tight hand on my forearm, gripping in a way that says *I'm not done yet.*

I swing around, wondering if this situation is urgent enough to slam my palm under his chin, but he's still smiling that easygoing smile, his free hand raised in faux surrender. The fingers clenching my sleeve are giving a pretty solid counter-argument.

"I don't mean any harm, Sugar. I'm just letting you know that I'm around."

He must be around the fucking bend if he thinks that this interaction would merit a second one. Jesus Christ. I rip my arm from his hand and he laughs again, like this is all good fun. He holds both hands up and then tips his head towards his van.

"I'll be over there if you want my number." He watches me from over his shoulder the whole way back to his car.

My brain is spinning and I feel like I might throw up. Are these the kinds of guys working on my mom's site? With the sole aim of putting distance between myself and the guy in the van I head over to the centre of the valley, my wandering almost aimless as I think about what just happened.

This is what they're like, my brain reminds me. *This is why we're shunning them now.*

It's a well-timed reminder seeing as Mitchell's level-headedness was starting to make me go mushy. What an idiot. They're all the same.

Even if Mitchell isn't the one who's a brute, by hiring one he's endorsing one. I remember my guise as the on-site 'supervisor' and I wonder if I should actually call my mom and tell her that we should think of hiring a different crew.

I stop walking and realise that I've stepped under the canopy of the now-empty workshop. The guys have retreated into one of the cabins so I walk cautiously around the benches, calming the erratic racing of my heart. All that I've done by coming here is trade off being in the vicinity of one good-for-nothing dude for a whole freaking bunch of them. I thought that I'd be happier here, away from it all. Will there never be any escape?

To distract myself I start rummaging through the box beside the nearest bench, wondering what the crew keeps in here. Power tool after power tool after power tool. It's kind of fitting.

I stand up from my crouch and my eyes land on the big bag of wood off-cuts that I watched Mitch throwing bits of timber into when I was stalk-watching him from my rooftop lookout. Maybe some physical exertion will help use up the adrenaline that's hammering through me. I look at the bag and contemplate hauling it over to where all of the others are, gauging the heaviness and whether I'll be able to carry it for the length of the trek.

Then I remember the laugh that the guy in the white van made when I justified my being on a construction site and all of a sudden my vision is turning red and I'm wrapping my hands around the handles and—

I realise my error the second that I begin to heave.

My body is deer-limbed, this sack of wood probably weighs about fifty of me, and the four-post canopy currently sheltering the portable workshop was only erected today. Meaning that, when we had the first taste of fall rain yesterday the grass got super muddy. Meaning that, when I dig my heels into the dirt as I try to haul the bag two-handed my feet are instantly sliding under, the weight of the sack about to collapse on top of me.

Suddenly a large tan fist swoops forward, gripping

directly between my own. I'm suspended mid-fall, my body tilting backwards, only just high enough from the ground to stop the wood from breaching the edge of the sack and raining down on top of me. My feet are still scrambling and my ass is mere inches from the dirt.

I stare wide-eyed into the face of my saviour, simultaneously horrified, surprised, and immeasurably grateful. He stares right back at me, the words *what did I just say* so evident in his expression that I almost hear them.

Then I *do* hear them.

"What did I just say," he bites out, his expression hard as he uses the strength in one arm to pull the sack of wood upright. My body lifts effortlessly right along with it.

"Get off my back," I snap, although I feel like I've just had a spiritual experience, ascending to a realm where I'm as weightless as a sugar granule.

His face glitches momentarily, heat rising up his cheekbones.

I think back to my phrasing and flush. Now we're both thinking about him getting *on my back*.

He recovers faster than I do. "I told you to let me do my job."

"And without me you wouldn't *have* a job. I wanted to help out. Sue me."

"If you keep pulling stunts like this someone *will* end up getting sued."

I tip my head back and growl in frustration, barely aware that Mitch is still holding me upright. It's only when I tuck my chin against my chest, looking up at him through my lashes, that I see his arm extended and flexing, the vein in his bicep bulging and protruded.

Oh. I blink slowly and my brain begins to loosen.

"Steady your feet," he commands suddenly. I look into his eyes and feel a little weak. "Put your weight into them and hold steady so you can regain your balance."

I do as he says and I see his shoulders relax in approval.

I swallow hard. Interesting.

"Now stand straight and let go of the sack."

Our eyes burn straight into each other's, bad thoughts aflame behind our molten irises. His mouth is a flat hard line, his jaw bunching with restraint.

I almost raise an eyebrow. *I know exactly what you're thinking, Mitch.*

I carefully regain my balance, shifting my weight so that I can stand upright and then letting go of my grip on the bag, my gaze resting on his strong, steady hand.

You couldn't be in safer hands.

"This doesn't change anything," I say breathlessly, trying to act more composed than I feel.

Mitch is looking at me through half-mast eyes, his chest heaving in fast pumps as he maintains his grip on the sack. His gaze stays on my parted lips for one long moment and then we're staring into each other's eyes again, alarm and confusion making our breathing quick, our cheeks ruddy.

I cross my arms across my chest, hoping that my jumper is thick enough to disguise what's happening beneath it.

He follows the movement, his body emitting pheromones that are drugging me comatose, but then his brow is dipping and his muscles are setting like steel.

"What's that?" he asks suddenly, his eyes unmoving from a spot on my sleeve.

"It's a jumper. You should try wearing one some time." Mitch's muscles can be seen from Saturn's farthest ring. I endure daily cardiovascular murmurs when I catch sight of his swollen biceps. My eyes stray briefly to them now and my heart pumps a little faster.

"No," he says, his eyes still staring intently at an area on my forearm. "I mean what's *that?*"

I look down at the lower part of my sleeve – the fabric fitted and an adorable baby pink – and I blink at it in confusion, attempting to see what he's seeing.

It takes me a moment.

Then I get it.

"*Ohhhh,*" I say, because I would very much like to avoid where this conversation is about to go. "It's nothing. Just a bit of dirt."

His eyes fix onto my own like he's ten seconds away from boiling point. Then they're back on the dusty brown hand-print marring my sleeve, his jaw muscles rolling as he silently takes it in.

I'm so overwhelmed by the past ten minutes that I try to lighten the mood with a light laugh and an easygoing, "Seriously, Mitchell, it's no biggie–"

"I'm starting to realise that you say that a lot, even when it comes to things that are in fact pretty big."

His neck is heating up and so is mine, both for different reasons. He's quietly getting angrier and angrier, whereas I'm becoming lightheaded with flattery. How is it that a man who doesn't even know me is more willing to come to my defence than people who I've been literally born and raised with? I try to think of that quote from the Bible, something about the people in your hometown respecting you the least. I'm starting to quite plainly see that there's more than a pinch of truth in that.

"Harper." His voice is low, restrained. "Did someone touch you?"

I keep my expression neutral as he tries to stare the truth out of me. My lashes flutter momentarily when his eyes dip to my exposed clavicle, the curve of my covered chest.

He tries again. "Did someone touch you on my site?" he asks. "Did one of my men touch you?"

I move over to the only bench that isn't carrying a saw. He throws the bag of wood down to his side and takes a few steps closer, following me.

"Um," I say, chewing briefly at my lip. My eyes flick towards the bungalows and the van is still sitting ominously up there. I don't want to cause a problem but I also don't like the fact that there's a creep on-site who now knows where I'm sleeping. I mumble an incoherent, "*I-guess-maybe-kinda.*"

"Who?"

"I don't know their names, Mitchell."

"Which one? Point him out."

I move my eyes back to Mitch's and he's so livid that he's swelling. Heaving. *Is he really angry for me? Does he actually care that someone just touched me?*

"Uh," I say breathlessly, a little dazzled by the intensity of his stare. "He's mid-thirties-ish, dark hair." Mitch narrows his eyes, raking through names in his head. I try to help him out, adding, "The guy who drives the white van."

His expression immediately shifts, a little confused. "None of my men drive a white van."

I nod my head as subtly as I can over to where the van is parked up. "I'm pretty sure that that's a white van."

He whips around and I watch as his shoulder muscles roll, his brow furrowing. He locks his hands together and cracks his knuckles. Then he turns back around and looks down at me. "That was the guy who touched you?"

"Yeah."

"Did you... did you want him to?"

I study his cautious expression, the slight redness touching his cheeks. He's still looking into my eyes but I can tell that he's uncomfortable now too.

"No," I tell him truthfully.

He grunts. Nods. Then he says, "He's not one of my team. I'm gonna go talk to him and tell him to get the hell out of here."

He doesn't even deliberate. He grabs the bag of wood, tosses it over his shoulder, and then he turns around, about to head straight up the grassy incline.

I'm startled, flattered, and amazed. But then I think about things like *male ego* and *fighting with power-tools* and suddenly I'm reaching out to him, the tips of my fingers brushing feather-light across the curve of his bicep.

He stills, eyes locked in on my fingertips.

Shit. I'm a hypocrite. Does that count as sexual harassment?

"Sorry, sorry," I say quickly, pulling back my hand like I just touched a flame. That seems about right – I can still feel his hard swell burning into my skin. "I just wanted to say that you don't have to say anything, there's really nothing we can do."

Mitch's eyes follow my hand as it leaves his skin, floating momentarily in the air before I imprison it in the front pocket of my jeans. Then he licks his bottom lip and meets my eyes.

"No-one gets away with that kind of shit on my site. He's not on my crew so he shouldn't even be here. I'm getting that asshole out of here and I'm gonna make sure that he doesn't come back."

"Mitchell, really, it's—"

"Don't say it," he growls. "Do *not* say that it's okay."

When did we move so close to each other? He's mere inches away from me, his heat sinking deep into my body. My eyes roam over his pecs and I hear a rumble sound in his chest. Wow. Then my gaze is moving over to my bungalow, thinking about other parts of him that I wouldn't mind sinking deep into my body.

He must be thinking the same thing because he looks across to my bungalow too, his body moving even closer until we're only millimetres apart.

Then a new thought dawns on him and a fresh wave of concern crosses his features.

"Did he see you leave your bungalow?" he asks, his eyes bright with alarm.

"Um." I can't be sure so I don't answer.

"*Shit*," he curses, swiping his palm down his face. I can see a plan forming behind his eyes as he stares back up to the van. "Okay, here's what we're gonna do. I'm gonna talk to that piece over there and tell him to stay the hell away. But if for some reason he's hankering for a bust-up and shows his damned face here again, I'm gonna give you my number and you're gonna dial me straight away. Then I'll sort him out, pronto." He looks down at me, his expression serious. "Is that okay? Does that sound alright to you?" he asks, his voice gentler now.

I'm a helpless damsel. I'm a trope from one of my own screenplays. But in this moment I don't mind being a storybook stereotype.

I nod up at him, the urge to touch him so strong that I grip my fingers around the edge of the desk.

He nods back at me and then turns to fulfil his promise.

Somehow I feel as though this changes everything.

CHAPTER 6

Mitch

I shouldn't care. She isn't even mine.

But the thought of what just happened to her instantly made me flip the switch.

I trudge across the site so that I can throw down the haul of off-cuts and then I start to make my way uphill, towards the curve in the valley where Harper's bungalow is set.

Clearly she can't stay here alone anymore, not when there are random guys illegally trespassing onto the premises and scoping her out like she's on the market.

My cheekbone twitches. *Is* she on the market? I refrain from incriminating myself by looking back at her over my shoulder – not that I'd need to, seeing as the image of her is thoroughly burned into my mind. The soft sun-kissed wisps that gently frame her face. The long delicate fingers that tentatively brushed my arm.

I roll the muscles in my back, trying to forget about our fleeting moment of contact. Did that even happen? I glance down at my bicep as if I'm expecting to see a poker-red burn mark, but it's just business as usual. I shake out my wrists and try to shove the soft scrape from my mind.

As I work my way over to the van and its unfortunate driver I mentally catalogue a way to extrapolate Harper from living on site. *Or*, my brain suggests, *a way for you to stay closer to the site, and therefore prevent any further unwanted incidents.*

Obviously it would be... potentially uncomfortable to move into the bungalow next door to her. I'm classifying the place as one-hundred percent hers and I'm not about to encroach on her womanly space. I'm not here to patronise her or tell her how to live her life. I mean, she can take care of herself, as a twenty-eight year old woman and all.

My subconscious snickers back at me. *You keep reminding yourself of that, buddy.*

Maybe it would be better if I could just temporarily relocate somewhere nearby for a while...

The van door swinging open is enough to pull me from my thoughts. Thank fuck. I've got some energy to burn.

"Hey man, how's it hanging?" he says. I'm met with a knowing grin and a uniform that sure as hell doesn't have the name *Coleson* written across it.

"Hey. You got a permit to be here?"

His bravado falters for a second and then he re-masks and shrugs. "I was just scoping out the situation."

"And what situation would that be?"

He nods down to the valley. "That's one big project you've got going on." He slides his eyes back to mine. "With such a small team."

Why is it so hard for people to keep to their own turf? Speaking of off-cuts, that's what this guy's after. Pine Hills is a bells-and-whistles cherry pie and he's after a slice all for himself. I check the words on the side of his van and it nudges to a distant memory. I've seen his name around but he doesn't have the kind of reputation that I've spent years building for myself. Which means he's either looking for a freelance job on my crew or he wants to take over the job entirely.

Neither of which are on the cards for him.

He notices my silent appraisal and he shifts on his seat, wiping dirty palms down his jeans as he starts feeling increasingly awkward.

Which brings me back to exactly why I'm over here.

There's no way to tactfully say this without getting straight down to the point.

"There's a woman on my site. I heard that you touched her."

His demeanour changes entirely and now he's grinning like a wolf.

"So she's *yours*," he says like *gotcha*. "Makes sense. Fine little thing."

I roll my bottom lip into my mouth and bite down hard. My eyes stray to the fingers that he's got curled around his doorframe and I imagine breaking every single one of them. "You're trespassing. Get the hell off my site."

His eyes are glowing with entertainment. "Which

bit don't you want me trespassing on exactly? The site or...?" He moves his gaze so that he's looking down into the valley. I shift my body so that I block his view of Harper.

"Let me put this into words that you'll understand. You set foot on my site again you'll be leaving with a souvenir. You put your hands on the *woman* on my site again you won't be leaving, period."

"Is that a threat?" he asks, grinning.

"Yes."

A little colour drains from his face but he keeps going because he's an idiot.

"You're a real tough guy, aren't you?" He laughs and gestures down the hill. "Whaddya gonna do, throw me in the cement mixer?"

"Don't give me ideas."

He blinks rapid-fire and then shakes his head. "She's not worth it, man."

"I've got your plate number, a motive, and about ten-thousand shovels. Hit the pedal, asshole."

He looks up at me from the inside of the van, the roof casting part of his face in shadow. He's contemplating whether or not I'll actually rough him up. The set of my jaw states my intentions loud and clear. *Touch her again and I'll break your neck.*

Verbally, I opt for a more diplomatic approach. "It's protocol. You can't ride in here."

I think that I've finally gotten through to him with the pacification speech but when I see him lean farther back in his seat so that his eyes can dip back to the valley I choose to check all the boxes.

"And yeah, she is mine. She's, uh, she's my girlfriend."

Not once in my adult life have I considered a woman that I'm seeing to be my 'girlfriend'. Once you get past a certain age it's just a case of dating, and then deciding whether or not she's about to become your wife. But I needed to use a label that would send this guy running and I couldn't exactly call her my fiancée when there's no ring on her finger.

Hell yeah I noticed.

The word 'girlfriend' bulldozes whatever plan he was cocking up right out of his head and he returns his gaze to mine, nodding once, pissed off but understanding, and I step backwards as he reaches to shut his door.

Good riddance.

I watch him punch the engine to life, pull a rickety three-point turn, and then the van is groaning to the entrance of the road diverging from the Pine Hills Nature Trail, the low metal gate already wide open from where he clearly lifted it without my knowing. I follow the tire tracks once he's out of sight and pull the gate across, clicking in the hatch as my eyes watch the now-empty road. I look down at the gate under my palms, re-checking the mechanism in the thick bolt attached to the chain. *So that's how he got in here.*

Time to get a couple new locks.

I pull out my notepad and pen and jot down a couple of thoughts, including that asshole's licence plate number and a one-item shopping list that just reads *bolts*. Plus I'll have to give Harper a key of her own for the new lock, so I'll have to get a couple spares cut.

When I turn to head back down towards the workshop my eyes land straight on Harper, whose boots have already brought her halfway up the grassy incline. Are those pink laces? I don't have the opportunity to stare at them for too long though because she's suddenly giving me a big perfect smile for the first time since she got here, her eyes sparkling with gratitude and her cheeks two rosy apples.

Holy shit.

Do not think of her cheeks. Of any kind.

"You really scared him, huh?" she asks, her grin making little dimples appear. "You are a very handy handyman."

A gruff sound rumbles in my chest as she gets closer, and we meet somewhere in the middle, on the precipice of her bungalow's front garden. She's looking up at me all cutesy, and my eyes are fucking dying to get another look at her bare left hand.

I change topics entirely.

"He won't be coming back here again. I'm gonna get a new lock and key for that gate though, so I'll get some spares cut for you ASAP."

She nods and smiles, her eyes unblinking as she looks wondrously up at me. I watch as she slides her palms down into her back pockets, her body arching forwards and releasing a wave of her sweet scent straight from where the little gap in her zipper is, right between her breasts. Hell. I reach an arm up so that I can scrub at the back of my neck but I think I just gave her a hormone-dousing of my own, and her eyes look up and linger on the curve of my lifted bicep.

"Well, thank you," she says, a little raspier than before. "And I'm sorry for being such a pain. I…" She looks down at the sleeve of her pretty jumper and dusts at the dirty hand-print. Instantly the cords in my neck are twisting a little tighter and I'm thinking about actually paying that guy a late-night visit. "I've learnt my lesson. It was kind of you to look out for me like that. I've had a hard month is all."

Suddenly I'm very interested in continuing this conversation. She's had a hard month? I'm guessing that explains why she's here. What could have gone wrong in this beautiful woman's life?

Did someone do something to hurt her?

She wafts a dainty hand in the air, dispersing her words between us.

"Not that that justifies anything. What I'm trying to say is that I'm sorry for being a pest and, after my little scare, I am now ready to actually stay out of your way and let you do your job."

Her little *scare*? She was scared of the guy in the van? Fuck. Now the last thing that I want is for her to stay out of my way. I want her *in* my way. I need her close by, so that I can keep on looking out for her.

"Harper—"

"Seriously. I'm really grateful."

I can tell that she's trying to now head back inside her bungalow, with her judgemental teddy and dick-thickening lingerie, so I quickly say, "My number, Harper. I promised you that I'd give you my number. Just in case."

She twists back around, eyebrows arched as if she'd forgotten. Of course she had. She's probably been thinking about lots of other things, including but not exclusive to *men her own age*.

I pull my notepad out of my pocket and quickly jot down my number. I write MITCH above it for good measure. Who knows how many guys are trying to get their digits in her pocket.

My blood boils at my own phrasing.

I rip out the page and she jumps a little. My eyes fly to hers, hoping that I'm not coming across as too much of a brute. To balance out the violent tear I gently fold the paper in half and then extend my hand, passing it to her.

She reaches for it, looks up at me, and then slowly lowers her hand to the paper. Her fingers brush softly over mine and we both stare, unblinking, until she's fully taken it.

I stand there dumbstruck, wondering how the hell that was one of the hottest moments of my life. I can still feel her cool fingers burning into me, stroking against my palm.

She gives me another smile and then she stuffs the number into the tight front pocket of her jeans.

I watch her walk away until the front door closes behind her.

*

It's almost the end of the week by the time that I can get a reservation on a room at the motel three miles from Pine Hills. I flip over how illogical it is to not just stay in the bungalow next door to Harper's – or, better yet, to not simply leave her alone like a normal guy would – but I convince myself that getting a little nearer to the site whilst simultaneously not infringing on her space is the safest option when there are potential hazards in the area. I don't think that our visitor will be coming back any time soon but I'd prefer to be only a few minutes away, just in case.

Motels are cheap and I'll be making sure that the heir to Pine Hills is out of harm's way.

It's a no brainer.

My son, Tate, stands in the foyer of my house, shrugging on a jacket as he watches me silently from under the dark shadow of his fringe. We just had a father-son dinner together because he'll be leaving the site a little earlier tomorrow, what with it being Friday and him spending the weekend heading up to his fiancée's campus during her term time. Her third year just started so I'm sure that he's more than eager to help her settle back in.

I'm pretty sure that his mom, Pam, never taught him how to cook but for some God blessed reason he's naturally skilled when it comes to working around a kitchen. Our arrangement when he comes round is simple – he cooks and I clean.

His mom and I were tight in high school, not as a couple but as kids who liked each other's company. When we got a little older we decided to experiment in the 'safe zone' of our friendship and soon Pam was pregnant. She didn't want to be in a relationship and there was nothing I could do about that but I was immediately dead-set on getting a full-time job so that I could pay for our kid. Despite the circumstances and the fact that I was low-key shitting it, deep in my chest I was stoked to become a dad. Having a family was my sole goal in life. Even though it took me my whole adult life to get to the stability and salary that I'm at now, and even though Pam and I were never meant to be, I wouldn't change a damn thing.

Regardless of the fact that Tate's always seen his mom and I as two separate parts of his life, I know that it might be weird for him to consider me having an interest in a woman who isn't his mom. I mean, my last relationship that he was aware of wasn't exactly the greatest for him to witness.

Just ask his fiancée. She would know, seeing as I was dating *her mother*.

I swallow that thought down and then take a deep breath to calm my mind. It was a head-in-my-hands moment when I found out that the first woman I'd decided to get to know in years was the mother of the girl who my son was in love with. It was for the best when we quickly realised that we weren't going to be the greatest match. Now she's doing her thing, I'm doing mine, and I want nothing but the best for her.

It's been – what – two years since my last relationship? So surely it's okay to start thinking about someone new now.

Not that I would have anything to do with Harper. I'm positive that whatever chemical imbalance I'm currently feeling is just a by-product of not having my needs sated for such a prolonged time. Hell, I'm six-four, two-hundred-and-fifty-pounds, and thrumming with testosterone. It's probably unhealthy to have gone without for as long as I have.

But I'm ninety-nine percent sure that Harper isn't the chick for that. One, she's only twenty-eight, and even though I'm aware that she's not wearing a ring, that doesn't mean that she doesn't have a boyfriend. Or boyfriends. I steel my jaw and try to push aside the thought of multiple guys trying to get near to her.

And two, I don't even know what I need right now. I've been out of the game for so long that I can barely remember if it was worth playing.

I feel a protesting flex down south. My body *definitely* thinks that the game is worth playing.

I'm left with two options. I either keep beating my meat on my own, or get out there and consider a hook-up. If Harper's an impossibility then I need to think of some other options.

I run a hand down my face and feel the scratch of stubble that I really ought to shave off.

I need to get laid, like yesterday.

I toss the hand-towel down on the counter after I put the last of the cutlery away and then I turn to face Tate fully, sensing that he's a combination of curious and unsure about my motives to temporarily relocate closer to the site, emotions that put a boyish look in his eyes. They make me see him as a kid again, rather than an almost twenty-two year old man with a fiancée who's in college.

"Let's hear it," I say to him, giving him the all-clear to voice his concerns.

He shifts a little, glances out of the kitchen window. Then he says, "You wanna… stay in a motel. Instead of" – he looks around the foyer – "your house."

My eyes crease around the edges. "Well, it sounds dumb when you put it like *that*," I say, my mouth slanting into a half-smile because I'm kind of messing with him. "I'm… sampling the local hospitality. Seeing if there's anything Pine Hills might be missing whilst we fix it up."

He stares at me blankly. I've already told him exactly why I'm relocating to a motel for a little while and I know that he'd do the exact same thing if he was in my position. And I know that because he literally travels to check in on his fiancée every weekend without fail.

"How long do you think you'll be staying in the motel? The reno still has a month and a half to go, minimum." His expression tells me that he doesn't like the idea of his dad staying in a stop-off motel for such a prolonged period of time.

"Haven't decided. Maybe a couple weeks, when I'm certain that our cold-caller's history. Ideally not the whole month and a half but I'll just have to wait and see."

He nods his head. Then, quiet and a little begrudging, he finally murmurs, "I guess I'd do the same."

I bite back a smile and say, "I know you would, kid."

I give his shoulder a squeeze before he heads out onto the porch and a sharp warmth spreads in my chest. I fold my arms and lean against the doorframe as I watch him take off into the night.

The apple didn't fall far at all.

CHAPTER 7

Harper

"You should come home, buttercup."

My mom's voice is kind but firm as it comes rattling through the tiny speaker in my cell.

I've walked all the way from the Pine Hills site to the nearby town instead of dialling for a cab like I usually would, and the journey seemed like a good time to have one of my twice-weekly check-ins with my mom. I had intended to exercise, call, and get some of that fresh small town air on route to buying my groceries, but now the sky is full of thick rolling clouds and I'm dressed in denim shorts and a short-sleeved v-neck. I give the sky another hasty glance and swap my phone from one hand to the other.

"That's not an option," I say, horror trickling through me as the first wet dots appear on the blacktop.

"What, because you'll see them? Because you'll have to face the reality of the situation? Yes, you will, but you can handle it, Harper. Do not throw away your career just because you're scared of bumping into two narcissists. If everyone did that then there would not be a single soul left in the whole county."

"I don't want to be there right now, and I'm not contractually joined to any projects at the moment. Maybe this is a good time for me to see what else this country's got to offer."

"In Pine Hills?" she asks sceptically. "And what is an artist like you going to spend her time doing in Pine Hills, for this length of time? It's been three weeks. Are you eloping?"

I tilt my head and roll my eyes. A fat raindrop does a hit-and-run down my clavicle. "I've been writing for seven years without a break, mom. I need this."

"Is that so." Her voice is drier than a paper towel. "Okay, sure, so how's the 'supervising' going?"

I bite back a smile. My mom is the person who helped me fandangle this arrangement in the first place, only she probably didn't expect me to actually stay here for longer than one night. She's the CEO of Ray Corp, making and maintaining a plethora of magical small town vacation properties, and I'm her workaholic daughter who ironically never vacations. I'm not the free-spirited mess with a personality disorder who puts her life's responsibilities onto everyone else around her.

My mom has another daughter to fill in that role.

"Aside from the time when I said that I was going to 'oversee' the project to the literal Project Lead, it's been fine. Good, in fact. Good and fine."

Her long silence suggests an eyebrow raise.

I wipe at the raindrops turning my cotton top translucent.

Then I hear a long inhale and a low, "Well well."

My cheeks burn pink.

"Isn't this an interesting development. You're fraternising with my employees."

I comb my fingers through my soft blow-out as I rush to correct her. "There has been no fraternising, mom. I swear. I've just been… admiring from afar."

I hear her breathe out a laugh. She's probably also drumming her nails on the top of her mahogany office desk whilst patting her cropped Marilyn curls and shaking her head.

"He wouldn't want anything to do with me, obviously. I look infantile in comparison to him. And he's probably at least ten years older than me. And probably also in a relationship."

I hear keyboard tapping in the background. "What's his name?"

I shield my face from the rain and laugh, "No, mom, you're not going to Google him."

"Too late, I've already pulled up the list of men working the project." There's a scrolling sound, then, "Ooh, yummy. So much tanned skin."

I squeal, mortified. "Mom, you are *married*."

"And? I am admiring from afar."

I rub the rain off my forehead and mumble, "Touché."

As I get to the main portion of the town I skirt down one of the back alleys, leading to the small parking lot of a medium-sized supermarket. I jog, water splashing at my ankles as I head for cover under the extended roof housing the trolleys. "I've got to go, mom. I'm getting groceries."

There's a little *tut* on her end.

"Think over what I said – you shouldn't have to sacrifice your life by running from your problems." She pauses and then adds, "And I expect a name in my inbox by 5pm."

I laugh. "Bye mom."

"A name, buttercup."

I disconnect the call, sliding my cell into the back pocket of my shorts whilst simultaneously collecting a basket from the front of the store. I get a prolonged stare from an employee behind a till. His name-tag reads "Joe" and his age could be anywhere between fourteen to nineteen judging from his gangly limbs and mid-puberty complexion. At first I think that maybe he's staring because of my cute blonde pouf, as I've realised that boys are like magpies and I am a shiny thing. But then I take a look down at my front and I realise it's because my shirt is now transparent. I give him a withering look before I descend down the first aisle.

The basket was a bad idea but I'm too stubborn to go past Pervy Joe again in order to swap it for a trolley.

Milk, tagliatelle, a small fillet of white fish. I turn the corner and contemplate a medium-sized baguette, then twiddle aimlessly with the fingers on my left hand. This should last me for a couple meals but what else should I get? Life in LA means eating out. A *lot*. I haven't been so active in the kitchen since I was in Home Economics class.

As I look down at my sparse basket I think of how I really ought to have got a cab here so that I could have carted more back to the bungalow. I won't be able to carry much more than this, which means that I'm going to have to do *another* trip here in the not so distant future.

For some odd reason, I don't actually mind.

I tally up the total cost so far in my head, well aware that after my Uber-insanity three weeks ago I should really try balancing that out with a little frugality. I put my hand in my front pocket to grab my purse but my heart suddenly stops in my chest. I look down at the flat area in my shorts and I squeeze my eyes shut, mentally screaming.

I forgot my purse? Who the hell goes shopping without *their fucking purse?*

I place the basket on the ground in front of me and I rub softly at my temples. *Idiot, idiot, idiot, idiot–*

"Harper?"

A low voice, gentle and surprised, sounds behind me, and I whip around like I was just caught stealing spaghetti. His usually stern expression looks a little calmer right now, perhaps because he's not currently managing a site full of grown men operating dangerous machinery.

I realise that this is the first time that I've seen Mitch off-site. Seeing him here in the middle of the food aisle, his uniform darkened with little speckles of rain, my own clothing so wet that it's literally see-through, is so out of the ordinary that I grab my basket just for something to do with my hands. Something that doesn't involve *rubbing them all over him.*

"Mitchell, hi," I say with a smile. Getting to peek a look at him before he heads home this Thursday evening is such an unexpected secret treat that I almost don't care about the fact that I'm going to go back to my bungalow empty-handed.

Re-remembering my transparent shirt situation I casually fold my right arm around my chest. Rainwater trickles down my legs as my bra cups squeeze and release. Mitch's eyes flick down for a beat, he realises what I'm doing, and then his gaze is back on mine, more heated than before.

I throw out a pleasantry to tamper the sizzle in the air.

"Small world," I say lightly. If he notices that I'm breathless he does a good job at hiding it.

"Small town," he corrects me, putting his own basket on the floor and gripping his hands around the belt that's keeping his cargo trousers in place. I quickly scan his basket, mentally calculating how heavy that many bottles would weigh. Little shivers tingle in the peaks of my chest.

"I didn't know you lived near the site," I say, as if I'm not about to now spend my evening logging into my mom's Pine Hills reno folder and stalk her documents until I find out exactly where he lives.

I'm feeling naughty – maybe it's because of the sound of the rain thudding hard and repetitively against the roof, or maybe it's because he smells so good that I can taste him down my throat – so I give him a shimmery smile and say, "Lucky me catching you doing your weekly shop."

His muscles swell and flex but he watches me, unblinking. "This isn't my weekly. This'll only last me a few days."

I look back down at the crammed basket and then up at him again. His cheeks are starting to flush and he's avoiding my eyes. Is he… self-conscious? About how much he has to eat to keep his giant body going? My eyelashes flutter as I contemplate our size difference. My mind whips up an image of him sat down at a table, legs spread wide, ready to feast.

Why is it so sexy to think of him refuelling?

I go a little lightheaded thinking about all of the ways he could use up that energy.

He swallows and continues, "I, uh, I live in Phoenix Falls. Usually. But it's a bit farther out so…" He scrapes his perfect white teeth over his bottom lip, as if he's unsure about whether or not he should say what he's about to. I keep my eyes on his but in my peripheral vision I can see the fast rise and fall of his broad chest. I wonder what that would feel like moving hard and fast up against my back. "I'm living closer to the site for a while. For convenience purposes," he adds quickly.

I've forgotten what we were talking about and my pupils have dialled out.

Mitch's eyes rake me up and down and in that deep voice of his he states, "You haven't called since I gave you my number."

But holy fuck have I thought about it. Mostly at night, when my body is burned red-raw fresh from the shower, and a cotton tee is rubbing over my sensitised skin. My fingers drift over to my phone and I contemplate calling him. Texting him. Sending him a *wish you were here* photo taken in the steamed-up mirror.

Instead I give him another little smile, a dimple popping in my left cheek.

"He didn't come back," I clarify.

He blinks as if confused. "Who?"

I laugh. "The guy? With the white construction van?"

It takes him a moment but then he remembers. "Oh. Oh yeah, that's why… that's why you'd be calling." He swallows. "No other reason."

I tilt my head, watching him curiously. Wait: did he want me to call him for a different reason? Does he… does he feel this too?

He rocks on the heels of his large workingman's boots, tongue poking at his cheek, unable to keep still. It takes me back to the morning in my bedroom, his thickly-muscled thigh bouncing fast and frenzied. He's restless. And I can think of a great way for him to expend all of that pent-up power.

Over and over and over again.

"I like your uniform," I say without thinking, my voice a little hoarse. "The navy. It looks good against your skin."

He scratches roughly at the back of his head, eyes on the tiny space between our boots. "Uh, thanks. We were… we were gonna go with khaki, but the website didn't stock them."

"You mean that they were all out of 2XL?" I say teasingly, giving him a small wily smile. But when the tips of his ears begin to turn crimson I realise that I've literally just hit the nail on the head.

Oh my *God*. Of course normal websites wouldn't stock clothes that fit him.

He looks nervously up at me and his cheeks are a little ruddy. I give him another encouraging smile and after a moment his eyes crinkle in response, his shoulders rolling back as if he's finally relaxing.

I think that that might be the Mitchell Coleson

version of a smile.

His eyes drop down to my basket and he jerks his chin at it. "Nice pasta."

I wonder how many tonnes of carbs it would take to satisfy a man his size.

"Oh, thank you. I don't know why but I only like the thick one. Spaghetti gives me the heebie-jeebies."

I think he breathes out a laugh but I'm not one-hundred percent sure. He's not exactly smiling, but he also doesn't look like he's trying to run away from me so that's probably a pretty good sign.

"And you're, uh" – he looks at the other items in my basket – "you're cooking fish."

I nod sagely, crossing and re-crossing my legs. "I know, I'm evil. I don't usually eat meat but I'm so iron-deficient that I'm literally anaemic. Not that fish will help with that, probably, but I'm like working my way up to a steak."

This time I do get a laugh and, bonus point, a sexy deep-cut laugh line in the tan hollow of his cheek.

Fuck me sideways. Literally.

"Do you like seafood?" I ask, before my brain can catch up with my mouth.

Then Mitch's eyes are darkening and flashing up to mine, a heavy sensation pooling deep in my stomach. But he doesn't make me feel like an idiot. He just rubs a hand down his mouth, eyes momentarily straying to my bare legs, and then he nods once like I just asked him a normal question. "Yeah." He swallows. "Yeah, I like seafood."

Is it hot in here? I feel like I'm spiralling on a Codeine trip. Images of the bed in my little bungalow flash through my mind, the soft sheets crumpled luxuriously under my back, and my thighs splayed backwards, knees bent and weightless over his large undulating shoulders. The rhythmic roll of his body as he works his tongue between my legs. Stubble scraping at my belly when he looks up to check on me. The unrelenting thud of the headboard against the wall when he decides that I've had enough and now it's his turn to take.

I'm so lost in my haze of lust that my body jerks a little when I snap back to the present, and the toe of my little boot accidentally nudges against his large one. He grunts, surprised, shifts his belt, and looks down at me. I take a big step backwards and quickly tuck a rain-dampened curl behind my ear.

"Sorry," I breathe out, waving my hand airily next to my face as if to say *don't mind me*. "It must be the change in the altitude. I'm not used to being this close to the mountains."

The heat of Mitch's testosterone is literally rearranging my chromosomes.

"Anyway," I say quickly, turning slightly so that I can shove the baguette back onto the shelf, "I should be heading back. I forgot my purse so I need to run back to Pine Hills. Get my cash, call a cab this time, yadda yadda yadda. The altitude, you know," I add on, a gratified shimmer spreading in my chest when I see that almost-smile of his again.

He shakes his head in a way that I would like to describe as endeared and he releases his clutch on his belt, pulling a battered leather wallet out of his side pocket.

"How much do you need?" He thumbs through a fat wodge of bills.

I blink fast, eyes on his thick fingers, the wad of cash, that one raindrop that's slipping pornographically slowly down the vein in his hard bicep. "Oh, no, that's okay, really. I have to sort out my own problems. Otherwise I'll never learn." Advice that my mom told me repeatedly throughout my childhood. Interestingly the words were never shared with my sister.

He starts pulling out notes. *One, two–*

"You're allowed a helping hand. You wanna call a cab back to the site?" His eyes meet mine and he's being genuinely serious. In LA sometimes you're lucky if a millionaire will split the bill with you. "Or I could… I could drive you back."

My stomach drops, warm and heavy. I've seen Mitch's truck and it's the sexiest vehicle that I've ever seen. It's so gnarly that I'm not even sure if it's even road legal. If he let me climb into his passenger seat right now after paying for my groceries and saving me from the rain I'm not sure that we would leave the parking lot, ever. The thought of clambering over the stick-shift and straddling his lap is enough to make me squeeze my legs together.

"That's too kind," I rasp, no longer smiling. He's pampering me and I don't know how to handle it.

He pulls out four notes and pushes them into my left hand, eyes lingering there momentarily before he reaches around me to retrieve the bread that I put back a minute ago. His chest is now about three inches away from my mouth and I'm dying for him to close the gap. Instead he steps backwards and places the baguette in my basket, the thick stick somehow looking small in his hands. Then he reconsiders and grabs one to throw in his own basket too.

My cheeks are aflame. "I'll pay you back," I say, suddenly shy, and looking up at him from under my lashes.

He picks up his basket like it weighs nothing.

"Don't," he replies and he takes another step backwards.

I don't want him to leave me. He looks begrudgingly over his shoulder and I start to think that he doesn't want to leave me either. When he turns back around he gives me a parting lift of his chin, his jaw muscles bunched tight. "I can afford your groceries, Harper. Fill up that basket."

I stay rooted to the spot as he walks away, both of my hands now clutching the handle of the basket, four bills crumpled in my left palm. He glances back my way before he turns the corner and a painful warmth spreads in my belly.

I whip around, my feelings all over the place, and haul ass to the check-out.

Free-Show Joe is manning the only till in operation so I unpack my basket with a violent flourish. His eyes stay on the scanner.

I pay for a carrier bag and then he reads out my total, so I absentmindedly hand over Mitch's notes as I pack away the food.

"Uh, ma'am?" he says suddenly, a fearful edge to his teenage twang.

I look up at the cashier and he readjusts his branded cap.

"You, um…" He turns back towards the reader, pressing buttons until the cash drawer pops open.

I frown. *Am I still under? Mitch gave me forty — that covered my total.*

But when he hands me my change I understand his bewilderment.

I look down at the cash in my hands and my lips part in surprise.

He really wasn't kidding when he told me to fill up my basket *and* to get a cab back to Pine Hills.

Mitch didn't give me forty dollars. He gave me four *hundred*.

CHAPTER 8

Mitch

I pull up to the site on Friday just after six a.m., knowing that Tate's going to be doing an early-start early-finish so that he can head off to spend a long weekend at River's dorm. He parks up right beside me and when I glance at him through my driver's side window he points up at the sky. It's a dark gloomy blue, yesterday's storm apparently only the start. It isn't drizzling right now but it looks like it will soon, so today is probably going to be an indoors kind of day, working on re-tiling and re-flooring the cabins, rather than filing down the furniture in the make-shift workshop space we erected a few weeks ago.

I get out of the truck as he locks up his Ford.

"It's grim as shit," I grumble and he breathes out a laugh. "I'm seriously thinking that the rest of the big pieces are gonna have to be made over at my place."

We both squint up at the sky and he nods his head in agreement. I've occasionally used the garage at my house to store my truck or, in the wintertime, Tate's motorbike, but more often than not I use it solely as a workshop.

"We'll make them, haul them in the back of the truck, cover them with the tarp, and then bring them up here as and when they're finished."

He shrugs his shoulders. "Easy."

Then we're walking over to the office to get the keys to unlock the cabins. As I unlock the door to the portacabin my eyes stray up the sloped valley, over to Harper's bungalow.

Usually by now her curtains would be open. Did she get a cab yesterday after I saw her in the store? Surely she wouldn't have walked back here in the rain.

I bite at my bottom lip as I push open the door, Tate waiting on the steps as I go to grab the keys.

Did she come back at all last night? I mean, how the hell would I know?

The only thing that I *do* know is the fact that she definitely didn't call me.

I should be happy about that, because that means that there were no problems, but I feel a tight twist in my gut. I wish that she'd open the curtains so I could just know that she got back safe.

And alone.

The thought of her pulling open those curtains and then seeing a guy cosying up right behind her is enough to make me slam the door harder than I usually would as I leave the office. Tate flashes me a look and I shake my head apologetically.

"Feeling a little rough," I tell him, as if he won't see

right through me.

He gives me a prolonged look and then says, "Sure. But just know that you can… if you want to, you can talk to me about it."

I can't stop the chuckle that rumbles through my chest. When your kid tries to sort out your problems? That is singlehandedly the cutest thing ever.

"Tate," I say, giving his shoulder a reassuring squeeze. "It's nothing, I promise."

Although, all things considered, out of the two of us he is the one with a long-term girlfriend-turned-fiancée. Three years apart and he still managed to get his chick back, and now he's got a rock on her finger blinding every dude who lays his eyes on her. Maybe I *should* ask him for advice.

I decide that that's a bad idea as I unlock the cabin that we're focusing on this morning. Tate's intentions are pure but I don't want to be inappropriate. Instead I pull out my phone and shoot a text off to my brother, telling him that I might need to give him a dial in a bit.

The crew all arrive and we settle back into the grind but my mind remains distracted at how quiet it is up at those bungalows.

During her first week here Harper was a little nightmare, 'overseeing' the site like a spoiled princess. But now that we've sort of… gotten used to each other, sometimes I get a smile, sometimes I get a wave. One morning she even opened the window and offered me breakfast.

But if I step foot in that bungalow there's only one thing that I'm gonna be eating.

I wipe my hand down my jaw. Fuck it. I need to see that she's alright.

I'm five paces out of the cabin door when I feel my cell vibrate in my pocket. Clenching my jaw to hold back a groan, I pull the phone out of my cargos and hit the answer button.

"Yeah, it's Coleson," I say curtly, eyes trained up on Harper's unmoved curtains. *What is happening inside that bungalow?*

I hear a snicker in the speaker. "Stole my line, man."

I shift the cell from one ear to another, suddenly apprehensive about this call with my brother. I need him to keep me on the straight and narrow, to prevent me from doing anything unprofessional.

I take a deep breath and bite the bullet.

"We need to talk about the chick."

"Fucking finally," he agrees.

I wait him out, hoping for a little advice. Then I realise that he's also waiting *me* out, thinking that he's about to get an update.

"Oh Jesus," he grumbles. I can almost see him rolling his eyes. "Don't tell me that you've been pining for three weeks without making a move."

"That's exactly what I've been doing, and that's exactly what I need to *keep* doing. I'm calling you so that you can punch some sense into me. Get my mind off of..." *The thought of her soft thighs locking tight around my hips, her back arching high off of the mattress. Her nails scoring red lines down my skin and those perky curves bouncing fast with every thrust.*

My silence doesn't go unnoticed. He breathes out an exasperated exhalation and half-scolds me, "Are you messing with me right now? The second that I saw that woman I knew that you were gonna be all over that. Get your head out of your ass and put yourself out there. What's the worst that can happen? Her saying 'no'?"

"What about getting charged with sexual harassment in a workplace?"

"A workplace that she doesn't have the paperwork to legally be at," he interjects.

Wait, what? I try to think back to when I gave her that first briefing in my office. Did she say that she had the docs to be here? I can't fucking remember. The only coherent memories I have of that morning involve red lace tangled over my digits and her panties poking out above the waistband of her jeans.

I shake my head. *Get back on track.*

"Or losing my job because I was hired by her *mom.*" I grip a fist in my hair. "Jesus Christ. She's almost young enough to be my kid."

"Only if you had a kid at, like, eighteen," he says consolingly.

I give him a long pause to think about what he just said. Then I grit out through my teeth, "Which I *did.*"

Okay, so she's not actually young enough to be my kid. But an age gap over ten years seems steep to me. She's twenty-eight. I'm pushing forty. Generationally we are worlds apart. I'm from the last group of guys that wants to court a woman before they bed her. Whereas she… God, just thinking about it makes a hot flame lap at the muscles swelling in my abdomen.

She's from a new generation, the type where sex comes first and thoughts about whether or not they want a relationship comes after. And that is not an arrangement that would work with me.

If it got to the point where I had her moaning on

my sheets I know for a fact that I wouldn't ever be letting her go.

"This is what I think," Jace says, after giving me the ten seconds that I needed to calm the hell down. "Is she on-site right now?" he asks.

"Yeah. She's in her... bungalow."

"Okay, perfect. Go over there, knock on her door, and then gauge how she seems when she opens it up. If she seems pleased to see you, come out with it straight. Tell her you wanna date her and see how she responds. On the flip side, if she doesn't seem happy to see you just tell her how far along you are with the reno and get the hell out of there. Find someone else to fill up your evenings. Well, someone else to fill *up* in your evenings."

"Watch it," I warn him.

"How old is she, anyway?" he asks.

"Twenty-eight."

He whistles. Then regrets it.

"That ain't too bad, man. Besides," he adds, "if you don't date her someone else will."

He's right and we both know it. I disconnect the call and take a long hard look at Harper's bungalow, promising myself that the second I finish up this evening I'm heading straight over there, consequences be damned.

*

I wait for the crew to drive off the site before I finally head up to Harper's bungalow, raise my fist, and knock on the wood.

I rap it three times.

Nothing but silence.

I take a step back so that I can glance at her windows again. Curtains are still drawn but I swear I can see a little bit of lamp glow in there.

I give the door another light pounding.

This time, there's movement.

I hear the bedroom door open and light steps stop on the other side of the wood. For the briefest of moments I think that she has knocked back, and I have to compose myself to fight off a smile.

Then I catch a tiny, "Who is it?"

Why's she being so quiet today? I feel an ache grip at my chest.

"It's me, Harper. It's Mitch." When the silence stretches on I say, "Noticed you stayed in today and I wanted to make sure that everything was alright."

I'm about to apologise for overstepping a boundary and turn back around to leave when the lock clicks and the door opens a millimetre. At first my heart catches in my throat, but then my brow starts creasing when the picture pulls together more completely.

I'm met with big round eyes, staring up at me through long pretty lashes, whilst she twiddles incessantly with her slender fingers. Her hair is stacked into a messy bun, little golden curls brushing against her forehead, and she's wearing an oversized white shirt and fuzzy pop socks. My first thought is *imagine coming home to this every night.* She's beautiful. But then I start to see the finer details and the frown fully settles on my brow.

She looks really pale, and her eyes are underscored with dark purple bruises, like she hasn't slept in the last twenty-four hours. There's a glittering sheen of sweat on her brow and her exposed forearms are shivering. She opens the door a fraction wider and makes a woeful sound as she leans against the framework.

I want to get in there with her and pull her into my arms, but instead I grip my fingers around the doorframe and ask as gently as I can manage, "Harper, what is it? What's wrong?"

"I–" She stops abruptly, eyes going wide as her body jolts.

Holy shit, is she going to be sick?

I am literally desperate to get my feet over this threshold but I keep it together and ask her again, "What's wrong, Harper? Tell me."

She winces hard and clutches at her belly, her shoulder pressed tensely against the wood. "I think..." She swallows and another convulsion rolls through her. "I think that I might have food poisoning."

My eyes fly straight over to the kitchen at the back, clocking an unwashed plate next to the sink as my mind flicks back to what she bought at the supermarket yesterday. *Seafood.* I mean, how could I fucking forget. She said that she was trying to eat more meat, implying that she's not used to cooking it, which means that there's every possibility that she didn't know *how* to cook it.

Goddamn. I run a hand down my face and try to think of what to do.

The site's empty which means that I could stay here to look after her tonight and no-one would know that I've essentially just shacked up with the boss's daughter. But we're going to need on-hand Dioralytes and sick buckets, none of which I'd bet she has stocked up in that small wooden cupboard.

She must sense what I'm doing because she shakes her head quickly before turning her back to me and making a little retching sound. When she faces me again cartoon birds are spinning around her curly bun.

"I'll be fine," she shivers. "I self-medicated."

Huh? My frown intensifies. "With what?"

When she remains stoically silent I peer behind her again, checking for a glass of water that's nowhere to be found. But you know what I do find?

"Is that a bottle of champagne?" I'm almost growling. Is she fucking serious?

Suddenly she's heaving again and then she's scampering like lightning into the bathroom. She leaves the door wide open in her haste and I watch her tremble and shiver over the sink.

Can I let myself in? This is a mitigating circumstance, right?

"Harper, I'm coming in," I say, one boot lifting to breach that threshold.

"Don't you dare," she whimpers, looking up at me through the mirror in front of her. My eyes stray to the backs of her legs as her knees wobble and quiver.

I should be standing behind her right now, holding her hair back with one hand and stroking her belly with the other. Passing her a glass of water to keep her fluids up before cradling her against my chest and taking her back to bed.

"Food poisoning only lasts a couple days but it'll go faster if you get the treatment that you need. Water, Dioralytes, rest." I check them off on my fingers. "Let me take care of you."

She gives me a sad pout. "Just let me die."

"Ah shit," I mutter, looking over my shoulder so

that I can see my truck across the site. I hear her rinse out the sink and I turn my attention back to her. "You don't have anyone nearby?" I ask, knowing damn well what her answer is going to be.

She shakes her head.

I take a deep breath. So this isn't exactly what I expected to happen when I knocked on her door two minutes ago, especially after Jason gave me that pep-talk about asking her on a date. Actually, this is kind of the antithesis of a date. But I don't mind. I want her to be safe and well and if I can give those things to her then so be it.

"I'm going to suggest something right now and you can say no if you think that it's..." I roll my shoulders, looking for the right word. "Inappropriate, or unprofessional. But if you'd like, I can... I could bring you to my place, to look after you until this passes. Or I could even, uh, I could even stay next door." I would camp out in the fucking woods if she asked me to. "I don't want you choking on your vomit or anything. I just want you to get better."

I swallow and straighten up, eyes locking in with hers. She's leaning against the sink now, legs clenched together and her eyes blinking rapidly. Sweat soaking the neckline of her top. Cheeks glowing raspberry red.

"What do you think?" I ask her, steeling myself for an eye-roll and a door being slammed in my face.

But instead she quivers on the spot and then gives me a little nod. I almost growl with satisfaction.

"Is that a yes?" I ask. "You're gonna let me look after you?"

Her brow is pinched in pain and she holds her hands tighter around the sink. "Yeah," she whispers.

"But can we please hurry? I think I'm gonna be sick again."

"I'm going to grab my truck and haul it up here – save you from walking all the way down the valley, okay?" I ask.

She nods, eyes closed.

Fuck it, I'm coming in. I head for her bedroom and rip the quilt off the bed, but as I carry it to where she's slowly sinking to the floor I realise that it's soaked with sweat. *Why didn't she call me? I told her to come to me if she needed anything.* I throw the quilt down and she crumples onto it facedown, scrunching the cotton under her belly in tight little fists. I notice that her toy bear was hurled during the upheaval so I pick it up, give it a scowl, and then toss it down next to her. One of her hands reaches out and she stashes it under her tits.

I tug my belt buckle as my shaft thickens in my boxers. I'm wanting, badly, but this sure as hell is not the time for it.

I tell the back of her head, "Give me two minutes, Harper," and then I'm heading back down the incline, ready to get this girl taken care of.

CHAPTER 9

Harper

It takes Mitch five billion years to get his truck from the bottom of the valley to the bungalows. The sounds of twigs cracking and the metallic wane of the gate to the Nature Trail being opened mix in with the autumnal rustling of the surrounding pine trees. He brings his truck off-road and parks it not more than six feet away from the door, eyes burning into my back as his door slams shut and his boots thud into my empty living room.

I feel the air shift and grow warmer as he crouches down in front of me. Heat tingles down my back, quickly followed by another wave of nausea.

"Truck's up, Harper. Do you want me to give you a hand?"

"Not exactly the appendage that I'm after," I mumble, muffling my words into the quilt so that he can't hear me. Then I lift my head an inch and a throb pulses in my belly. My face is completely level with his groin.

"There's a bucket on the floor in the passenger side and we'll keep the windows rolled down."

He holds out a hand for me to pull myself up with and I study it like a foreign object. It's large and tan with the tendons extended from his unending shifts of manual labour. He watches my perusal and a shadow crosses over his features, hardening them in the dimming light.

I flatten my palms under my belly and heave myself up, groaning as the blood rushes erratically from my head. He pulls a pained face as he watches me and he lifts himself in time with my movements, hands hovering nearby in case I decide that I do need him to steady me.

Which I do. So badly. But I don't want to finally indulge in this runaway-vacation post-break-up fling and then, part way through, cut it short because I'm about to vomit.

He walks beside me as I make my way to his vehicle, his eyes wary as he debates with himself about whether or not he should be holding me upright. I don't even put a pair of shoes on. My fuzzy socks are sacrificed in exchange for the prospect of more water, rest, and *sleeping in Mitch's house*. I tuck the seatbelt between my breasts and he watches me silently, chest rising and falling in heavy pumps as his hand grips the roof above my head. I slot in the lock and tuck my knees under my chin. Then I look back at the still-open bungalow door and spot something.

Mitch can tell.

"What is it?" he asks. His voice is huskier than before and when I glance up at him I can see that heated thoughts are flickering behind his irises.

I stare intently at a spot in the living area. "You're forgetting someone," I murmur.

He turns to glance at the bungalow. Then he shoots me an irate look. "You're kidding."

I make a sorrowful sigh.

One minute later Mitch has locked up the bungalow, I've got my teddy bear in my lap, and he's driving through the forest like he's got a pregnant woman in his passenger seat. Every branch that we crunch over has his eyes flying my way, checking that I'm not about to heave. When the air streaming through the window laps at my cheeks I shiver unconsciously and he leans over me to roll it higher up.

He smells so good that I think I audibly moan. He misreads the sound as one of anguish and he says to me in a deep gentle voice, "Give it fifteen minutes, Harper. Fifteen minutes and I'll be taking care of you."

My stomach makes another vicious contraction and I squeeze my thighs flush against it, aching everywhere. The only balm to my pain is the sight and the scent of him. I imagine that if he pulled over, got me in the back and pushed inside of me, he would have just found nature's cure for food poisoning.

"Did you really drink champagne to try and alleviate the symptoms of food poisoning?" he asks suddenly, his brow furrowed and his voice a low scrape.

I narrow my eyes on him, wounded and defensive. It almost distracts me from the sloshing sensation in my brain. "Yes. Did you really give me four hundred dollars to pay for my shopping in the grocery store?"

Now it's his turn to look uncomfortable. He scratches roughly at his stubble as his cheeks stain crimson. "You needed money for a cab, too," he says quietly. Then with more bite he adds, "And I told you to fill up that basket. I didn't want you going hungry, Harper."

"And I told *you* that I was going to run back to Pine Hills to get my purse. I'm not a charity case and – before you start making assumptions – I pay my own bills with the money that I made. Okay, my mom put me through college, but I paid her back the second that I could. I'm not a helpless mess."

This last line is followed by a sudden full-body shiver and then a series of painful heaves over Mitch's bucket.

"And I didn't spend it," I add, sliding my eyes over to him with a defensive scowl. "I kept it on the counter in the kitchen. I just forgot about it when all the dizziness happened."

"I bet the champagne helped," he deadpans, as if I'm not *this* close to tossing the bucket on him.

"I'm from LA," I say, angry enough to semi-shout despite the ringing happening in my ears. "We aren't exactly renowned for sensible behaviour."

You know what really isn't normal to me? Being taken care of when something bad actually happens. It's not as if anyone from my hometown came looking to check up on me when I fled my now-ex fiancé. My now-ex fiancé who I helped to get cast in the movie that *I wrote*.

If I asked him, I wonder if Mitch would help me

bury a body.

I look over to him and realise that the car has stopped. He's pulled up onto a wide driveway with a cute porch to the left and a large garage to the right. Curiosity wins out over the need to stop throwing up so I tentatively turn in my seat so that I can look out the back and scope the neighbours' houses. Their porches are all glowing with sconce lights, and jack-o-lanterns are lining their steps. I twist back to look at Mitch's and see that he hasn't decorated for Halloween.

"You don't like the holidays?" I ask, watching his jaw muscles tighten and relax. He unfastens his seatbelt and silently gets out of the truck, rounding to my side and then holding the door open for me.

"I told you before – I haven't been back here for a while. I've been living closer to the site." Reiterating this confession makes him blush for some reason.

When he directs those penetrating eyes on me again I suddenly remember what I'm holding and I try to hide the bucket from him.

"Pass the bucket, Harper. I promise I won't look."

I frown deep and my throat constricts, my stomach preparing me for another onslaught.

"Yes you will," I murmur, horrified. I'm touching base with delirium and the champagne in my bloodstream isn't helping. Pin-pricks begin stabbing behind my eyes and my oesophagus tightens as if I'm about to cry.

He regards me with consoling patience, eyes thoroughly assessing, and then he nods his head and opens the door wider. "Okay, Harper, that's fine. Just leave the bucket next to the truck and we can deal with it later."

I know that he's lying but I do it anyway, placing it carefully just outside of the vehicle before stepping out on wobbly legs. The autumn pinch in the air makes me wrap my arms over my chest. A second later I feel a warm unzipped jumper drape snugly over my shoulders, and then Mitch is directing me up the porch steps as he slips his keys from his pocket.

Once he's got the door open and me inside he's on an immediate mission for warmth and light, turning on heaters and lamps when I'm barely past the threshold. Whilst he's got his back to me I nuzzle my nose into the collar of his jumper and the scent of his skin obliterates the last iota of common sense from my mind.

I follow him into the kitchen which is set to the right of the entryway and he immediately fills up a glass with water, handing it to me and watching me drink the whole thing. I pull an expression of distaste when I finally finish it and he makes an apologetic face in return.

"We have to flush it out, Harper, I'm sorry," he says as he turns slightly so that he can fill up the kettle. When he sets it to boil he gestures that we should leave the room and I tag behind him like a stray. "I would give you a tour but now probably isn't the best time," he murmurs, something like regret lacing his tone.

I shake my head and try not to vomit in my mouth. "Just show me where you keep the shovels and I'll let the earth reclaim my body."

He gives me a withering look and then jerks his chin at the stairwell. I cling to the banister and drag myself upwards. "That's not funny," he grumbles. "I don't want you saying things like that. I want you to get hydrated, rested, and then–"

"And then you want me to get the hell out of here, I know, I know."

At the top of the stairs he stops next to me, looking down into my eyes with a harsh crease on his brow. "I wasn't going to say that at all, Harper. I…" He shakes his head, runs his hand down his jaw. "I wouldn't have offered you to stay here if I didn't *want* you here."

"Because I'm the boss's daughter." I say it like a fact, eyes sharp on his own.

He narrows his gaze in return and reaches behind me to hold onto the ball at the top of the banister. The combination of his warm skin and the traces of his cologne make my eyes slow-blink and my knees wobble. He gives me a hard look before he leans in a little closer and tells me, "That's one of the reasons why you *shouldn't* be here."

Then suddenly we're walking again but my mind is still levitating at the top of the staircase.

"What do you mean?" I ask petulantly. "What are the other reasons?"

He pulls open the door to one of the rooms and my heart jolts in my chest.

This is a man's bedroom. This is not a room that is shared with a woman – there are no touches of prettiness or femininity. It's dark and seductive, all brown and navy. My eyes are unable to move away from the king sized bed pressed up against the wall, covered in a plumped up quilt and a haphazardly discarded navy comforter.

"Why are we in here?" The words come out of me

in a hoarse whisper.

"I thought…" He clears his throat and then tries again. "I thought that you could sleep in here. I wouldn't have you on the couch, and the room upstairs isn't technically…" He trails off, not finishing the thought, leaving me unsure.

"I should sleep on the couch." I say it firmly, so that maybe one of us will believe it. Then I'm pressing the back of my hand against my mouth and keeling over on the threshold.

Five seconds later Mitch is back with another bucket, ushering me over to the bed with the basin held out in front of me. He risks a glance at the centimetre gap between my knees and his bed and rasps out, "I can change the sheets first."

He could but I don't want him to, so I give in to the need to slide my knees onto the mattress, kneading the softness with my hands and splaying my thighs out slightly. I hear his breathing catch behind me so I turn around to look at him, settling in on my butt. Then I fall face-first on his mattress and his quilt bulges up around me.

When I see that he's still watching me, a restrained expression on his face, I say, voice gravelly, "It's almost exactly what I expected."

His cheek ticks up for a split second. My heart racketeers in my chest.

"Almost?" he asks, clicking on a bedside lamp and illuminating the room in a campfire glow.

"I was backing a mirror on the ceiling," I whisper.

He laughs, loud and bright, and for the briefest moment I see a flash of his full undisguised smile. Those perfect white teeth against his deep bronze tan, twin creases in his cheeks and an amused sparkle in his eyes.

"Okay," he laughs, turning his face slightly so that I can't get the full whack of the smile he's trying to tamper down. "I'm gonna bring you water and an electrolyte tablet, and then I'll leave you until you need me. The bathroom is next door" – he gestures at the wall facing the bed – "and I'll be up as soon as you need anything. Just shout for me, or knock on the wall or something."

"Are you a light sleeper?" I ask quietly, turning on my side and cuddling his quilt up between my thighs and against my chest.

His eyes linger there momentarily, and his face loses the light-heartedness that was colouring his features only a second ago. Then he says, "I'm not going to sleep yet. It's only seven, Harper."

Time is not a concept to me in Mitch's sexy bedroom. All that I see is navy softness surrounded by deep brown furniture, all of which I'm pretty sure he made with his own two hands. Every available surface is hard polished wood and the only light amidst the darkness are his sharp diamond eyes.

I'm sweating and shivering on his beautiful cotton quilt and the only concern on his face is that I get well soon. He doesn't care that I literally vomited for half of the car journey and he's gotten over the fact that when I first met him I was a pain in the ass. For a second I consider telling him everything – why I came to Pine Hills and how infatuated I have become with him – but then I'm hit with a deep cramp and he's out of the room, storming down the stairs so that he can grab me a glass of water as quickly as possible.

When he comes back I sit up on one elbow and sip tentatively at the glass that he hands me. I notice that all three buttons at the top of his *Coleson Joinery* shirt are now undone, an extra inch of deep tan skin now exposed in the dark navy V. He's winding down after a hard day's work, but he's still managed to fit me into his busy schedule. I snuggle down into that luxurious thought and finish up my water.

"So if I call your name you'll come?" I ask him politely.

He gives me a long look, his jaw working overtime. "I'm here to help you with anything you need," is what he manages to say, gruff and tense.

Oh, but what about your *needs, Mitch?*

I choose to change the subject, mostly because I'm now seeing two of him and my thoughts have become so outrageous that I'm scandalising my own psyche.

"I'm sorry for, like, everything, by the way," I say quietly. Embarrassment mixed with food poisoning is one hell of a depressant. "For the mood swings that I came here with, and for the stuff that I say literally all the time – for someone who has spent the past seven years writing you would think that I'd learned a thing or two about communication. But the reality of the matter is that it's the most isolated job in the world."

A look of perplexity crosses his face. "You're a writer?" he asks, a crease deepening against his brow.

I forgot how little I have actually told him about myself. All he knows is that I'm a spoiled princess from LA – how the hell has he tolerated me these past three weeks?

I shake my head because this conversation is not for right now. "It doesn't matter," I mumble, tightening my grip on his quilt as my shaking begins to mercifully subside. "I'm just sorry, okay?"

Compassion sparkles in his eyes. I wish I could pull him down here with me.

"You don't need to apologise for anything. Just get better for me, Harper."

My chest squeezes, warm and tight. I'm not used to this hands-on care and it's making my body react in the most painful ways. I clench my legs tighter and he takes a big step back.

"Don't go truffle-pigging in those drawers whilst I'm gone," he warns me, mock-stern, a thick finger pointing at the small bespoke cabinet beside my head.

I bite into my bottom lip, smiling, and nod my head even though I'm a little liar. The second that he's out of this room I'm going through those drawers like I'm digging for gold in the Outback.

A flicker of an almost-smile touches his cheekbones. Then he gently closes the door.

I'm asleep before my hand reaches the first drawer.

*

The lamp has been turned off when I open my eyes, and from the absence of any streetlight making its way in under the drawn curtains I gather that it must be the middle of the night. I'm stiff, my body is cold with sweat, and my arms feel heavy as I struggle to right myself. If I had woken up ten minutes later I think that I would've ended up having an episode.

My sleep paralysis affects me only rarely but I've worked out that it's triggered when I don't lie in the right position. When I go to sleep on my back I tend to wake up okay, but it's hit and miss. The numbness pervading through my chest and arms makes me shudder involuntarily until my stomach bug is resuscitated, making me lean over and grab the bucket.

After my little retch suddenly last night's adventure hits me like a lorry and I shoot bolt upright because *I'm in Mitch's bedroom.*

I fumble for the lamp switch and then squint when I turn it on. My breathing is laboured and adrenaline is coursing through my body. I'm nervous. Excited. Then my mind wanders to how I would be feeling if Mitch was in here with me right now…

I look back to the cabinet that's housing the light and I see that Mitch brought me another glass of water, setting it on a coaster that I don't remember being there yesterday evening. My wrist feels weak so I lift the glass slowly and take a few small sips.

Then I look at the drawers.

Why would he ask me specifically not to go through his drawers? Okay, other than for obvious privacy reasons. If anything he simply drew my attention to them harder. Now I'm dying to find out what he keeps next to his bed.

I put the glass down and sit on my hands, restraining myself.

One drawer. Just one, I reason with myself.

Hm. Sold.

I lean slightly over the edge of the bed and tuck the drawer knob between my middle and pointer fingers, easing it forwards so that it slides quietly. Just a few inches, then I stop and peer in.

It's empty bar one inconspicuous black box. I can't read it under the shadow cast by the top of the dresser so I gently pick it up and hold it under the lamp.

It's glossy, like the kind of box that an expensive cologne would be in. I flip it over and run my fingers over the small raised text, written in gold script. In the centre is the word *MAGNUM* and then in small font beneath it is the word *Plus*.

I gasp when the words finally penetrate my 3a.m. brain.

MAGNUM? As in the largest condom size that's manufactured in the world? Followed by the word *Plus?!*

I squeeze my thighs together and pant. Is he joking? I scrabble for the lid seal and pull it open, shaking a mass of foil packets out onto the bed in front of me, checking that they are in fact real. I pick one up and hold the large square up to my face, a circular ring punctuating the surface beneath it. This must be part of the food poisoning process – hallucinations. But then I blink down at all of the wrappers between my legs and I'm having a hard time believing that they're just a figment of my imagination. I pick up a handful and let them fall between my fingers. Good God. I'm more than half-tempted to rip one open – I'm not even sure why – but then suddenly I realise that Mitch having condoms next to his bed, in his top drawer no less, means that he's having sex. In this bed. And the thought of that makes me shove all of the evidence back where it came from and stumble off the mattress, clutching my belly and heading straight for the bathroom next door.

Dark images flash behind my eyes as I hurl painfully in his bathroom sink. Another woman lying backwards on his navy comforter as he stands between her thighs. Not an oversized t-shirt or a fluffy bed sock in sight, her hair any colour other than my own. She's in bespoke lingerie and he's shoving his boxers down his quads – thickly muscled and rippling with the need to expend, to release. He pulls open the nightstand and grabs the first wrapper he can reach. She reads the words *MAGNUM Plus* on the foil as he tears it open. He rolls the rubber down his length with nothing but satisfaction on his features. He's never seen her vomit. This moment is nothing but sex in its rawest form.

The sound of a light clicking on downstairs draws me back to reality and I quickly rinse the bowl before another wave washes over me. A tube of toothpaste sits on the side of the sink and I squeeze a streak onto my finger, lick it, then spit. Sweat has trickled into my eyes and it's burning so bad that I'm sobbing quietly, my brows pinched together as I struggle through the painful hysterical embarrassment of this mortifyingly ridiculous moment.

Two hands suddenly reach around my face and scoop the fallen tendrils from around my cheeks, pulling them into a ponytail at the back of my head and holding it securely. I shield myself from his view as I cup water in my hand to rinse my mouth, and then I look up at him in the mirror, backlit by the faintest glow from downstairs.

He's wearing flannel pants and a grey t-shirt that's moulded obscenely to his expansive chest. When he speaks his voice is low early morning gravel, the deepest that I've ever heard it.

"It's okay, Harper. Get it all out."

I bend back over the sink as my stomach contracts

and the movement has me arching directly into his groin. I'm already lightheaded and dehydrated, but the sudden firm press has my body boneless. I moan quietly over the bowl, my hips moving mindlessly against him.

He chokes on his breathing and moves one fist from my hair down to my hip, preventing my grinding.

"No – shit, no." His reprimand is gentle, pained. "You're not feeling well. I'm trying to make you feel better."

I look back up at him through the mirror, his hips positioned strong and steady behind me. His shoulders shield the doorway, blocking most of the light, and his body is so tall that he had to stoop to get under the frame.

"I can think of something that would make me feel better," I mumble.

He lets go of my body and stumbles backwards, shoulders hitting off both sides of the jamb. I turn around to face him and my eyes catch on the bulge beneath his waistband. He notices what I'm seeing and he covers it with both of his hands.

"Shit, I'm sorry," he says, angry and breathless. Then he thinks back on what I just confessed and he heaves out, "That's the champagne talking."

I steel my jaw to try and stop the tremble. A month ago I was engaged and thinking about red carpet events for the movie I wrote. Now I'm single, curdled with food poisoning, and tears are threatening behind my eyes. I swipe at them quickly, brushing away any evidence.

"That won't even be in my system anymore and you know it. You're giving yourself a get-out."

"I'm giving *you* a get-out," he argues back.

"Why?" I demand, incredulous. A guy is turning down a no-strings hook-up? If my head wasn't throbbing I would be shouting at him, but as it is we remain to be having the world's quietest argument.

"Let's not go there, Harper."

"I've seen you watching me when you're on your site and I don't think that I'm so bad at reading people that you don't actually like me. I'm in your house, and you're letting me throw up in your bathroom for Christ's sake. So what's the issue?"

I put my hands on my hips. He glances briefly at my fluffy bed socks.

"Don't think you can control yourself with a hot young thing like me?"

"Yeah. That's exactly the issue. That and the fact that *you have food poisoning.*"

"Fine. If you think that I'm incoherent with illness then I may as well ask anyway. Don't you feel this?" I defiantly keep my chin up despite the spinning in my head, the weakness in my body. "Is there something happening between us or am I really on a roll for the worst luck of all time?"

He closes the gap between us and I shut my mouth tight. "You want honesty? Okay *baby*. When I came over tonight I was going to ask you on a date."

The shock on my face must penetrate the darkness because his mouth curls into something almost resembling a sneer.

"You... I... what?" My voice is nothing but a whisper. After all of my provoking and teasing, I think that ninety-nine percent of me didn't actually believe that he'd reciprocate any romantic interest.

I was going to ask you on a date.

I can't remember the last time that I was asked on a date and, up until a month ago, I was literally engaged.

He licks his bottom lip, hands twitching at his sides. His eyes stray to my chest, covered by the cotton of my shirt, but that doesn't stop him from appraising the curves and points shielded beneath the surface.

Every atom in my body is screaming for him to touch me. He swallows hard and his Adam's apple rolls.

"But that's irrelevant now," he finishes. "We just need to get you better."

He turns ninety-degrees in the doorway and gestures for me to leave the bathroom. When I enter the corridor he walks silently with me until I'm sat upright in the centre of his bed, very dazed and very confused.

He goes to reach for the glass of water when suddenly his gaze catches on something – his top drawer, slightly ajar. His eyes slide over to me, studying me for a moment, until his chest finally heaves and he shoves the drawer shut.

Shit. I swallow and hold my hand out for the glass, trying to distract him from the fact that I just behaved like a truffle pig.

He hands me the water and watches me in silence, the light from downstairs making his shadow eclipse me fully. I'm completely shielded, with *MAGNUM Plus* protection. When I finish the glass he takes it from me and returns half a minute later with it refilled. He sets it on the cabinet but his eyes are on mine. We said way too much tonight, feeling untouchable in the darkness.

Finally he says, "Get some sleep, Harper."

I nod and shuffle backwards on his bed, jolting a little when I feel the wetness from where I've been sweating.

His thumb runs back and forth on the top of the dresser and he watches me with a crease on his brow as I tuck myself under his quilt.

He opens his mouth to speak, stops, then starts again.

"About what just happened in the bathroom…" he begins, his other hand scrubbing at the back of his head.

Which part exactly? I want to ask him. *The part where I told you I wanted you to have me, the part where you told me you wanted to take me on a date, or the part where I rubbed my ass against your supersized hard-on?*

I blink at him innocently.

"It was a heated moment. I shouldn't have said those things." He winces and looks away from me, apologetic and ashamed. "I guess maybe you won't remember any of this in the morning, anyway," he says quietly.

I give him a small smile even though my heart just dropped like a tonne of bricks.

Trust me, Mitch. I will.

CHAPTER 10

Mitch

How the hell do people wear pyjamas? I grip at the neckline of my shirt and tug it away from my neck. Then I think *fuck it* and rip the damned thing off.

Harper is upstairs sleeping on my bed and I'm on the rug in the living room because I'm too big for the sofa. I toss the shirt on the floor next to me and then run both hands back through my hair, trying to mentally suppress the muscle that's thickening in my pants. My body's a compass and it's pointing north. I lean back on my palms and look up at the ceiling, aware that Harper is currently directly above me. I swallow hard, imagining how things would be if the situation right now was different – if she wasn't ill and in need of recovery time, if I hadn't followed up my *I wanna date you* confession with a dumb-ass *I shouldn't have said those things* backtrack. And – fuck – did she really start grinding that beautiful little ass up against me last night? Thank God I had some restraint, because if the opportunity presented itself to me right now, I'm not sure that I could behave so gentlemanly.

I readjust my shaft as I get to my feet and I make my way over to the kitchen. It's Saturday but I'm up at half-five regardless, so I flick the coffee maker to life and grab a mug from the cupboard. Then I head over to the dining room table, open up the paper that I found through the letterbox yesterday evening, kick out my legs, and settle back. By the time that it's seven I've read the news cover to cover and I'm just about to get a breakfast going when I hear the bedroom door click open upstairs. A scuttle, followed by the sound of the bathroom door. Then, thirty seconds later, that door's being gently eased open, like she's trying not to wake me.

I put the bagel down, not wanting the smell to trigger another episode of sickness, and I move to the bottom of the stairs, watching Harper appear on cautious feet. She peeks hesitantly around the banister.

"Good morning," I call up to her, jerking my chin at her to signal that she should come down. Then, after seeing how unsteady she looks, I ask, "You need a hand?"

I'm already mounting the stairs when she shakes her head, but I walk backwards with her anyway, keeping just in front of her in case she stumbles.

"Thanks," she says breathlessly, but she keeps her eyes averted. Her cheeks are flushing pink and she's twiddling non-stop with her fingers.

I frown, trying to work out what's wrong. Then I look down at myself and I realise what the problem is.

We're standing about two inches away from each other, I'm shirtless, she's bottomless, and now all of a sudden she's flustered as hell. Can't deny it, that makes my chest swell with pleasure. *It's 7a.m., a beautiful woman's in my kitchen, and the sight of my naked body is getting her going.*

"Sorry," I manage gruffly. "I'll grab a shirt–"

She shakes her head adamantly. "Don't be silly, it's your home, I'm just… immature around, uh… men like… um, men like…"

My eyebrows raise. *Men like me?*

She turns to the sink and starts running herself a glass of water, and I watch her from behind thinking through everything that I know about her so far. I know where she's from and how polished that type of environment probably is, so maybe this *is* her first time being around a man like me.

She keeps sipping at her drink but she turns her head over her shoulder so that she can look at me, her hair a little matted against her neck from last night's cold sweats. We're back to almost the exact same position that we were in last night, only she seems perkier this morning with a sparkle in her eyes. Her eyes flicker down my torso making me involuntarily flex and still, and I swear she arches back a little, hiding her face behind her shoulder so that I can't see her naughty little smile.

I'm damn well tempted to get my hands around her waist, rub her back until it's nice and warm, and then murmur into her neck that maybe we should finish what we started. But I know that that thought is coming directly from my sac, without an ounce of common sense in sight.

You know what else could be coming from my sac?

I squeeze my hands into fists, trying to alleviate the energy that's getting hotter and faster as it courses through my body. Jesus, bringing her here was a bad idea. Did she really say that I would "make her feel better" if I gave it to her last night? Whilst she's literally ill?

I rub a hand over my mouth, not believing my own brain.

She finishes her drink and then faces me fully, eyes on her socks because the inappropriateness of our actions, *especially* after that surreal 3a.m. champagne fantasy last night, is starting to hit home. I might be the boss at the Pine Hills site but Harper Ray is practically my employer. That would be a legal nightmare as is, but add in the fact that I've got so much riding on keeping Ray Corp sweet and then this is suddenly even more serious. I wouldn't be exactly shocked if it turned out that Harper's mom didn't like the idea of her employees cosying up with her hot twenty-eight year old daughter.

Yeah, fine, I'm dying to ask her out again, but I don't want to cross that line without a direct all-clear.

Restraining the urge, I change the topic completely.

"How're you feeling this morning?" I ask her, and my eyes stray over to the bagels. I don't know about Harper but I sure as hell need to refuel. "Do you think you could handle some plain foods today? Or are we keeping to having just fluids for now?"

"Uh…"

I look down to see her panting up against the sink, eyes raking all over my exposed pecs, and then the swollen muscles of my abs. Damn baby. I can't remember a single instance in my life where I've been so keen for a woman, and if she's not hiding the attraction that's happening here anymore then I'm not going to either.

I step a little closer and watch as her breathing catches in her throat, one hand pulling at a soft blonde curl and the other smoothing out the creases in her top. My eyes slip down her neck and land right on those tits, small and soft under the cotton of her shirt. Her nipples are pebbled into small hard peaks and I rake my teeth over my lip, wanting those gorgeous curves in my mouth this damn second.

But then I notice that her shirt is clinging to her belly, meaning that she's sweat so hard that her top is literally soaked, and it's the slap across the face that I damn well needed. I back up and nod my head at her top. She looks down at it and tries to peel it off her abdomen.

"We need to get you a clean shirt," I say hoarsely. I'm trying to act like a gentleman but the fact of the matter is that I know exactly where this is going. Harper stripping in my bedroom, followed by one of my shirts getting hands-on with her tits. I should be so fucking lucky. "You wanna use one of mine?" I ask. "Or," I swallow hard, "I could drive back to Pine Hills and get some of your stuff. Bring you some tops of your own."

She shakes her head. "You don't need to do that, but thank you. I'd borrow one of yours, if you… if you really don't mind."

I really, *really* don't mind. We walk back upstairs into my bedroom, the sheets still fluffed up from where she left them a couple of minutes ago. Keen to not get distracted I head straight for the drawer where I store my shirts and I pull out whatever's on the top. I unfold it and see that it's one of the work tops that I didn't pack for the motel so I hold it up for her, waiting out a yes or a no.

"Oh, sure, yeah, that's great." She's breathing heavy and I can't tell if it's because of how exerted she is from being sick last night or if it's because she wants my name scraping over her chest as badly as I do.

I place it gently on the bed and then give her a wide berth as I make my way out of the room. I turn slightly and catch her rubbing her thumb over the fabric.

"I'll get another drink ready for you but, uh, come down whenever you're ready. Or just call for me. Either works."

She laughs a little, scrunching her nose. "I've never been so hydrated in my life," she jokes.

My mouth ticks up slightly, giving her almost a half-smile, but then I think about how *dehydrated* she had to have been last night to start offering herself up to me and the smile vanishes as quickly as it came. She must've been out of her mind.

Or *was* she? Because, now that I think about it, she seemed just as interested this morning.

It's the lack of food, I tell myself as I turn and start heading down the stairs. *She's not functioning properly because she doesn't have the right nutrients in her system.*

When I reach the kitchen I slice up a bagel and slot it in the toaster, but my mind is completely distracted. All of my thoughts are upstairs, in my bedroom, where Harper's stripping down with the door still ajar. I swallow and run a hand down the back of my neck.

We're going to have to talk about this – whatever

"this" is. The flirting, the taunting… I need to know what her intentions are, I need to know if she's as into me as I'm into her, and I need to know it yesterday.

I pop up my bagel before it chars, topping it with some spread and wolfing it faster than I should. My eyes flick incessantly up the staircase, wondering if and when Harper's going to show herself. I'm so hungry to see her in my work shirt that I scarf down another bagel.

I'm about to go up there and check on her when there's a knock at the front door. I free the latch, pull it open, and then I'm met with the sight of the neighbourhood's delivery guy giving me a quick wave from halfway down my drive, a small brown box sitting on the welcome mat. I spot the sender's name on the side of the cardboard and my cheek ticks up a little.

I give him a jerk of my chin, and then collect the package and bring it inside.

I get a welcome of my own.

Harper looks up at me from underneath her lashes, my navy shirt hanging loosely on her body to mid-thigh. She told me in the supermarket that she liked the way my uniform looked on me, but I fucking *love* the way it looks on her. The contrast between the dark blue cotton and her soft golden skin is addictively hot – and I'm the only guy in town who's gonna get to see her wearing it.

I realise that I've been standing stock still for the last fifteen seconds, my pupils dialling out as I soak in the sight of her, so I steel my jaw and snap myself out of it, blinking hard away from her and walking over to the counter beside the stove.

I want to tell her how insanely gorgeous she looks, how the way she's wearing my shirt is literally blowing my mind, but I kick myself back in check with a couple of teeth-gritting reminders. Namely, that my job here is to work for her family, not to try it on with their hot young daughter.

"The shirt fits," is all that I manage to rumble out, eyes on the drawer that I've just pulled open as I look for a Stanley knife. When I find it I quickly slash it across the top of the box, piercing the brown tape, and then I toss it back to where it came from and shut the drawer.

I'm about to open the package when I notice how quiet Harper's being. I glance over at her and her eyes are glued on the box in front of me, her brows creased as she reads the cursive *Return To* address on the side of the cardboard. My eyes flick back to River's name and address and I can't help but feel that paternal warmth spread out in my chest.

My son's fiancée was a little headache when I first met her but even then I knew that she was going to be part of our family. She had a spark inside of her that I knew Tate would never stop chasing, and everything seemed right in the world when he finally got a ring on her finger.

That being said, God knows what she's sent me. She's more of a gift-ee than a gift-er, so I'm a little tentative as I tug open the boards and start pulling out the crumpled wads of tissue paper.

When I get to what she's hidden in the centre I shake my head and breathe out a laugh.

It's a small eight-inch pumpkin, painted completely baby pink. *You know me so well*, I think dryly. I pick it out of the box, weighing how small it is in my hand, and then I set it down beside the kettle so that I can snap a photo of it on my phone and send it to her with a *thank you* text. Plus I can show it to Tate when he pulls up to work on Monday because I know that River's little stunts make him snicker.

I squash the cardboard and paper, tossing them into the corner so I can take them to the recycling bin out the back when I next go out there, and then I turn back to Harper.

Her cute pink blush has drained from her face and her eyes are boring dead straight into the pumpkin. I look back down at it, frowning, trying to work out what the issue is. *Is she allergic to pumpkins or something?* When we pulled up last night it kind of seemed like she was into all of the fall décor that my neighbours had going on.

Before I have a chance to ask her what's up she says, "Who... who sent that to you?"

Understanding instantly dawns. She's just seen me open up a parcel from a chick, pull out a present, and then text a photo of it to her – all immediately after probably one of the most vulnerable nights of her life, wherein she's in a town that she doesn't know, staying in a stranger's bedroom, and she was so freaking delirious that she gave him a midnight feast, grinding those perfect little buns all over his fully-erect stiff.

Fucking hell, I'm an asshole.

"Harper, I swear. This is not what it looks like."

She's shaking her head and backing away. "I'm... oh my God, I'm an idiot. I didn't know... I promise, I didn't know that you had a girlfriend. If I'd known, last night I wouldn't have – I wouldn't have–"

Is she thinking about last night? Does she remember what happened?

Was that a conscious non-illness-related action?

"I don't have a girlfriend," I say firmly. Then, "Do you remember what happened last night?"

She ignores my question, blinking fast and no longer backing away. "You... you don't have a girlfriend?"

"No," I say immediately, swiping my hand through the air for emphasis.

She looks sated for a moment but then her eyes bulge. "Tell me if you're married, right now."

I hold up my vacant left hand.

"Some people don't wear a ring," she says, narrowing her eyes.

"I've never been married, Harper. You seen any wedding pics around my house?"

She thinks about that briefly, then twists to glance into my dining room.

"I want to talk about last night," I repeat, eyes dropping to my name on her chest, sitting right above the teasing point of her nipple. What I really want to do is ensure that she's recovering and then show her how *men like me* give it to their woman.

She turns back to me, a red glow on her cheeks. "I don't want to talk about it right now," she admits, her voice soft and quiet. "I feel a lot better today – thanks to you, keeping me hydrated and everything – but I'm still kinda unsteady. And, to be honest, I'm not ready to talk about how freaking insane I've been over the past three weeks. Please know, I'm not usually so unhinged – you just happened to meet me during" – she makes an un-funny laugh – "extreme duress."

Extreme duress? My jaw hardens.

"Who's putting you under extreme duress?" *Give me their name and I'll sort them out, no problem.*

She shakes her head, eyes faraway. "He's not relevant anymore," she says.

He? My brain almost explodes in my freaking skull.

So there's evidently a guy in her life who's causing emotional distress. I drop it for now so that she doesn't get uncomfortable.

"My priority right now is making sure you're feeling better – I don't want to talk about bad stuff either. But I can't deny that, once you're recovered, I do want to talk about what happened last night." I roll my shoulders and decide to go for brutal honesty. "I want to talk about how much I liked it. How much I'm liking right now, with you in my kitchen, wearing my shirt." *How much I'm liking you up against my counter, eye-fucking my bare chest. You millimetres away from me, squeezing your thighs together to relieve that ache.*

Her eyelids grow heavy and her head tilts back a bit, like she doesn't have the strength to keep upright anymore. "Okay," she murmurs, fingers fumbling with the bottom of her shirt. "When I'm better we can…"

I nod at her, arms rigid at my sides in an attempt to keep my hands to myself. *Keep this clean, Coleson.* I try to realign my thoughts with the here and now.

"Water and then back to bed?" I ask her, somehow managing to not suggest getting in there with her and holding her until she's asleep.

She nods up at me so I walk her upstairs. I stop outside of my bedroom doorway, but I know it in my bones that she wants me in there with her too.

*

At 6a.m. on Monday morning I'm shoving my feet into my work boots whilst Harper slips her long legs into a pair of wellies. I stop what I'm doing so that I can watch her, dazzled by how lithe, how feminine, she is. She needed something to put on her feet to prevent those fluffy socks getting irreparably dirty because it pissed down last night and the driveway is fully slick, so rain boots seemed like the most appropriate call.

That makes them the only appropriate thing to happen this weekend.

Getting Harper well again consisted of her snuggling down in my sheets on Saturday, followed by her snuggling into my sofa on Sunday, whilst I made her various plain soups to try and get her belly full again. After all the sickness passed it could've technically been one hell of a romantic weekend, but I kept my hands as far away from her as possible, busying myself in the workshop whilst she worked her way through my entire DVD collection.

It gave me thinking time too, which is why when she looks up at me now wearing my work shirt, my boots, and *no damn bra* I pass her a jacket to put on and rumble out, "I had a thought."

She slides her arms into the sleeves, looking up at me as she adjusts the collar and then fastens the zip, leaving nothing but those smooth thighs on show. God, she's sexy. Add on that sore-throated recovery rasp and it's no wonder that she's had my pipe throbbing all weekend.

"Yeah?" she asks, tucking her hands into the

pockets. Then she frowns and removes her fingers, pulling out a receipt, ten tonnes of keys, and a fat wad of cash. She raises her eyebrows and gives me a look that reads *uh…?*

I hold out my hand and she passes me all of the crap that she just found.

"Yeah," I tell her, tossing the receipt aside and putting the keys and cash in my cargos.

I'm hesitant to tell her about what's been playing on my mind because I'm still not entirely sure about where we're at or how she feels. But I want to hear her opinions so I suck it up and come out with it.

"I was thinking about the bungalows on the site, and how I've been staying in a motel, and how you came up here this weekend because there was no-one on hand to look after you. Not that you need looking after," I add on, quickly. "Just that it's better to have someone with you when you're unwell. Not 'you' specifically! It's the same for everyone."

Jesus Christ. I scratch at my forehead, hoping that this is making some kind of sense to her.

"What I'm trying to say is that if I'm not staying here during the reno then maybe I could occupy the vacant bungalow next door to yours. If something was to happen on the site" – *or to you* – "then I'd be right there, no travel time." I pull a jacket off the rack for myself and sling it over my forearm, looking down at her now to gauge her reaction.

She's being unusually impassive. I narrow my eyes.

"So," I finish up slowly, "how does that sound to you?"

She tucks her hands back inside the coat pockets and her eyes flash briefly over to the kitchen – or, more specifically, to River's pumpkin. I tug at my lip, knowing that there's a lot of stuff I haven't told Harper about myself yet.

She breathes out a shaky breath and then looks up at me, her eyes big and bright.

She's been ill all weekend and she still looks beautiful.

"You wanna move into the bungalow next door to mine?" she asks.

"Yeah," I tell her, shoving my hands deep in my cargos.

"So we'd be neighbours until you finish the reno," she continues.

I swallow and nod. "Yes."

She watches me cautiously. I think I'm about to sweat. Then a small smile appears on her pretty mouth and she says tauntingly, "Well, I guess that would make it a lot easier for us to have that conversation that you've been dying to have with me."

I grunt and nod. Yeah, it *will* make it easier to find a moment to tell her how much I want to get her on a date.

And it could facilitate a hell of a lot of other stuff too.

"That a yes?" I ask her, trying to ignore that naughty glint in her eyes. *Not yet, baby. Let me wine and dine you first.*

She turns her smile up to full-watt. "Yes," she says, and then she brushes her body right past me, pressing firm and deliberate to rile me up.

She opens up the door and I turn around to step out with her, but then we both stop in our tracks.

Great.

It's less than a week until Halloween so it's no

wonder that it's chucking it down.

I take my trucker hat off the rack and place it gently on her head. She looks up at me with those big beautiful eyes and I look back down at her, giving her an almost-smile.

Then we hightail it to the truck and head back to Pine Hills.

CHAPTER 11

Harper

The wall between our bungalows is thin.

Our bedrooms are situated headboard to headboard and every groan of Mitch's mattress has me clutching at my sheets. Every time he pads to the bathroom and twists on the shower, I know about it. And Mitch takes *really* long showers.

I'd wrongly assumed that having Mitch next door would facilitate and enable my interest in getting to know him, but it turns out that it's had the opposite effect. Since we got back to Pine Hills and Mitch relocated from the motel to the bungalow next door, all that it's enabled is Mitch working overtime. Instead of finishing up at the site at 6p.m. at the latest Mitch is in his office until at least half seven, and then he's pulling out of the site so that he can buy groceries in town. Admittedly, Mitch being next door has lead to

Mitch bringing me dinner every evening, most likely in an attempt to prevent me furthering my adventures with food poisoning, but when I offer him to come inside and eat with me he's all red cheeks and heavy breathing. It makes me unsure about whether he's feeding me because he likes me or because he thinks that I'm incapable.

Maybe both.

But by the start of November I've stressed so hard that I now fully believe that Mitch's decision to move in next door had nothing to do with getting closer to me and everything to do with finishing up the reno ahead of schedule. It doesn't matter that when we were at his place he told me that he wanted to take me on a date – in fact, I was so out of it that I can't be sure that I didn't hallucinate the whole thing.

The final nail in the coffin for my withering confidence is a call from my mom on her lunch break, gently urging me to head back to LA ahead of my movie's upcoming press tour.

It's 5p.m. and I'm sat cross-legged on the roof, watching Mitch and his guys as they finish hauling in the bespoke furniture my mom commissioned for the cabin bedrooms, joking together as they pick up cabinets and panels like they weigh nothing more than a marshmallow.

I clutch the phone tighter in my right hand, my left hand pressing against the ache in my chest.

"I can't come back, mom. Not right now." I sound like I'm pleading even though this argument has nothing to do with her. Of course I don't want to face Evan and, in this context, it would be even more humiliating.

"You wrote the damn movie, Harper. Why are you letting him win? He doesn't have half as much right to be there than you do."

"Does your other daughter know that you're talking about Evan like this?" I ask her, aiming for a low blow because I know that she's right. I should be there, but instead I'm acting like I don't exist and letting Evan take all of the limelight. I've been writing movies for a long time and I've always loved falling in love with each new character, but after what happened with this last one, it really sucker-punched the passion out of me.

"Holly did a shitty thing, Harper, I know. But there's nothing that we can do to align other people with our own moral compass. Most people are inherently selfish, and last month you got a master-class in that. It's shocking and it's upsetting, but I promise you that seeing their true colours now will be so much better for you in the long run." She deliberates for a moment and then tacks on, "Honestly, thank fuck that spoiled little prince is finally out of your life. I never understood what you saw in him anyway, Harper."

"I bet you haven't said that to—"

"No, you're right, I haven't said that to her, Harper. But it's not because I'm hiding the truth from her. It's because they're the perfect narcissistic match."

There's a finality to her tone that stops me from arguing back. I take a deep inhalation, allowing the oxygen to refresh my body and my mind, and then I breathe back out, closing my eyes.

"You're right," I say, nodding. "I know you are. But I think that I'm better off staying in Pine Hills for a bit, and just missing the press tour. I... I really don't want to see him."

"Why not? Maybe the time apart will have given you a new perspective that you didn't see coming." I hear tapping on a keyboard and then she says, "How's your handyman, by the way? Don't think that I've forgotten."

I open my eyes and look out down the valley, where Mitch is leaning against one of the cabin railings whilst one of his crew lights up a cigarette beside him. I feel a sparkle in my chest when I realise that his eyes are already on mine.

When I forget to formulate words my mom says, "In case you were wondering, I've narrowed down the selection to the ones that I think you'd go for." Then she mumbles, "I know who I'd be going for."

"How's dad?" I ask her sharply.

She laughs. More key tapping. "If you're staying in hiding then you may at least have some fun. Please."

I do some rapid blinking, trying to work out if that was thoughtful or weird.

"LA is messing you up," I say to her. Mitch's thumbs are now tucked behind his belt, his rippling forearms on full display.

"Don't I know it," she mutters back. The line crackles as she moves the phone from one ear to the other. "You know what, maybe you were right in leaving for a while. Has the change of scenery given you any creative inspiration?"

I get to my feet on shaky legs, my eyes blacking out as I look at my source of inspiration.

"It's been..."

Mitch cocks his chin at me from across the site and

the pool in my belly is suddenly throbbing.

"I've got to go," I say quickly, and I can almost hear her eyebrow raise through the line. I'm stepping backwards towards the latch, my head feeling heavy as I watch him watch me. "I'll call you tomorrow, mom – bye."

I hang up before she's finished talking, my feet already racing down the steps, slipping into my flip-flops, and then out of the front door, chest rising and falling in double-time as I make my way down to the cabins.

When he sees me approaching Mitch pushes himself off the railing and starts heading towards me, his friend looking at us curiously with an amused glint in his eyes.

"Hey," he says as he stops a few inches away from me. I'm eye-level with his chest and feeling very lightheaded.

"Hey," I breathe back, my voice the ghost of itself.

He gives me a brief once-over. *Fuzzy jumper, denim shorts, flip-flops.* I try not to pass out.

"It's been a busy week," he admits, running his hand across his forehead. "Sorry I've been AWOL."

I tear my eyes away from the thick column of his throat and move them upwards to meet his icy gaze, gorgeously striking against his tan skin.

"That's okay," I say.

I don't know what's going on anyway so don't worry about it, is what I don't say.

He's watching me intently, jaw flexing as he decides how to take it from here. I lace my hands behind my back so that I can fidget. His eyes narrow as he follows the movement.

It was the incentive that he needed.

"I want to take you out tonight, Harper," he says, and my heart hitches in my chest. He watches me cautiously, both of our cheeks beginning to blush. "I wanna, um… I wanna take you to one of the places in town. There's a couple nice restaurants, cafés, and, um, there's a country bar too–"

"A country bar?" I ask, intrigued.

He pauses, his brow furrowing a little. "Yeah, there's a country bar," he says slowly, "but I was thinking that a restaurant might be more–"

"I've never been to a country bar before," I admit, and my mind begins concocting images of Mitch swapping his uniform for a pair of denim jeans and a tight-fitting shirt, muscles bulging beneath the cotton as he dons himself a cowboy hat.

"Uh," he says, laughing slightly and shifting his bodyweight. "You, uh… you want to go to a country bar?" He gives me a prolonged look. "Instead of a restaurant?"

"I mean…" I toe my flip-flop back and forth in the grass. My silence screams *YES*. He hears it.

"Okay, yeah, sure. We can go to the country bar tonight. If that's what you'd prefer," he adds on, eyes burning into mine. I think that he's trying to get me to change my mind but I've never been able to indulge in small town novelties before, what with never living in a small town. I want the full-blown IMAX experience.

I glance over to the guy on the railings, his eyes still trained on us, and I give him an eyebrow raise. *Look away, Smokey.* After he chuckles and turns to give us some privacy I look back up at Mitch, a warm sensation spreading in my chest. I love that he's willing to compromise, to facilitate whatever he thinks will make me the happiest.

I watch him work the muscles in his throat as he waits for me to give him the green light, stoic and patient even when he's still on the clock. I give him my best girl-next-door smile and his eyes drop to my lips, colour flushing up his neck. His chest swells even larger.

I decide to toy with him a little. "Let me just check my diary," I say, holding up my pointer finger and flipping open my notebook.

His eyes dip down to the pages as I flick through page after page of nothing but delirious plot concepts handwritten in size 0.4 font, because he actually thinks that I'm being serious – he actually thinks that I'm checking my diary. It's so adorable that I have to bite back a smile and I tuck the book back into my pocket because I can't take it anymore.

"Looks like I *might* be able to squeeze you in," I say, unable to stop myself from smiling up at him.

He grunts and nods, then jerks his head towards the bungalows. "Collect you at seven?" he asks, his voice low and brusque.

I think for a moment, then ask, "What do I wear to a country bar?"

He's about to answer me but he abruptly pauses, followed by his eyes slow-dripping down my torso and lingering on my bare legs.

"Layers," he says gruffly. "Lots of layers. It's probably gonna be cold tonight. I can give you a jacket."

I try to restrain the golden sunshine feeling in my chest, but the knowledge that he wants me for his eyes only is something that pleases me on the most innately feminine level.

"No to the shorts then?" I tease him, stepping back a bit and cocking my hip.

His eyes are locked on my thighs, pupils swallowing up those cut-crystal irises. "Uh…"

I smile, chewing at my lip a little. "I'm messing with you, Mitch," I finally whisper, when I realise that he's so captivated that he's literally stopped functioning.

His eyes flash to mine and he gives his hair a quick tug, licking at his bottom lip. "Sorry," he murmurs, shaking his head. "Got distracted." He takes a few deep breaths and then says, "Seven o'clock, I'll come get you."

Pleasure ripples through my belly as I smile up at him. "Can't wait."

CHAPTER 12

Mitch

At six-fifty-nine I'm on Harper's doorstep, fist raised to the wood and giving it three quick poundings. It's fall so it's dark out, the sky the same shade of navy as my on-site uniform, and hazy white moonlight streams in from behind. It flashes right off Harper's *Head Office* plaque. My abdomen clenches tight.

When I hear movement from behind the wood I stand a little straighter, tucking my hands into the front belt-loops of my jeans and swallowing hard as I wait for her to open the door. I already brought the truck up through the Nature Trail so that she wouldn't have to walk down the valley in order to reach our make-shift site car park, and I glance over to where it's sat, safe and sturdy on the gravel. Then the door clicks open and my attention is immediately drawn to Harper.

As soon as I get a look at her my pupils are dilating, my jaw's turning slack, and I'm running a hand down the back of my neck as my mind turns blank, speechless. I grip at my belt with my other hand, the pace of my breathing suddenly increased.

"Harper, you look…"

My voice comes out in a bass rumble, pulsing need fogging up every square-inch of my brain. I drag my eyes up those denim jeans, locking in for a couple seconds on that tight section at the apex of her thighs, and then forcing my gaze to travel further, over the sweet curve of her waist and then right on those perky little tits. She's wearing a high-neck top, completely covering her chest, but it doesn't stop me from imagining ripping it clean off her body, then finally getting to work on her.

Her left hand moves to her waist and she cocks out her hip. My eyes flash up to hers and I'm met with a self-assured smile, kind of smug and sexy as hell.

"I look…?" she prompts me, her eyebrows raised in a mocking arch. She wafts her other hand in the air as if to teasingly say *get on with it.*

I swipe my tongue over my bottom lip, nod, and take a step backwards. I'm used to seeing her in her sweat-tops and little shorts, so this slightly more formal version of her, dressed up for my benefit, is really doing it for me.

"You look beautiful," I manage to rasp, nodding my head over to the truck and taking another step backwards as she joins me outside, her body turning around so that she can lock up.

I can't help it. My eyes drop straight to her ass. Suddenly my jaw is hardening, my muscles are swelling, and my head's getting heavy with all of those pre-sex chemicals.

I must have moved a little closer to her, my body drawn to hers like a magnet, because the second that she moves back around to face me she's knocking right into my chest, a surprised gasp leaving her throat as her breasts brush my abs, and her hands quickly grip at my pecs in an attempt to steady herself.

My hands swoop down to her lower back, stabilising her, and then as soon as she's rebalanced I release her. It would be damn tempting to keep her locked in my arms and see where this moment could go, my pheromones pouring all over her and her bedroom only ten steps away, but she needs to know more about me before I can start breaching her physical territory.

She drops her hands from my chest, interlacing them behind her back and giving me another little smile. I run my gaze over her face and a pleasurable burn ripples through my abdomen – she's excited, I can tell, so I take another step back and gesture for her to walk on in front of me as we make our way down the narrow gravel path towards my truck.

"You ever been to this bar before?" Harper asks, turning her head so that she can look at me over her shoulder. The soft light from the moon lands on the pillow of her bottom lip, catching on the sparkly balm that she's got on, and making my head go blank for a couple of seconds. Then I remember that she just asked me a question and I shake my head to say *no*.

Because no, I haven't been to the country bar in the town up the road from Pine Hills, but that doesn't mean that I didn't scope it out quickly on my cell, making sure that we'll be there early enough to leave before the two-stepping starts.

Yeah I want to give her the small town experience, but that definitely is not about to involve her getting propositioned by every man in town who wants to get his hands on her.

I walk to the passenger side with her and before she can get her fingers on the handle I reach around her shoulder and click open the door. She looks back at me, surprised, and then silently dips into her seat. When her legs are tucked in I shut the door gently, and then I make my way to the driver's side, ducking in, strapping up, and then punching the truck to life.

I can feel her eyes hot on my face so I glance over at her before I get the vehicle moving, sensing that she wants to say something.

She wets her lips, making me shift on my seat, and then she says, "I love that shirt on you. That shade of dusty blue... it really brings out your eyes."

Now it's my turn to be surprised. I look down at my torso, covered in a simple long-sleeved top. It's a big size so I didn't expect it to be so fitted, but I didn't try it on before I bought it. Hell, I'm so used to wearing the same shit most days that I hadn't actually tried it on before this *evening*. I bought it in town when I was psyching myself up to ask Harper out and I only just ripped off the tags.

This is its first outing.

"Thanks," I grunt, and then I tear my eyes off of her so that I can actually get us to town without ending this date prematurely, by pulling her up onto my lap and showing her all of the things that you can do inside a truck.

We crawl cautiously down the Nature Trail, all the way until we're out onto the main spread of blacktop, and then it's a steady cruise upland to the town, the truck's headlights the only source of brightness before the road reaches the more populated centre. I drive slow and keep my boot gentle on the pedal, hoping to hit some red lights so that I can divert my attention back to the beautiful woman beside me, but we get green lights the whole damned way. The thick border of pine trees disappears into spaced out suburban housing, which leads directly to the town square, the buildings short and squat, with signage straight out of the silver-screen era. A couple dry cleaners, a cinema, and that godforsaken country bar.

I park up right in front of the restaurant that I wanted to take her to – the restaurant that I decided to still make a reservation at, in the hopes that Harper would see its romantic potential and suddenly change her mind – but the pull of the neon cowboy signpost and the subterranean hum of soft country music lures her right towards the bar. She's out of the truck before I've even disentangled myself from my seatbelt.

I slap my door shut, lock up, and then jog a couple of paces to catch up to her, a jacket slung over my arm in case she wants to put it on when we leave.

I guess we'll save the restaurant for another time.

She smiles up at me when I reach her and my heart skips a beat in my chest.

"Are we going to see some dancing?" she asks me hopefully, one hand twiddling with the end of a blown-out curl.

I take a glimpse through the large windows facing out onto the square and I can see that there are already couples milling about on the square patch designated for swaying. I grimace as I look back down at her and she laughs at my expression. My face reads: *not if I have anything to do with it.*

"Didn't you have to learn this stuff in cowboy ethics or something?" she asks, her voice teasing, but I can see that twinkle of curiosity hiding behind her eyes.

I breathe a laugh and nod because, yeah, I'm not a cowboy but these parts are so rural that we actually *did* do cowboy ethics when I was in high school. Which was a long-ass time ago. And which I have no intentions of reminding her about.

"Yeah, we were taught fundamentals. Theoretical fundamentals," I hasten to add as we step up the curb and I reach for the door. The second I pull it open I'm met with the sex-me-up twanging of country strings.

Maybe this wasn't such a bad idea after all.

"Are you not much of a… uh, a mover?" she asks, eyeing me up a little more shyly because I know what she's implying.

I look down at her as we head up to the counter and her eyes are trailing over the swollen peaks of my pecs. I almost laugh. *Don't mind me, baby.*

"Sure, I'm a mover," I say, regaining her attention. "But I don't do it in front of other people, and I don't do it with strangers. If I have a partner I don't want her jiving with any other guy on the floor – and I definitely don't want my hands on any other woman."

I look over to the dancers again and I pull a disgruntled face, absolutely steadfast that Harper is not going over there. The thought of other guys putting their hands on her waist? Not on my fucking watch.

When I look back down at her she's watching me curiously so I give her a shrug and say, "It just doesn't sit right with me."

She blinks up at me, a little dazed, and then she nods in understanding. I pull a menu from beside the cash machine and hand it over to her.

"Are we eating?" she asks, splitting her concentration between watching my face and scanning the laminated card in her hands.

Eating out was my initial intention, hence the restaurant, but I'm not about to force her to eat diner style food in a place where cowboy hats are the literal wall décor.

"Whatever you want, Harper," I say, and I scope out the room, checking for a vacant booth. I clock the one in the corner parallel to the end of the counter, and I'm instantly manoeuvring us over to it before it gets snapped up. My palms encase her exposed shoulders and she stifles a gasp, shivering.

She slides onto the pleather and then looks nervously up at me, wondering where I'm going to choose to sit. If I sit next to her then I'll be able to touch her, but if I sit across from her then I'll be able to look at her. Damn it, I want to do both. I opt to sit next to her whilst she picks what she wants, and then when I get back from paying I'll move to the seat in front of her.

That was the plan at least. It turns out that I take up most of the bench, and I let out an embarrassed laugh when I'm forced to keep one thigh sticking out of the booth, my lap spread wide unlike Harper's daintily crossed-legged position. She leans one arm on the table, resting her chin on her palm, and she looks up at me with something like amused omnipotence as my face gets hot. Like she just knew that I was a fucking dork.

I drop my coat over onto the bench-seat opposite and then I hold up the menu in front of us, Harper tipping her head to the side as she begins to browse it with me. I take the reprieve from her scrutiny to let my eyes trail down her throat, long tendons poking out beneath the surface and her skin a soft golden colour. Then when I realise that she's suddenly flushing I turn my attention over to the menu, scanning for what's caught her eye.

I find it between the chillis and the grits, written in bold cursive as if it didn't have enough emphasis on its own. I fight back a smile, looking down at that sweet scandalised expression on her face. Her eyes re-read the phrase "*Doggie Deluxe*" over and over again.

"It's just a hotdog, Harper," I tell her quietly as she begins gnawing on her lip. She glances up at me and then returns her eyes back to the menu, a concerned crease in her brow. "We can just get drinks if you prefer. Or we could go to that restaurant—"

"Okay, just drinks for now," she agrees, moving her body so that she's sat with her back straight up against the chair, her fingers twiddling in her lap. When she sees that I'm still watching her she admits in a rush, "I haven't done this in a while is all. I'm a little nervous."

I hate that she feels nervous but I love the fact that she's crossed her leg so that it's almost wrapped around my calf, ensuring me that she wants to be here and that her nerves aren't to do with my presence. I pull my wallet out of my jeans and slip a card out of the leather, before pushing the wallet back inside my pocket so that Harper doesn't see what else I've got in there.

"What do you want to drink?" I ask her, absentmindedly drumming the edge of the card against the tabletop. Then a thought comes to me and I almost smile, leaning a little closer to her so that I can murmur, "I don't think that they do champagne here."

A startled laugh leaves her chest and she quickly scrunches up her nose and knocks her thigh against mine. "You must think that I'm such a princess," she says sadly, shaking her head.

I return the thigh press, gratified when her breathing catches in her throat. "Why are you saying that like it's a bad thing? I do think that, and I like it. I like the fact that you're into girly stuff."

"So you won't judge me if I say that I don't want to drink anything alcoholic, and that I'd rather get a milkshake?" she asks, avoiding my eyes as her cheeks burn brighter.

I wrap my left arm around the back of her seat and reply, "All I'd say to that is: what flavour, baby?"

She ducks her head away from me, hiding her cute dimples as she laughs.

After a moment she looks up at me, eyes bright, and says, "Okay, um, maybe a... a strawberry milkshake for now, please." Then she takes a shaky breath, leans up towards my ear, and whispers, "But maybe we can try the Doggie Deluxe later."

I grunt and spread my thighs wider as my muscles suddenly flex, my hand dropping the card to the table so that I can squeeze a tight fist. She pulls away from me to watch for my reaction and I look down at her with a warning in my eyes.

Is she trying to kill me? We haven't been in here for two minutes and she's already trying to get me excited?

She uncrosses her legs and my gaze automatically falls into her lap, my body tensing as I imagine how warm and ready she is down there.

Jesus fucking Christ. I practically throw myself out of the booth, snatching up my card and the menu before pinning her back with a piercing stare. She doesn't look too nervous now that she knows how insanely badly I want what she just suggested. I roll back my shoulders, trying to burn off a bit of adrenaline, and she bites back a smile as she watches me struggle.

"Behave," I tell her, and then I turn away, storming over to the counter.

My head is practically in my hands as I wait for the guy behind the counter to whip up a milkshake and get me a non-alcoholic beer. I keep my eyes completely averted from the booth over to my right, refusing to look at Harper before I've managed to fully cool down.

So she wants me as much as I want her – I'm pretty confident of that now, considering the fact that from the few words we've shared this evening they've all been fairly suggestive. Over the month or so that I've known her she's given me a hell of a lot of whiplash, but now I'm thinking that that has less to do with me and more to do with whatever she came to Pine Hills to get away from in the first place.

I tap my card above the reader as the server rings up the till, and then I slot it between my teeth, taking the milkshake in one hand and the "beer" in the other.

Harper eyes the bottle in my fist with an

apprehensive frown as I set down her milkshake and slide onto the bench in front of her, her fingers shoving a red and white striped straw straight through the mountain of whipped cream. She slides the cold glass closer to her body and then after locking her lips around the straw she takes a quick suck. She narrows her eyes on me as I watch her, like I'm suddenly the world's biggest jackass.

I pick up the brown bottle in front of me and face the label her way so that she can read it.

"It's non-alcoholic, Harper," I tell her, and her expression instantly softens.

"Oh," she says with an embarrassed smile as she slips the straw from between her lips. "Sorry, I just… assumed. Thank you for, uh, for not drinking whilst I'm your passenger."

I shake my head to tell her that it's no worries and then I take a long pull on the bottle, bitter liquid coursing down my throat. About half of the contents has disappeared by the time that I place it back on the table.

"That's the whole point of tonight," I say to her, meeting her gaze with mine. "No more assumptions. Whatever you want to know, I'm happy to answer. And I'd love to hear every detail that you're happy to share with me about yourself, too."

She flutters her lashes as she holds my stare, eyes only dipping momentarily so that she can have another sip of her milkshake.

"What do you want to know?" she asks me, pulling out her straw and then stabbing it back into the cream.

"Everything."

She pulls a face. "Like career stuff? Family stuff?"

she asks.

I shrug, picking at the label on the bottle in front of me. "Yeah, that sounds like a good start. You said you were a writer, I know that much."

Her eyebrows rise in shock, but she smothers it quickly.

"You remembered?" she asks, blinking fast as she surveys me. She's trying to play it cool but her irises are molten under the warm string-lights.

"I remember everything you say to me."

Why the hell would she think that I wouldn't remember?

Heat climbs up her neck and she glances over to the dance floor. I gather that she doesn't want to talk about herself and that she'd much rather be getting her sway on, so I try to give her a little comforting encouragement. With my thighs spread wide beneath the table I move my boots further forwards and then cross my ankles behind her feet. Her eyes fly to mine before she takes a quick peek under the table, her cheeks glowing pink as she lets me subtly envelop her. We're like two kids in a classroom behind the teacher's back.

She tucks her hair behind her ears with flustered fingers and then drops them into her lap, beginning her incessant twiddle.

"Okay, fine. I guess you know some of the details since you're employed by Ray Corp, but I'll give you the brief Wikipedia summary. I was born and raised in LA. I don't mind it there but I haven't exactly missed it much since coming out here. There are things that I'd love to do there – like camping in the nature valleys and stuff – but I mainly just miss the orange trees. They look so cute when they get those tiny oranges," she laughs, but then she shakes her head as if she's trying to get herself back on track. "My mom's the CEO of Ray Corp, my dad's the head of the books. She met him when she was scouting for an in-house accountant and I guess he fit the bill. She's…"

Harper's eyes flick back to mine, assessing me for a moment, unsure about whether she should go on. I feel like she's getting to the meat of it but she's clamming up, so I gently rub the back of my calf up against hers, telling her it's safe to continue. I get another flutter of those pretty lashes and then she's sitting on her hands, eyes on the table.

"My mom's the breadwinner, so I always knew that I'd have big shoes to fill. After high school she put me through college, and then from the age of twenty-one to twenty-eight I worked pretty much non-stop as a screenwriter – and by that I mean that I worked hard enough to be able to pay my mom back for my tuition fees after my second year as a working woman."

Jesus, she's impressive. I give her another rub and she goes on.

"It was slow at the start because I wrote a movie for a friend from college. She was doing her directorial debut but, regardless, it kind of went viral. In an instant cult classic kind of way. And there was a lot of negativity from the… how do I put this nicely? Um, the *lower intellectual echelons*. But then the right people found it – big production houses, insane producers – and they loved it. And then the negativity that had happened didn't seem to matter so much. Because then I compared the lovers to the haters and I was like, *well shit – not only are the lovers so much nicer to listen to, they're also the powerhouses that literally run the whole industry.*

151

One thing led to another and then I was signing a three movie deal with this huge production company, and from then on it's just been…" She shakes her head, eyes far away. "Writing, and writing, and writing. Nonstop. And it was literally like heroin for me, until…"

The straw goes back between her lips, putting a full-stop on her suspended sentence.

"Until?" I ask, prompting her.

She looks up at me, her soft blonde curls framing her vulnerable expression. I sit back against the bench and roll my shirt up my forearms. Then I rest them down on the table between us and rub my thumb around the base of her glass.

"Sounds to me like your mom raised you real good. You're smart, accomplished. Unthinkably beautiful."

Her lips part and a little gasp leaves her throat.

Why is she always so surprised when I give her a compliment?

I know that she's got a confident streak in her – you've got to when you're working in a cut-throat industry. But is all of that confidence coming solely from within?

Has there never been anyone to tell her how amazing she is?

An even worse thought crosses my mind. *Has there been someone in her life actively suppressing her flame?*

I narrow my eyes on her, trying to get to what she isn't telling me.

"So here's what I'm wondering," I tell her, crossing my legs a little tighter behind her calves. "Why did such a gorgeous young successful woman set up camp in the middle of a construction site, in one of the coldest parts of the country, right bang centre in the middle of the holidays. Halloween, Thanksgiving, Christmas," I tick them off on my fingers. "We've passed October, so that one's already gone. And from what I'm gathering, you have no intentions of leaving before the Pine Hills job is completed. You don't sound mad at your parents, so I can't imagine that you're avoiding them. Which leaves me with about three possible conclusions.

"One, you have some other family members that you aren't telling me about, and maybe they're jealous of your success or something. But then I'm thinking that I'm not sure that that's a strong enough reason to keep someone as determined as you out of the city that you were born and raised in. Two, you're having a creative block, but that one doesn't really sound right either, because you're always writing in that notebook of yours."

I take a deep breath and watch her eyes widen in shock. I'm about to hit the nail on the head. We can both feel it.

Might as well get this over with.

"So that leaves me with option number three. There's a guy. The guy who you claimed to be irrelevant, but who has done something so bad that it's worth you fleeing your home, your job, and your family in exchange for a solo cabin retreat in the middle of a winter reno."

She watches me in total silence, her body stock-still.

"Don't think that I haven't noticed the way you can't leave your fingers alone for five minutes. You had a ring, didn't you?" I ask her, my jaw a little tense because that thought didn't seem real until I finally said it out loud.

Goddamn it. Some bastard really managed to make this woman his fiancée and then he blew it before he got her down the aisle?

His fucking loss.

Then a horrible thought crosses my mind and the words are out before I can stop myself. The blood pounding in my ears is roaring louder than any country song ever could.

"Is that why you keep saying sexual stuff to me? Is that why you wouldn't let me take you to a restaurant?"

My brow furrows hard and I see her throat gently bob as she swallows.

"Are you trying to make me a rebound?" I ask her finally, the hurt in my voice betraying my stoic expression.

It's about a minute before she speaks up, her beautiful lips quivering, her eyes wide with shock. Then she removes her fingers from under her ass and tentatively puts them on top of mine.

Somehow, even after sitting on them, her skin is still so much colder than my own.

"You really want to know?" she asks me quietly.

My hands are tingling, the feel of her touching me, consoling me, spreading through my veins like a drug. Fuck alcohol – give me this every night and I'll be high for the rest of my life.

I grunt. "Yeah, I wanna know."

"It's confusing," she warns me.

"Confuse me," I tell her.

"I was seeing someone for two years. We got engaged last year and we broke up last month. I met him through work – I was the screenwriter, he was the actor. I knew him for a while before he finally asked me out, and he was always friendly so I thought it would be a good call.

"The last movie that I wrote… it was my favourite. It was a romance, so who better for me to base the lead guy on than my boyfriend at the time, right? Obviously, the second that the production house and the director looked at the script they wanted Evan for the part, because it *was* him, or it was at least all the best parts of him."

She swallows and looks away. I'm not sure who's more uncomfortable right now. All I know for certain is that now the name *Evan* is at the top of my kill list.

"The issue came when we were casting the female lead. That detail that I omitted from my life story? It's that I have a sister, Holly. Ridiculously cute name, right? LA born and raised, the same as me obviously, only she wanted to be in front of the camera instead of behind it. Do you see where this is going?" she asks me, the delicate pulse in her neck hammering double-time.

I'm not sure that I do. All that I know is that her hands are still on mine and I don't want her to ever let go.

"She wanted the part," she says, squeezing her eyes shut, "even though I told her that it would be really fucked up. It's bad enough having your boyfriend-turned-fiancé kissing any other woman on-screen, but having him kiss your sister? That's just weird. Bottom line, I put my foot down, got in touch with casting, and I didn't let her get the part. Not that she would've gotten it anyway, but I expressed my reluctance about having her involved with this role in this project. In turn, she decided to do me one better. She suddenly became Evan's best buddy. All through our engagement she was just... *there*. She wouldn't let it go. And then at the end of September, after we'd finished filming and we got the Christmas release date that we were after, Evan comes to my place one evening and tells me, 'Hey babe, I heard the movie's gonna be huge, so thanks for the role of a lifetime. Oh, and by the way, that weird friendship that I have going on with your sister? It's more than a friendship. We're fucking. Bye!'"

My jaw practically hits the table. Harper's eyes are back on the couples, her fingers stilled on mine.

"That's why I'm here," she admits, a curl dropping loose from behind her ear. "Because I found out that the guy I gave a big break to decided to give me a big break of my own."

She laughs dryly and shakes her head.

"We have our release week and press tour all through December and he's going to be there for the whole damned thing. So I'm not going. I'm hiding away from the billboards and the paparazzi until this movie blows over, and then, after that, I'll see if I can continue writing about idiots in love."

"Harper–" I start, but she cuts me off with a look.

"Enough about me," she says, scrunching up her nose to try and hide the fact that she's got tears in her eyes. "I want to hear about you. Unless you realise now why I've been such a neurotic nightmare and you'd rather not get involved – which I totally understand. I can walk back to Pine Hills if you want."

I stand up, reluctantly letting her hands drop from

mine, and I move around to her side of the booth in three large steps. Then I sit my body down on the pleather, wrapping one arm around the small of her back and using the other one to take her hands, both delicate enough to sit perfectly in my palm.

"They didn't deserve you," I say to her, looking straight into her eyes and hoping that she can see how deeply I mean it. "You gave them a chance and they fucked it up – it's their loss, Harper. They'll never deserve you."

Her brow arches in the middle and she re-crosses her legs so that she can drape a toned calf over one of my thighs. I let go of her hands so that I can run a palm up the outer side of her jeans, right up to her hip, and my fingers gently press, squeezing her ass.

Fuck. I hadn't even intended to do that, but then she lets out a little mewl and grips her fingers around my belt loops. I quickly glance over my shoulder, checking that no-one's watching, and then I turn back to her, shielding us with my shoulders. Keeping her body out of any peeping creep's eye-line.

Like I told her, I don't do stuff with an audience.

"Do we have to keep talking?" she asks me breathlessly, her eyes lingering on my mouth.

I can't help but smirk at that one. "You aren't gonna ask me any questions in turn?" I ask. "Makes me feel like you just want me for my body or something."

She wets her bottom lip and suddenly I don't care if she only wants me for my body. I don't even care if I'm her rebound. For Harper, she can use me any way that she wants.

"You have, like, one minute to fill me in," she says,

hands sliding dangerously low in my lap.

I grunt, trying not to imagine *filling her in* as I attempt to recall any details about my life before the past fifteen seconds.

"I'm a joiner," I tell her simply. "I started my own company a while back after working for other guys my whole life. My old boss retired so I decided to build something on my own. Already had the tools, the skills, the clients. My brother Jason has a construction company so we're often working different bits of the same gigs. Entered the workforce straight out of high school because—"

I stop myself short, unsure about how Harper will react to this particular piece of information. She doesn't notice my pause, too distracted by my hand that's now rhythmically kneading her ass.

I swallow hard and say a prayer that this won't change how she feels.

"I have a kid," I say gruffly, pausing my hand in case this is a deal breaker for her. "When I was in high school I was…" I shake my head, hating how cliché this is going to sound. "I was a jock. The stoic silent one who no-one dared get in a fight with."

I look away from her and breathe out a laugh. I don't usually travel down memory lane so this is weird as shit for me.

"Basically, I was a teenage kid with needs like any other, but I wasn't the type to fuck around. That wasn't my scene. I was close with this cheerleader – Pam – and we decided to just…" I pull my hands off of Harper because it feels inappropriate to touch her when I'm discussing another woman. A surge of relief courses through me when she keeps her leg crossed over mine. "It was essentially friends-with-benefits before the phrase friends-with-benefits existed. We were just two friends, experimenting, but I guess we experimented a little too well. I loved the idea of having a kid and Pam did too, but she wasn't interested in a serious relationship. Didn't matter – I knew what I needed to do anyway. I finished up high school and got a job straight away. I wanted to be the best dad ever – make sure that Tate and his mom had loads of money – but I didn't get to see him the most during his earlier years. So I filled my time away from him with nothing but work, until I finally started my own company and, when he was old enough, he chose to live with me. Now we work together – you'll have probably seen him at the site."

I think for a moment and then say, "That pumpkin that got delivered to my house last month? It was from his fiancée. She has a…" I search for the right words to describe River. "An interesting sense of humour."

I roll my lips into my mouth and rub my hands over both of my knees as I wait for Harper's reaction. After ten silent anxious seconds I reach across the table and take another swig of the fake beer.

At last she says in a wispy voice, "Experimented too well."

I almost snort my drink out of my nose, smirking as I turn to face her. "That's the bit you're honing in on?"

She shrugs, looking kind of shy. "I don't mind that you have a son," she says quietly. "And I guess a lot of kids don't know about protection when they're in high school."

I shake my head, looking down at her as I take another drink. "We used protection," I say, as I set the

159

bottle back on the table.

She sputters on her milkshake. Blinks rapidly up at me. "I'm sorry, what?"

"We used protection," I repeat.

"You used protection... and she still got pregnant?"

I shrug my shoulders and nod. "Yeah. That's how it goes."

She looks like she's glitching, little pink and blue sparks flickering around her temples. "That is not how it *goes*," she hisses, eyes flashing around the bar behind me as if she's suddenly learned dangerous information. "If you use protection you're not supposed to get pregnant. What the hell kind of protection were you using?"

I'm trying not to smile now as I gauge her expression, a nice combination of mortified and impressed. "She was on the pill," I admit.

Harper's brain erupts. "Isn't that the *safest* type of contraception?" she asks, horrified.

"Not for me."

I can see what's happening behind her eyes. She's thinking *if I let this man bed me, am I sure-fire going to get pregnant?*

I try to ease her concern, my voice low and quiet to keep this conversation private. "If I bag it, it should be fine. And, you know, trying to avoid your ovulation period might be beneficial too."

Harper looks like she's ten seconds from passing out. "Mitchell," she says, like she's not so sure.

I take this as my cue to get my hands back on her body, one massaging her ribs and the other reclaiming its place on her behind. "Does it bother you?" I ask her, dipping a little closer.

"Which part? The part about you making a baby with another woman, or the fact that you're so virile you defy scientific intervention?"

I breathe out a laugh, pressing my forehead against hers. "Both," I reply.

She swallows, her hands hesitantly finding their way up to my abs. Her fingers rest there for a nervous moment and then they begin roaming up across my chest.

I bite back a smile. I love how hot she is for my pecs.

"I'm scared that if I let you near me you're going to knock me up," she admits in a whisper.

"I'll bag it, every time," I whisper back, moving my hand around her ribcage a little higher, just enough so that I can get my hands on those–

"We should head back to the bungalows," she says quietly, her intentions crystal clear in the pretty facets of her eyes.

I give her ass a little squeeze and she makes a sound that has my abs clenching tight. "Not tonight," I tell her. "I need to wine and dine you first. We need at least, I don't know, five dates under the belt before we get to that point."

She throws her head back and lets out a little howl. I laugh and dip my mouth to her throat, pressing a kiss right on the curve.

She tastes milkshake-sweet. I kiss her a little harder.

Her hands find my hair, her body arches into mine, and suddenly I'm not laughing anymore.

Yeah, she's right. We should head back to the bungalows.

CHAPTER 13

Harper

We didn't kiss in the bar. Well, technically Mitch kissed me, but I didn't get to kiss him back. I lift my hand so that I can delicately press my fingertips over the area where his mouth met my skin, and a deep tingling sensation sparkles in my belly.

He's staring intently out of the windshield, jaw tight, and his hands gripped around the steering wheel like he's about to rip it clean from the dashboard. I'm curled up in his passenger seat, watching him like he's my favourite movie.

The sound of my voice breaking the silence makes him suck in a quick breath, like he's on the verge of losing his composure.

"Did you shave your stubble for me?" I ask, when my eyes suddenly note the fact that his usual sharp coating of scruff has disappeared, his laugh lines and deeply tanned jaw now stealing the show.

He scratches at the back of his head, eyes still on the road, then he wraps his fist back around the wheel.

"Yeah," he says, his voice low and deep. "Thought you might–" He bites his lip and shakes his head, as if he's embarrassed by whatever he's thinking.

"You thought I might...?" I prompt him, my brow arching curiously.

He swallows and stretches his neck. "Thought you might prefer it," he says, his face turning hard, as if he doesn't like what's coming out of his own mouth. He clicks the indicator with a little extra vehemence as he makes the turn off the main road. "Thought it might be more like what you're used to."

My eyebrows rise involuntarily. Wow. And I thought that *I* was the over-thinker.

I lean closer towards him, resting a palm on his thigh, and I watch his jaw clench. Then I move my hand slightly higher and a gruff sound reverberates in his chest.

"I like you exactly as you are," I tell him. "I'm not into pretty boys anymore, if that's what you're worried about."

When he still doesn't look down at me I rub my thumb into him harder, making his chest swell and heave.

"Mitch, I'm serious. Even when you're covered in dirt you're more clean-cut than any of those shallow-ass motherfuckers could ever pretend to be."

The truck comes to a smooth, abrupt stop and I realise that we're already in front of the gate at the top of the forest's Nature Trail. I was so distracted by the sharp angles of his jaw, the thick cords in his neck, that

I hadn't noticed how quickly we'd made it up bank towards the bungalows.

Mitch uses one hand to un-strap his seatbelt and the other to clasp his fingers around mine, his eyes moving from the opening up ahead to stare deeply into my own. In the shadow of the cab roof with only the moonlight and his car beams to illuminate the gloom, his eyes have never looked so striking.

It's the blue shirt. That soft dusty blue against his unbelievably deep tan, drawing my eyes straight up to the only other source of brightness: those candy-crystal irises.

"You say the sweetest stuff," he murmurs, his thumb stroking firmly up the back of my hand. We instinctively both lean closer, me lifting up and him ducking down, but then his gaze sweeps back through the front window and he lets out a low curse. "Let me just... the gate... once I've opened the gate–"

I nod adamantly – anything to get us through the gate and over to those bungalows as quickly as possible. Anything to speed up the process of getting his mouth on mine.

He heaves himself out of his door and storms over to the gate, the truck headlights giving me a clear view of his large bulk striding to the latch, and his hands practically ripping the chain from around the wooden pole keeping our metal obstruction in place. He tosses the chain and shoves the gate wide, wiping his hands on his jeans as he makes his way back over to me.

He's the hottest contradiction that I've ever seen. Protective yet threatening. Light yet dark.

He ducks back into the driver's seat, quickly shutting the door, and then he puts his foot down hard on the pedal so that we can get out of the truck as soon as possible.

Once he parks up beside the bungalows he unfastens my seatbelt and gives me a heated look as he says, "Stay here."

I watch him as he leaves the car, shutting his door after himself and jogging back towards the gate so that he can lock it up again. He picks up the chain and it clanks in loud repetitive twangs as it hits off the metal and thumps against the wood, only dropping into silence once he's got the lock in place and he's retracing his steps towards the truck.

A few moments later he's pulling my door open and holding out his hand so that I can take it as I dismount the step. Once I'm on the ground he shuts up the vehicle behind me and suddenly we're back to that moment in the bar. That suspended second of stillness. Our hands are hesitantly hovering beside our bodies as we gauge what we can and can't do.

The car lights are off, the bungalows are in total darkness, and the only source of light is the soft beam of the moon. I look up at Mitch, feeling a combination of sexually desperate and nervously unsure, and he looks back down at me, his eyes half-mast.

Quietly he says to me, "I owe you a dance."

We stay totally still for a few long moments and then suddenly I'm being warmed, his hands pressing firmly into the arch of my lower back. I tuck my fingers into the front belt-loops of his jeans and his mouth curls slightly into a grimace, like he's losing his gentlemanly control.

"Couldn't do it in that room," he admits gruffly as he closes the gap between us, pressing his hard abs up against my breasts. "But we can do it here, so no-one else gets to see when you…" His hands slide to the sides of my hips and he grips into them hard, making them move in a provocative sway. "When you do that," he finishes, his face set hard like he's ready to snap.

My lashes flutter as I look up at him, my body turning weak and lightheaded. I lift one arm so that I can encircle his neck and it enables me to press my chest against his body harder.

"Christ," he grunts, and suddenly my back is against the side of his truck, his hard thighs are knocking my knees apart, and he's settling himself right against my heat, hands tight on my ass as he starts to grind me.

I gasp quietly but it only encourages him to move a little faster, a little deeper, his fingers impatient as they knead and grope.

"This is how you dance?" I ask breathlessly, tilting my head back as he dips his face into the warm curve of my neck. "Good job we didn't do this in the bar. We would've been banned for life."

A huff of laughter hits my cheek and then he's looking down at me as he rolls his body firmly against mine. "Gonna let me kiss you?" he asks, his eyes on my lips, then my throat, then my slightly bouncing chest.

I can't help but smile as I watch him become hypnotised.

"Where do you want to kiss me?" I whisper back at him.

Something like a snarl leaves his chest and he presses his forehead fervently against mine. "Harper, for Christ's sake, I'm trying to not get too carried away. Please don't give me any more reasons to let myself get carried away."

I arch slightly backwards and let him rub my nose with his. Then I subtly nod my head and he makes a low groan of relief.

"Thank you, baby," he murmurs quietly, and then he ducks down to press his mouth against mine.

At first it's soft and gentle, the light press of something respectful, him wanting to make sure that I'm as okay with this as he is. I move my hand from the back of his neck to grip at the firm line of his jaw, and he breaks the kiss for a second so that he can look into my eyes. Then he dips straight back down, taking my lips again.

The second time it's harder. The immediate pressure of his mouth on mine has me moaning into him, incentivising his hands to grip and squeeze more roughly at the soft curves of my behind. When I pull his belt-loop as close to my body as it'll go he slides one hand down my thigh and suddenly hitches my leg up around his hip, pinning me to the truck with the pressure of his hardened groin. He turns his head to the side and the movement makes me gasp, giving him the opening to slip his tongue inside. It's soft and warm as he laps gently around mine, but the anguished moan that leaves my throat makes him growl and rub our tongues together harder. Faster. Soon we're nothing but a frenzy of him pounding my crotch against the side of his truck and his tongue stroking wet and relentless, deep into my mouth.

My mind goes blank, sputtering and fizzling until I'm nothing but physical sensation. I slide my hand from his jaw so that I can pull hard at his hair and he makes a gruff noise in response, his hand landing a quick spank against my ass.

My body jolts right into him, my breasts jumping up to meet his pecs, and he tears his mouth away from mine, breathing heavy as he stares down at me.

"We have to stop now," he says, his voice a thigh-clenching command.

I shake my head.

"Yes," he orders. "Otherwise we're going to end up screwing over the hood of my truck."

"That doesn't sound so bad to me," I reply, my voice a quiet vixen rasp. I watch heat stain his cheekbones and decide to taunt him further. "Don't you remember what I asked for in the bar? The Doggie–"

He presses his palm over my lips and I lick a tiny stripe up his hand.

"Stop it," he says firmly. "You only just learned about my past. In the morning you might decide that a guy with a kid doesn't hit the spot for you."

When he removes his hand I murmur, "I bet you could hit my spot all night long."

"Harper," he says warningly, one of his hands moving to his jeans so that he can rearrange the situation trying to push its way out of the denim. "And we need to talk about our age difference, too," he adds on gruffly.

I roll my eyes. "Go ahead. All that's going to do is turn me on harder."

"Harper," he grits out, his eyes dark and aflame.

"Fine," I submit. "We'll stop for tonight. But I know all you're going to do in your bungalow is picture me on my bed, naked. You take really long showers, Mitch."

He licks his bottom lip, his hands both back on my hips rubbing gentle circles.

"You sleep naked?" he asks me.

"I will tonight," I say wickedly.

His mouth lifts into a smirk and he presses another hard kiss against my lips. Then he murmurs, "I sleep naked every night."

I shove at his chest but he doesn't move an inch. *Tease*, my mind thinks. The next time I shove at him he's so comfortable that he starts sucking on the lobe of my ear.

"I'll deny you," I threaten him, my arms now looped around the back of his warm neck.

He smiles against my cheek and then gently nips at my jaw. "I'll enjoy it," he taunts back.

"I know what you want, and I won't let you do it," I continue, and suddenly his movements slow down, like he's trying to work out how well I've read him.

"You won't let me do what?" he asks quietly, his hands slow-kneading my ass cheeks in an unending spread and circle.

"That," I say, like it's obvious. "That thing that I mentioned in the bar? From the second that I saw you I knew exactly how you'd be – you're the big bad boss who likes to be in control."

He pulls away from me now and stares down into my eyes. I use the moment to take the reins, turning my body one-eighty and arching my ass as hard as I can up against his crotch.

He lets out a hard exhalation and presses his chest against my back, my hands gripping the roof of his truck as his palms fly up to my breasts, massaging me.

"I know you want me from behind," I whisper, amused by how right I was but too aroused to fully revel in my glee. Because the fact of the matter is he *is* the big bad boss, and he's currently grinding two-hundred-and-fifty pounds of solid muscle against my soft little behind. The knowledge that he could take control of this moment at any second rings like a shotgun in the silence of the night.

I cover his eager hands with my fingers and he grunts against my neck.

"Yeah," he murmurs. "I want that. I..." He moves one hand up to my jaw, turning my head so that he can kiss me, slow and deep. He doesn't stop until I'm whimpering. Then he pulls away as flushed as I am and says quietly, "I wanna hit it from the back."

I almost lose all control of my body. I stabilise myself against the truck and then turn around to face him, our chests rising and falling embarrassingly hard.

"Okay, you're right," I say quickly. "We... we should stop for tonight." *Otherwise I will literally go into cardiac arrest.*

He nods in agreement whilst simultaneously scooping a hand under my ass, but this time he uses the position to lift me from the ground, holding me against his side as he walks us up the short path to my front door. When he deposits me on the ground both of his hands move to my jaw, cupping it gently as he leans down to kiss me again.

"You're going to make me change my mind," I whisper against him, "and you should know, I'm a fighter."

He grins, a flash of perfect white in the darkness as he pulls away. I give him an irritated glower before turning around to unlock the door.

As I push it open I feel his hands move back to my hips, his groin rubbing rhythmically against my ass, and a deep grunt coming from somewhere above my head.

I glance up at him over my shoulder, his eyes already locked on mine.

"You're going to make *me* change *my* mind, looking this damn beautiful all the time," he warns me. I tip my neck all the way back so that my head is resting in the centre of his pecs, and one of his hands climbs over my waist, all the way until it's wrapped gently around the front of my throat. "Knowing I got all this right here? Knowing that you're my neighbour?" He dips down and whispers against my cheek, "Knowing how you're going to let me pump you?"

I shiver hard against him and he presses a firm kiss against my jaw. Then he lifts up, releases me, and I turn to face him, his feet just behind the threshold.

"Lock your door," he instructs me.

"As if you wouldn't just break down our adjoining wall. What's it made of anyway? Papier-mâché?"

"Sheetrock," he growls. "And don't tempt me."

I bite back a smile, leaning against the frame as I murmur, "I was only kidding."

He flexes his jaw and his eyes burn into mine. "I wasn't."

I suddenly feel limp, his strong body less than a foot away, and he senses it in the air between us. He takes a large step backwards, trying to clear the fog from his brain. It's too late for me – my whole kitchen is steamed up with red smoking lust.

He nods his head at me and I'm gratified to see that

he's as begrudging about this departure as I am. Then he jerks his chin over to his own bungalow and we both smile at the ridiculousness of it.

So close, yet so far.

"Goodnight Harper," he says finally.

I kick off my boots and smile. "Goodnight Mitch."

CHAPTER 14

Mitch

"You got any big weekend plans, boss?"

I pull off my gloves and look over at my latest recruit, Jared. He's been finishing up an en suite re-tile and appliance affixation in the cabin that some of the crew members and I are currently standing in.

My son Tate glances over to me as he ditches his own gloves, vague curiosity momentarily crossing his features.

"Uh…" I clear my throat as we head into the living area space and then I pull open the front door to get some air into the room. Is it just me or is it suddenly hot as hell in here? Hail pellets hit the deck outside the entrance in quick little smacks, and my eyes follow the peaks up the valley until I'm looking up at Harper's bungalow.

After date number one I decided to implement a

kind of strategy, partially so that I could stay somewhat focused on finishing up the huge project that her mom hired me to do, and partially so that I could subtly persuade her to go steady with me instead of jumping straight into the haystack. Not that I don't want to jump straight into the haystack – I've been ready for that since the moment I laid my eyes on her. The reason why we're waiting is because I'm giving her the chance to end this before it gets serious.

So we've been doing the traditional thing. One date a week, every Saturday night for the past three weeks, meaning that we've had four official dates, including the one that was at the country bar. I tug at the collar of my shirt when I think about the fact that tomorrow is date number five – the number that I plucked out of thin air in the bar that night when I told her how long we should wait at a minimum before we got closer.

I run a hand down my jaw and I take a deep steadying inhalation.

"Yeah," I say at last, eyes still zoned in on Harper's bungalow. "I have some pretty big plans."

The second that the guys follow my gaze up the valley Harper appears at her door, shutting it quickly behind herself, and then holding an arm over her head as she begins to leg it down the hillside. She's wearing her statement flip-flops-and-short-shorts combination, but it's even better this time because my jacket is slung around her body, protecting her from the impaling impact of the hailstones. Warm pride spreads through my chest and I almost smile at the sight of her wearing it.

Jared lets out a low whistle when he takes in what I'm looking at, putting two-and-two together, and my attention is briefly drawn over to him.

He instantly raises his hands in a kind of surrender, as if he's committed a misdemeanour.

"Sorry, that was inappropriate. My bad, man," he says quickly.

I shake my head in understanding. Harper's so beautiful it's crazy, so I'm not surprised that he's impressed.

"All's good," I tell him, giving him a brief nod when he starts heading for his truck at the edge of our make-shift lot. "Have a good weekend."

When Harper's about twenty feet away from us Tate jerks his thumb over his shoulder to the inside of the cabin that we've just about completed and he says quietly, "I'm gonna grab my stuff and head out."

I nod at him before he re-enters the cabin and then I turn and walk the final few paces to close the gap between Harper and myself.

Her jog stumbles to an abrupt stop as she hits into my chest, and I look down at her with my heart going double-time as I wrap my arms around her back. But the second that she looks up at me I can tell that something's wrong.

The sound of Tate trudging out of the cabin has my head snapping to the side and he pauses briefly, as if he's seeing something that he shouldn't. He blinks at me for a moment and I release Harper from one of my arms, torn between not wanting my kid to see me cosying up to a woman that isn't his mother, and not wanting to let go of Harper when her face has blanched of all colour.

She misreads my movement, thinking back to when I told her that I like things to be private, and she quickly covers for me, making my heart clench painfully in my chest.

"I just, uh," she begins, taking a step away from me, much to my absolute dismay. "I just thought I'd come and see how the cabins are coming along. Almost all done," she adds, followed by a quick swallow.

I look down at her and ask teasingly, "Are they up to my supervisor's standards?"

She gives me a little glower and some colour flares back into her cheeks. That gives me a moment of relief. *Maybe whatever's happened isn't too bad.*

She lifts up on her tiptoes to try and scope out the interior through the open door, and Tate moves out of the doorframe so that his body doesn't totally block the view. Tate and I share a wordless look, both of us not sure about what to think of this moment.

"Did you make that?" Harper asks suddenly, pointing over to the newly installed kitchen cabinets.

"Yes," I say.

"And that?" she asks, now gesturing to the smooth wooden table sat in prized position at the centre of the room.

"Yes."

"What about that?" she continues, and I breathe out a laugh, not even bothering to look at what she's pointing at this time.

"Let's just assume that I made everything you're currently looking at. Including him," I add on, jerking my chin at Tate. I guess I'd be introducing him to her at some point, so it might as well be now.

Harper's eyes fly up to mine, her lips popping open, and then she looks quickly back over to Tate, giving him a stunned once-over. She lingers for a few extra seconds on the large cross tattooed around his bicep, the name etched across his knuckles. Then she gives him a quick nervous smile and moves closer to me again, making warmth spread through my chest as she lets me circle her shoulders with both of my arms.

I slide my gaze over to Tate and he's squinting back at me, his lips pressed together as if he's trying to stop himself from laughing. We share a father-son look. Mine says, *so this is the woman I've been seeing.* His says, *please dear God leave me out of it.*

I half-laugh and he shakes his head, an almost-smile playing around the deep-cut dimples of his cheeks. I think that Harper's gone into shock, so this is probably the extent of their introduction for now.

Tate gives me a quick shoulder nudge, spares Harper a 0.2 second glance, and then he jogs easily over to his truck, head tilted slightly to shield himself from the pelting rain.

I bring my attention back to Harper and my eyebrows raise a little when I take in her flushed expression.

I think she's turned on. She likes the fact that I made a kid – a solid six-four kid – and she's finding it impossible to hide it.

"That's your son?" she asks, looking up at me through her lashes. I lift one of my hands above her forehead to shield her face from the harsh weather.

"Yeah," I say back to her, dropping my other hand to her ass and giving her a gentle squeeze.

Her breathing catches in her throat.

"He's so… big," she says finally. "I didn't think that he'd be, like, a whole adult man."

I nod as I start walking us onto the cabin porch,

under the new wooden roof that Jace fitted a few months back. "Yeah, he's a big guy."

"Like his daddy," she says quietly, dropping her eyes to my pecs.

I laugh a little as I move my other hand away from her face, so that I can firmly caress her lower back. "Like his daddy," I concur.

I can feel Harper's energy waning. I glance up and watch as Tate's truck disappears from view, saying absentmindedly, "He's heading out for the weekend to see his girl."

Then I look back down at Harper and say, "What were you running over here for? You know that I always come to see you after I finish up."

The soft pink glow dims down a watt in her cheeks. I narrow my eyes, not liking that reaction.

"Speaking of this weekend," she begins, and my stomach drops like a load of lumber. I swallow hard, already not liking where this is going.

We had plans this weekend. Date number five. *The* date. The date where she tells me how she actually feels and she can decide whether we end this here or we make it official. Whether or not I get to claim her as my own.

I steel my jaw, preparing for the worst.

"I got a call from my mom," she says, looking up at me again. Now I'm a little less worried but a lot more confused. When she drops her eyes I look out across the valley and my gaze lands upon the portacabin less than thirty feet away from us. Warm and protected from the cold lashings of the hail.

I tuck two fingers under her chin, lifting her face to mine, and I finally give her a long, slow kiss. Her nails grip into my pecs as I slide my tongue inside and I give her slow unending strokes until she's moaning and trying to climb me.

"Let's go to my office," I say to her, and she nods up at me.

I lock up the cabin and then hitch Harper around the side of my body, tug up her hood, and run the distance over to the cub, quickly mounting the steps and pushing us inside. I drop her gently to the floor and close the door behind us.

When I turn around I'm met with her reaching her arms around my neck, standing on her tiptoes so that she can get another kiss.

I give it to her, a little harder, a little faster, walking her backwards until her ass is up against the side of my desk, and then shoving my jacket from her shoulders to reveal a skimpy tank top beneath. I pull away to get a look at her. Under the little top I see her push-up bra, her soft perky tits all but spilling out of it.

I stumble backwards and grunt, running one hand through my hair and using the other to grip the thickening happening at the front of my cargos.

"Jesus," I curse, breathing heavy and turning around. "If we need to talk, maybe you should put the jacket back on for now."

I'm not so arrogant as to think that I can actually multitask. Maybe some men can concentrate on a conversation whilst they've got a pair of perfect tits a couple inches away from their mouth, but I am one-hundred percent not that kind of man. My brain is already turning into a pile of smoking ash. If I get one more look at what Harper's got for me, our five date rule is about to get annihilated, repeatedly, over a desk full of paperwork.

I hear the scrape of the jacket zipper, give her an extra second just in case, and then I turn back around, my head spinning from my sudden tumult of testosterone.

"Sorry," I rasp.

She shakes her head as if to say that it's okay and I move around the desk so that I can heave myself down into my seat. I run both of my hands through my hair, giving it a rough tug to try and refocus on our conversation. I briefly consider jamming a pen lid into the side of my quad again.

"Sit wherever you want," I say to her when I realise that she still hasn't moved from her position at the side of the desk. I gesture vaguely to the chair facing mine on the opposite side of the desk, then to the tabletop, and then, after a moment, I spread my thighs wider and give her a look that tells her, if she wants to, she can sit in my lap.

She takes a step towards me and I swipe my tongue over my bottom lip. Christ. She's actually going to sit on my lap. May as well have kept the jacket off, because I'm pretty certain where this is going to go.

But instead of putting a bookmark in our conversation and straddling me until I can't take it anymore she turns around and lightly perches her beautiful behind between my thighs, steepling her fingers on her knees and dropping her head down as if she's feeling shy. I shift forwards so that my front's up against her back and I tug at the neckline of her jacket so that there's just enough room for me to rest my chin above her collarbone. She shudders when my stubble stabs into her skin and I entwine our fingers in her lap, waiting for her to tell me what's on her mind.

"So my mom rang me," she begins, a slight tremble in her voice.

I'm not liking that at all. The only times that I've ever seen her acting like this was when she was talking about a certain piece of shit that I haven't yet gotten around to finding the home address of.

I hold my tongue, waiting for her to continue.

"At first we were talking about the upcoming press release week, the promo tour we're doing, and I told her that I didn't feel comfortable going because of the Evan thing. And then, because I'd already mentioned him, she used that as her cue to tell me some news from home, and she told me that... that..."

I lean around her and watch as a big warm teardrop trickles over the curve of her cheek. It plops right down onto her bare thigh. Horrified, I keep both of her hands in one of my palms and I move the other so that I'm caressing her exposed leg, rubbing my thumb over the tear until all traces of it have disappeared.

Her voice drops to a whisper, her eyes scrunched shut and tears running silently down her cheeks. "She told me that Evan and my sister Holly broke up. Which means that it wasn't even a real relationship in the first place. Which means that my fiancé broke up with me for literally just a fling. But then, on top of that, because only my family and the crew knew about the break up in the first place, because it hadn't reached the press yet, apparently he's still wearing his engagement ring. As if we're still together or something, which then puts this weird pressure on me, especially with the movie coming out, to act as if everything's fine. My mom made me check my emails and there were literally hundreds from the crew, and super urgent ones from the board at the production house. They don't want their leading hero looking like an asshole ahead of the release, so they want me to—"

I keep my voice deadly calm. "If you tell me that they want you to get back together with him, or even to pretend to be with him, I'm going to lose my mind."

She turns around to face me, her eyes the brightest that they've ever been, flushed with her tears.

"I'm obviously not going to do that – but I do have to go to the final stop of the press tour. I'm going to have to see him again if I want to save face, to stay in the company's good books."

I try to unclench the steel screws in my jaw. "I'm going with you," I tell her.

She shakes her head. "I'd never ask you to do that for me."

"I know you wouldn't," I say. "Which is exactly why I'm saying it. I'm saying it for you, so you don't have to."

She leans up to me and I instantly swoop down to take her lips with mine. She moans the second that my mouth presses against hers and I kiss her in a wild frenzy – pissed off at her colleagues, fucking furious with her ex, and most of all damn determined to remind her that I'm here for her, I'm right for her, and I'll pledge to take care of her for as long as she'll let me.

I move my hands to unzip the jacket and she arches back against me as soon as I have her uncovered. My hands move immediately to her tits, kneading them in fast frantic circles.

"Mitch," she whispers, and I start kissing at her cheeks. She tastes like salt from her tears. Her tears about her ex fiancé. And that makes me so damn angry that I have to remove my hands from her for a moment and sit back in my chair, staring unseeingly at the wall to my left and counting slowly to ten.

Then she decides to punch in another blow.

"There's more," she says quietly.

My eyes snap right back on her. *Is she fucking with me right now?*

"What more is there?" I ask. My tone is level, as if I'm not fantasising about going out into that forest and digging a nice big Evan-sized ditch.

Hell, she said that she used to like pretty boys, so it probably doesn't even need to be a big one.

"My mom said that Holly is devastated and really angry – angry at *me*. But apparently she got a role in some series that's shooting somewhere past Colorado so she'll be passing by here when she travels to set this weekend. So my mom told me that she talked Holly into stopping by, here, so that we could talk about what happened and maybe clear the air."

I can feel the hot red anger burning all the way up my neck. I give Harper a long look and say, "She's not stepping foot on this site."

Her bottom lip wobbles dangerously. "She's my sister."

"She's disloyal. Family doesn't do that to family."

We maintain eye contact for ten long seconds, Harper threatening another cascade of tears whilst I try to mentally persuade her to cancel her sister's visit.

No such luck.

"Fine," I submit, bowing my head against her

shoulder. I don't want her crying again and if she wants to maybe make amends with her sister then so be it. Doesn't mean that I'm going to be happy about it, but I'm not going to make this any harder for her than it already is. "When's she coming?"

"Tomorrow. I'm to set up, like, a dinner for her tomorrow evening."

Tomorrow evening. Our date night.

She's cooking dinner for the woman who fucked her fiancé behind her back on our date night.

I nod my head, a numb anger coursing through my veins.

"Okay," I say quietly, my voice void of emotion.

"Mitch," she says, twisting so that we can look at each other. "Don't be mad at me," she begs.

I shake my head and then brush my palms over her cheeks, wiping away the remnants of her tear stains. "I'm not mad at you. I'm mad at everyone else."

I lean down so that she can reach my mouth and this time when we kiss it's gentle. It's me saying that I know we didn't agree on this one but I still want to comfort her in any way that a partner can.

Which reminds me.

"You don't have any furniture in your kitchen," I murmur, pulling away from her.

She pulls me right back down and parts her lips, making it damn well impossible for me to not slip my tongue right inside and rub her up in the way I know she needs.

So much for gentle.

"No table, no chairs," I say hoarsely as she tugs at the neckline of my work shirt to try and get a look down at my pecs.

"Make me some?" she asks breathlessly, and it's so sweet, so Harper, that I can't help but laugh, nodding my head and dipping back down for another kiss.

"I'll get them to you first thing, baby," I murmur against her.

"And maybe... maybe stop by? Tomorrow evening?" she asks. "She'll probably be here from six 'til eight, that time-frame roughly. So maybe just before she leaves you could... come round? For a bit of moral support. Unless that's stupid, in which case–"

"I'll be there," I rasp, and then I give her our last kiss of the evening.

I've got some work to do.

CHAPTER 15

Harper

I pay the cab driver and then shuffle out of the back seat, pushing the door shut with my hip and beginning the trek from the bottom clearing up to the bungalows at the top of the valley. I keep my steps fast because one look skywards tells me that we're probably in for a snowstorm. A rainstorm at the least. That odd winter stillness, almost akin to summer humidity, is hanging cloyingly in the air and I can practically taste the imminent onslaught. The clouds are thick and grey, and the cool pause in the air heightens the scents of the pine trees.

Mitch brought me something to eat yesterday evening and then told me that he was heading to his place in Phoenix Falls so that he could access his home workshop and get me some furniture finished up for today. I'd been overwhelmingly tempted to say screw it to the whole endeavour, to tell my mom to tell Holly that she's most definitely not welcome here, and then to grab Mitch by his collar and tell him that we're still on for tonight. For date number five.

Instead I wrapped my arms around his neck and reached up to press my lips against his, letting him push me up against my doorframe as he kissed me slow and deep.

I told him I was sorry. He told me he wouldn't let me down.

I drop the grocery bags on the step outside of the bungalow, fishing out my key and then quickly opening up. I move everything over to the kitchen counter and then start organising what I bought.

Dishes to cook in, kitchenware to plate up on, and, most importantly, all of the food. I don't know why I let my mom talk me into being so hospitable but I'm here now so I may as well get this over with.

I wash and peel a bunch of vegetables and leave the pre-cooked chicken resting on the counter, hoping that I'm not about to make the sequel to food poisoning part one. Then again, giving my sister food poisoning wouldn't exactly be unjustified.

Don't be petty, I tell myself. *You'll cook, she'll talk, and then you can part with a happy-family story to tell mom about on Monday.*

I've got all of my dishes labelled, ten timers set on my phone, and I'm looking undecidedly at the new bottle of champagne in my fridge when there's suddenly a three-thump rap pounding on my door.

I hastily close the fridge, hiding the champagne like illegal contraband, and then I scrunch my fingers through my hair, hoping that it has a little *va-va-voom*

187

bounce as I pull open the front door.

Mitch's truck is pulled up outside with the bed facing our bungalows. He's turned away from me as he throws down the back of the bed, and then he reaches in, spreads his feet and lifts.

When he turns around he's got a medium sized kitchen tabletop gripped over his forearms, the cords in his neck protruding from the weight of it, but his face is as calm and controlled as ever.

He jerks his chin at me and I quickly step out of his way, freeing up the doorway so that he can walk the large wooden top through it sideways.

"Sorry it took so long," he says, his voice low and tight as he lowers an edge of the tabletop to the floor and then leans the underside against the wall. "I made a bunch of parts back home but we've been assembling them on-site, in the cabins. Last night I remembered that I'd have to build the table inside the bungalow, 'cause the wood's too big to get through your entryway. Got the chairs in the back and they're upholstered real nice. You like red, right?" he asks over his shoulder as he walks back to his truck to pull out two beautiful carved chairs, their seats made up with plump red padding.

"I like red," I reply, watching him carry the chairs in, one in each hand. "How did you know that I like red?" I ask, and he lets out a low grunt as he drops both of the chairs down by the kitchen counter.

He wipes his hands on his cargos and walks out again, avoiding my eyes. When he comes back with the final pieces for the furnishings – legs, stabilisation planks, and screws to finish off the table – I see that his cheeks have turned ruddy.

Have I forgotten something? I let the thought rest when he shakes his head, drops his equipment and mumbles out, "Just a guess."

In less than a minute his thighs are splayed, he's half-straddling the underside of the table, and he's screwing the metal bolsters in place, aligning the legs against them before he gets to the drilling.

I send off a text to my mom to tell her that I've done my prep and that I'm all set for my sister's arrival. Then I toss my phone onto the dresser in the bedroom and I unashamedly lean against the kitchen wall, watching Mitch as he works. He grips a leg into place and twists a bolt inside of it, in a fast rhythmic rotation of his fist.

He glances up at me when he catches sight of my legs in his peripheral vision, still in my jeans from my quick stop into town, and he stares for a moment at the top of my thighs, his hand moving a little slower as he lets his mind wander.

Then he swallows, blushes, and drops his eyes back to his work.

"You aren't using an electric drill?" I ask him, watching his bicep bulge with each curl of the tool.

He shakes his head. "Used an electric drill for the holes, but when it comes to screwing the pieces together I don't need anything battery-operated. Manual tools let me screw it in tight and precise, whilst keeping total control."

"I don't use anything battery operated either," I say to him.

His work instantly pauses.

He glances up at me from his splayed position on the floor and he licks his lips as his eyes trail down my body again.

"You don't?" he asks, his voice hoarse.

I shake my head.

He nods, his jaw clenched.

"I like that," he says finally, and then he drops his drill to the ground, standing upright and stepping back to survey the table.

It's upside down with four bespoke legs erected high in the air. He suddenly grips two of the legs and heaves them towards himself, enabling the table to lift onto its side, and then he wraps an arm over the top and pulls it down with a thump so that it's standing upright. Dust particles jump into the air, sparkling when they catch in the white light streaming in through the open doorway.

He grabs a cloth from his back pocket and rubs down the surface of the table, only looking up at me again when it's so clean that I'm reflecting in its dark polished surface.

"Why do you like that?" I ask, looking at him from the other side of the top.

He rolls a shoulder as he stuffs the cloth back into his pocket. "I like putting the work in."

I raise my eyebrows. Then I reach out an arm so that I can poke a finger on the table, moving it to test if it wobbles. It doesn't move an inch.

"Sturdy," I say simply.

He nods his head. "It needs to be."

I look away from him, turning my head so that my hair covers my glowing cheeks. I hear him move across the room and then the dull scrapes of the two chairs being placed at opposite sides of the table sound in the quiet room.

"Only two chairs," I acknowledge, my brow suddenly creasing. "You're not coming?"

He wipes his hands on the back of his pants and then walks around to my side of the table. His hands encase my hips, automatically moving our bodies flush together, and he dips down so that he can give me a light kiss.

"I don't need a chair because I'm not eating with your guest," he says, a hard flash behind his eyes when he mentions my sister. "But trust me, I'll be coming," he says firmly, and my belly whirls, warm and throbbing.

*

With every timer turned off and everything cooked, I lean nervously against the new table, my fingers gently skimming the polished edge. When I look up through the front window of the bungalow, the valley outside darkened by heavy winter evening clouds, I see my reflection crystal clear.

I'm wearing a high neck dress in baby pink, its hem floating just below the knee, with a soft cream cardigan to insulate my arms. My hair is in a blonde cotton candy blow-out and my cheeks are a little more flushed than usual after my hours at the stove.

I look like a little Battenberg.

I walk quickly across the floor, my pointed satin kitten heels clapping swiftly against the wood, and I rip the curtains shut to block out the mirror image. Then I head back to the table, pedantically realign the kitchenware, and check my phone for the time. It's 18:43. My mom said that Holly would be here most likely between six and seven but the lack of communication is making me itchy.

In an act of daughterly goodwill I unblocked my sister's number on my cell, expecting an onslaught of apologies from October, followed by maybe some kind of explanation at the time of their "break up", but what I actually found made my chest ache even more.

There was nothing. She hadn't sent me one message, from the time that she started sleeping with my ex fiancé to the time that they split.

I stare blankly at my phone, the frown on my forehead battling with the stinging behind my eyes.

I mean, obviously this dinner was a terrible idea for *me*, but maybe it'll give Holly the opportunity to…

I struggle to come up with a word to justify or defend her actions. If my mom hadn't asked me to do this then there's no way that I'd be even considering forgiving her tonight.

By seven o'clock I'm so hyper-alert that I've taken to pacing, my hand rubbing desperately at my chest as I try to think of what I'll say to her when she arrives. I think about it for a solid ten minutes and not one expletive-free sentence comes to mind.

At half seven I'm pretty much numb. I've been listening out for the gravel-crunch of a cab, the clipped tap of designer heels mounting my step, but all that I get is the faint whistle of the wind coursing heavily through the pine trees. I shudder, cold, and I finally allow myself to sink down into the chair that Mitch spent last night upholstering for me as the truth hits home.

She's not coming. I was jilted by my ex and now I'm being jilted by the woman that he cheated on me with. My own sister, no less. She's standing me up, and she was the one in the wrong in the first place.

I press my fingers against the centre of my brow and the oven suddenly hums to life, snapping me out of my depression spiral. I glance over to it, checking that it hasn't randomly turned itself on, and a cringing pain tightens in my stomach as I see all of the dishes and ramekins keeping the food warm in there. I close my eyes, wincing, and then I let myself arch back in Mitch's chair, the soft red padding supporting my body like a hug.

A loud rap hits the front door and my eyes fly over to it, my heart stilling in my chest.

Three raps. His usual.

Oh God. I glance around the room, the untouched table set-up, the foil wrapped dishes inside the oven, and mortification makes my blood turn cold.

He can't see this. He can't know what happened.

"Harper?" His voice is low as he calls my name through the wooden panel of the door. For some reason I can tell that he hasn't smiled in the past seven hours. Maybe longer. "You in there?"

I stay still on the seat, hoping that he'll go away. I can make up a lie tomorrow, maybe say that everything got patched up nicely – anything to prevent him from finding out that my sister just broke my heart for a second time in two months.

"I can see that your lights are on, Harper."

Goddamn it. I push back the chair and the sound of wood scraping against wood rings loud in the silence. Then I make my way over to the door and rest my hand on the knob. Count to five, steeling myself, and then I pull open the door.

The past two hours of misery momentarily disappear.

He's standing just behind the step, his hands tucked into the front pockets of a pair of deep navy suit pants, razor-sharp lines pressed down the centre of each leg, and the muscles of his quads make the fabric cling obscenely. My eyes move upwards to take in his white shirt, pulled across his pectorals in an expansive stretch. It's rolled up over his forearms and opened slightly at the top, as if his large body just couldn't be contained.

The wind howls violently around him but he stands completely still outside my door.

When I finally peek up at his face his gruff coating of stubble and the hard look in his eyes almost makes me lose my balance. I have to take a long inhalation to get some oxygen flowing through my brain.

I make a small coughing sound as my eyes drop back down his torso, the sight of what he's wearing making my breathing turn shallow.

"Are you… are you wearing suspender braces?" I ask him, my voice rasping.

He pulls his hands from his pockets and runs his thumbs up the backs of the belts. Then, after a moment, he suddenly lets them go with a harsh *twang* and they snap hard against his pecs in a loud erotic smack.

I blink fast, trying not to stare so obviously.

"Yeah," he says simply. Then he looks over my head for the first time and his expression turns blank. He looks back down at me. "Am I early?" he asks, confusion in his tone.

I remain silent for a good ten seconds, my eyes on

the pink points of my shoes. When I look back up at him I catch the exact moment that understanding dawns on his face. His brow drops and his jaw steels hard.

He looks so angry that I actually take a small step back.

"She didn't turn up," he says flatly.

It's a statement, not a question, and my chest burns painfully. I rub at the sting and his eyes briefly flick down to my trembling fingers.

He nods slowly and then, after a beat, his eyes flash over to the gate about twenty feet away to his right, opened in preparation for Holly's cab. Suddenly he's cursing, storming across the gravel, and shoving the gate shut, the chain wrapped around his fists as he leashes it around the pole and entwines it through the gate.

Then he's hulking back over to me with a face more thunderous than the weather behind him.

I chew on my lip as I try to will away the prickling behind my eyes, keeping my gaze averted whilst I pull myself together. When Mitch finally gets his arms around me and I look up at him, his expression has recomposed completely. He's calmed down in the space of ten seconds, collecting himself so that he can take care of me.

I release my bottom lip and make a little sniff.

"You do all that cooking back there?" he asks me quietly.

"Yes," I say breathlessly, reaching my arms around his neck and gripping my fists around his suspender braces, where they're cutting firmly into his engorged shoulder muscles. His pecs are swollen, hard, and only a millimetre away from my mouth.

He glances behind me again, over to the oven, and he nods his head. "You did a great job."

I shake my head weakly, my energy melting into nothingness as I take in the scent of his warm beautiful skin. *He got dressed up, the most formal that I've ever seen him, to hold my hand whilst I said goodbye to my sister.* That knowledge alone was worth the effort I put in.

"I probably did too much," I admit as his hands stroke over the soft back of my cardigan.

"Looks perfect to me."

"Would you... would you like to come in?" I ask him nervously.

He looks back down at me, first at my eyes, then my lips. Then he grunts, "Yeah."

We walk backwards, me almost stumbling over my kitten heels and him sturdier than an army Major. He knocks the door closed with the back of his bicep and when we reach the oven he pulls it open. A puff of steam comes out. He scopes the spread, lifting away the scorching foil with the backs of his fingers, and he makes a gruff sound of approval.

Then he closes the oven door and looks down at me.

"Harper–"

I pull away from him, and quickly sweep a curl out of my eyes.

"This is embarrassing, I know it is. She fucked me over before and then I let her fuck me over again. Maybe you should go. Pity will only make me feel worse."

He closes the space I'd put between us, pulling me roughly against his body as he locks his eyes in with mine.

"I already told you, Harper – they don't deserve you. You gave her a chance and she blew it. But I'm not even mad about it anymore. All that she's done is free up your Saturday night for *me*."

I feel his large palm as it slowly slides down my lower back and then, when he's fully cupping my behind, he waits a beat before squeezing my ass. A small gasp leaves my throat and my eyelashes flutter as I look up at him.

"You don't mind that I blew you off on our date night?" I ask.

His hand grips a little harder and he presses his torso firmly against mine. "I'm not angry, baby. It all worked out, anyway."

"Do you, uh, do you wanna eat?" I ask.

He glances warily over to the oven, probably thinking about words like *food poisoning* and *uncooked chicken*, but after a moment he nods his head and says, "I could eat."

Mitch lifts the trays out of the oven and I serve up the food on the counter, so as to not scorch the top of my shiny new table. He watches my knife-wielding hand with a steady gaze as I carve the chicken, and I place three pieces on both of our plates. I look up at him and I point the knife at a leg, silently asking if he wants more. He slides his eyes over to mine and nods.

Then I point at the other leg.

He nods again.

By the time that Mitch is carrying our plates over to the table he basically has a whole chicken on his plate, plus mashed potatoes and an assortment of vegetables that were at one point caramelised but have since seen the depths of Mordor.

He waits for me to sit and then he pulls out a chair of his own, dropping down into it with his legs spread wide. I swallow hard and thank God that I put the glasses and a bottle of champagne on the table. It's been out of the fridge for so long that it's body is sweating. Which is relatable.

Mitch sees the bottle and raises an eyebrow at me. He's thinking about my "self medicating" incident and my subsequent behaviour.

I don't even blame the champagne for that – that was all me.

"Could you open it for me?" I ask him, scooching a little closer to the table and watching his eyes drop to my chest. Watching me bounce. He gives me a curt absentminded nod, his gaze unabashedly preoccupied, and he pulls the bottle into his lap, pointing the head away from me, over to the corner to my left. His left hand is gripping the base of the body and his right is clenched tight over the head, his arm lifted slightly so that he can wrench it, fast and clean.

I feel like I'm watching champagne porn. With a swift tug of his wrist he yanks the cork free, releasing a quick low grunt and then reaching for a glass to fill the initial overspill into.

He fills it so that the foam is just below the rim and he passes it over to me before setting the bottle back on the table.

"Thank you. Don't you want any?" I ask, braving a tiny sip, to relieve myself of the cloying heat he seems to be permanently putting me into.

He shakes his head, his fists gripping his cutlery but still waiting for me to take the first bite. "Not really my thing."

"I have other things," I say.

His eyes dip to my lap and he licks his lips. His hands tighten around his knife and fork as if to say *I bet you do.*

"In the fridge," I clarify, warmth staining my cheeks. "I bought you something, in case you were to come over."

His eyebrows lift in surprise and he gestures to the fridge, silently asking permission to get up and check. I nod and take my first mouthful of chicken, which is not pink, thank God. He watches me chew for a moment and then he pulls himself away from the table, heaving himself up and over to the fridge.

When he sees what's inside I see his tan cheekbone tick up in amusement.

"You really got my number, baby," he says with a half-smile as he tears at the cardboard that's joining the six bottles together, and pulls out a beer for himself. He uses his thumb to push off the lid, a fast *hiss* leaving the neck, and then he tips the bottle back, taking a savouring pull. I forget about my food as I watch his Adam's apple roll.

When he rejoins me at the table my food is almost as untouched as his.

"You don't have to eat all of it," I say as he raises his cutlery, poised to tuck in.

He glances up at me as his fork works a sweep of mass destruction around his plate. Without another word he shovels it in.

I raise my eyebrows in amazement.

His throat works as he swallows. "Why wouldn't I eat all of it?"

"Um." I watch, entranced, as he folds a piece of meat over with his fork, spears it thoroughly, and then wolfs it down. He chases it with a swig of his beer, his eyes on mine as he drinks from the bottle. My eyes stray to the bottom of his throat, the deeply tanned V of exposed skin at the top of his chest, and I watch as it heaves with each of his swallows.

When he places the bottle back on the table he jerks his chin at me so that I look up at his face. "It's really good, Harper. You're a good cook."

I squirm on my seat, secretly pleased, and I give him a little smile as a gold shimmery feeling sparkles in my chest.

"Thanks," I say, and I look down at his plate as I take a tiny sip of my champagne. He's literally cleaned half of it already. I look down at my own and say without thinking, "You can have mine if you'd like. I got a sort of anxiety adrenaline rush earlier so I'm not very hungry."

He shovels in another mouthful and glances across at my plate. Gestures at it with his fork, swallows, and then says, "Eat, baby. I need you to get your energy up."

The cutlery in my hands clatters shakily as I move it over the porcelain.

"Why do you need me to get my energy up?" I ask, forcing my fingers to saw a piece of chicken and take it in my mouth.

Mitch looks at me, long and hard, without saying anything. Then he moves his gaze back down to his plate and shoves in another forkful.

We eat quietly for a few minutes, the only sounds the high-pitched whistle of the wind outside as it rushes through the pine trees, and the repetitive scrape of metal cutlery as it grazes at our plates.

He finishes about ten minutes before I do, and he sits back in his seat, legs kicked out as he watches me over his beer. When I'm down to my last piece of chicken I look up at him from under my lashes and gesture to it in an offering.

He gives me a smug kind of grin and pushes back in his chair, taking his plate over to the sink and then coming over to my side of the table. I stand with my almost-empty plate and he takes my fork, spearing the meat and then consuming it like a Viking.

He takes the plate from my hand and places that in the sink too, squirting washing-up liquid on a sponge before running the tap and starting to wash.

He must be able to sense that I'm about to protest because he looks down at me from over his shoulder and says, "You cooked, I'll clean."

At least something in this place is about to get clean. Our height difference means that my eyes are permanently level with his giant pecs and I don't think I've had one clean thought in my head for the past eight weeks.

"You did such a good job tonight, baby," he says quietly again when he notices that I'm beyond verbal communication. He finishes up the washing and dries his palms on the towel.

"I didn't make dessert," I admit when we're facing each other, his hands re-rolling up his sleeves and mine twiddling with a button on my cardigan.

He says nothing, his eyes burning into mine like I'm missing something. When they begin to trail over the curves of my body I realise what he's thinking.

I'm dessert.

He wraps an arm around my waist and walks me backwards towards the table, leaning slightly over me so that he can pick up his bottle of beer. He watches me as he tips back the rest of it and then he sets it on the floor, freeing up both of his hands.

I arch backwards, allowing the backs of my thighs to hit off the wood of the table, and the slight jolt of my body makes Mitch grip his hands around the sides of my hips.

"Thank you for dinner," he murmurs, leaning down slightly to close the space between us.

"You're welcome," I whisper up at him. I wrap my hands around the front belts of the braces and add, "I wouldn't have wanted tonight to go any other way."

He stills for a beat and then, for perhaps the first time since I met him, he gives me a real smile. Perfect white teeth against deep tan skin, sharp cut creases in both sides of his angular cheeks. He leans down until we're forehead to forehead and a satisfied growl rumbles in his chest.

"You're so sweet," he murmurs as I lean up to rub my nose against his. "You're just so darn sweet."

He's too close to me to not have my mouth on his so I give the suspenders a rough tug and it has his eyes fluttering open, looking down at me in surprise before dropping his gaze to my lips.

"You're really gonna cook me dinner and then let me make out with you?" he asks incredulously, his fingers splaying slowly wider until they're encasing both of my butt cheeks.

"Well, you did do the cleaning," I whisper back with a smile.

He grins and shakes his head. "I'm dreaming."

"Do I usually make an appearance in your dreams?" I ask, pulling the braces tighter so that they bite hard into his shoulder muscles.

He grunts, his neck arching back at the burn, and he nods down at me.

"Yeah, you've been in my dreams."

"And what kind of dreams are they?" I continue, my breath catching in my throat when he presses the front of his pants up against my belly. He's so hard and thick that my eyes roll backwards.

He lowers his mouth to my neck and gives me a gentle suck. So gentle that I moan and my nipples pinch beneath my clothes.

He breathes a laugh against my skin and then rises so that he's towering over me again, pulling me up with his forearms so that my lips are only an inch from his.

He waits until I settle and then he finally whispers, "They're the kind of dreams that I have to wash the sheets after."

A delighted giggle bursts out of me, Mitch clutches me closer, and then he finally presses his mouth down on mine. His hands knead my ass rough and fast, and he grunts with pleasure at the feeling. Then he slants my mouth open and slides his tongue inside, with a long hot stroke.

I moan, no longer laughing, and my legs automatically move to wrap around him. He dips down so that he can shove up the bottom of my dress and then he hitches my thigh high up around his waist. I clutch at the tops of his biceps as his hips pin me to the table, at first grinding me hard against the edge, and then lifting me onto it completely so that both of my legs are off the ground.

He slips his tongue around mine, rubbing and licking until I'm whimpering, and his palms knead my thighs until I'm splayed, wanting and boneless.

"Mitch," I whisper, rubbing my breasts up against him.

He pulls back to look at me, his face set hard with masculine appreciation. The skirt of my dress has bunched in the middle, hiding my underwear, but my legs are fully exposed and he admires them blatantly. I wrap my ankles around his ass and use his hard muscles to help me kick off my kitten heels.

He breathes out a laugh and clasps my ankles in his palms when I'm finished, rubbing them so gently that I have to sit back on my elbows to stop myself from succumbing to total limpness.

"I like your... top," he says gruffly as his eyes rake up my arms and over my chest.

"It's a cardigan," I say breathlessly, tugging him closer against my lap when he releases my ankles.

"Cardigan," he grunts, like he's never heard of one before.

"Do you wanna see what's underneath it?" I ask, lifting one hand from behind my body so that I can toy with the buttons running from my breasts to my belly.

He makes a low sound and encases both sides of my waist with his hands, his eyes on my chest.

"Yeah."

I slip the soft fabric off one of my shoulders and I watch as his eyes cloud over, taking me in.

"Other side," he rasps, helping my arm out of the

sleeve and exposing one half of my baby pink dress, stretched tight across the rounded curves of my upper body.

I sit up and hold out my other arm. He rolls the cardigan down it gently and then, when it's completely off, he folds it neatly, his eyes on mine.

"Are we…" He struggles to find the appropriate words but his hands on my hips and his groin rubbing my heat tell me exactly what he's thinking about. "Are we… going to stop? Or…"

I lean up, wrapping my hands around his biceps, and I rub my thumbs over the hard swells, looking up at him from under my lashes.

"Do you want to stop?" I whisper.

He smirks down at me, pressing his crotch more firmly between my thighs. "That feel like I wanna stop to you?"

I press one of my palms flat on the table behind me so that I can keep my balance as his arousal obliterates my bodily control.

"It feels… it, uh…"

"Yeah?" he asks, pressing against me even harder.

I squeeze my eyes closed, the thick length of him making my belly pound and pool with heat. "Big," I finally whisper. "It feels… very big. I'm too small for you."

He breathes a laugh. "I'll get it in, trust me."

I drop down onto the table, my thighs hitched high around his waist. Mitch leans over me to collect the champagne and my glass before depositing them on the floor, and then he kicks out the chair beside him so that he has more room to position himself against me at the table.

He pushes my dress up so that the little skirt is over my belly and he looks down at my newly exposed underwear, a pair of simple navy blue cotton briefs with a small bow in the centre.

His cheek ticks up at the side as he rubs a thumb over the bow.

They're not exactly sex panties but he seems to like them all the same. I didn't know that this would be happening tonight since I had had other plans but when Mitch meets my eyes I can see the unspoken words sparkling in his irises.

You got navy panties to match my uniform, he tells me.

I can neither confirm nor deny, I tell him back.

He smirks and then his thumb presses lower.

"*Oh,*" I gasp, as he rubs his thumb firmly down the cotton and over the swell of my clit.

He drags his thumb up and down and his eyes watch his work, entranced.

"You're wet, Harper," he murmurs. "Wet through your panties. You know what that means?" he asks, and I shake my head, too over-stimulated to understand the nuance of what he's thinking. He looks down at me, his chest rising and falling in large controlled heaves, and his fingers suddenly slip beneath the cotton of my underwear and press firmly against my swollen little nub. I arch my back in surprise and he gently rotates his confident press. "I'm gonna glide inside so easy you'll think that I was made for you."

He pulls his hand away from my sex and asks, "How do I take your dress off?"

"Zip," I whisper, sitting quickly upright and getting shakily to my feet. He steadies me with his hands on my shoulders and I pull my hair to one side as I turn my back to him, exposing the long zip that travels down from my neck to the centre of my waist.

He grips one hand around my throat and the other pinches the tag of the zip, sliding it seamlessly down my back in one strong pull. He brushes the short sleeves down my arms and the top falls away from my body, until it pools around my waist in a little pink pouf.

"No bra," he murmurs from above my head, staying still as he waits for me to turn around.

"I was wearing a cardigan," I remind him as his hands encase my bare waist.

"Can I touch them?" he asks me quietly, his palms gripping into me with need and excitement, desperate to finally feel me without any barriers in the way.

I don't reply. Instead I move my hands to press against his and I drag them slowly upwards until he's fully gripping my breasts.

"Fuck," he grunts, no longer needing my fingers to guide him. He pushes them up with his eager palms and then lets them drop, towering over me so that he can watch them bounce firmly back into place. I tip my head back against his throat so that I can watch his expression, a hard sneer of desire set firmly on his mouth.

"Look at those babies," he rasps, getting another handful and bouncing them. I whimper and he starts caressing my nipples with fast relentless circles. "I'm not gonna be able to keep my hands off them."

I move my trembling hands quickly to my waist so that I can shimmy out of my dress, letting it drop to the floor and leaving me in nothing but my underwear.

I press my ass up against his crotch as he kneads at my breasts and he makes a low dangerous snarl as he moves a hand to the front of my panties. He dips his fingers beneath the gusset and rubs firmly against my clit, making me arch my back against him.

"The key to your bungalow has been burning a hole in my pocket for almost eight fucking weeks, Harper," he growls as I wrap my arms behind his neck, writhing against the pace of his fingers. "You and that smart mouth, and now I've got you all to myself. Got the whole weekend to show you what I've been fantasising about doing to you. Got the whole weekend to work this little pussy."

He turns me around and helps me back up onto the table, ducking down to kiss me and sliding his tongue instantly inside my mouth. He keeps one hand squeezing my ass cheek and the other flies up to my chest, claiming my breast with a rough grope. His tongue rubs against mine with warm long strokes, working me up until I pull away, moaning in agony.

"Mitch, I need it," I plead with him, my eyebrows arching as I watch him lower himself to my breasts and take a nipple in his warm mouth. He sucks it hard and firm as his hand teases my other one, and he moans in pleasure, like this is as much for him as it is for me.

"Softest little tits," he grunts when he lifts himself up again, eyes on mine as both of his palms massage my breasts. "Jesus, Harper."

Then he removes his hands from my chest so that he can yank down the suspender braces from around his shoulders, the belts snapping against his shirt as he rips them from their taut position. He watches me with a steady gaze as his large fingers work their way down the buttons, exposing more and more of his warm tanned skin.

"Do you have a condom?" I ask him as he undoes the final button, shucking the shirt off his shoulders and tossing it to the floor. He reveals his thickly muscled abdomen and those large swollen pecs. My mind goes blank as I take in the breadth of them.

He pulls his wallet from the pocket of his suit pants and flicks open the leather flap. My eyes drop to the contents. I see a thick wad of cash and five glossy black squares. He pulls out a condom, tosses his wallet to the edge of the table, and then holds the square up for me to read. I'm met with the familiar golden script of *"MAGNUM Plus"*. My cheeks heat up, remembering what I did.

"Look familiar?" he asks me, his eyes locked in on mine.

"Um." I look up at him as innocently as I can manage but his gaze is so ruthless that I squirm a little on the table.

"That morning back at my place in October," he says. "Noticed a drawer slightly ajar and decided to take a look. Was interested to find that my box of condoms had been ransacked and strewn all around the place. Any explanation?" he asks me.

I press myself against him but he doesn't waver, the condom still held perfectly eye-level.

"I didn't mean to," I say beseechingly. "I was out of it, remember? I just wanted to look in one drawer and then when I saw what it said on the box…" Suddenly I frown, remembering my thoughts from that night. "I was thinking about how you had a box of condoms

209

next to your bed, which meant that you were sleeping with other women."

I move to pull back from him, awash with renewed irritation, but he grips me tightly against his abs.

"I bought those condoms because a hot twenty-eight year old chick had just taken up permanent residence on my building site and I knew that I was gonna need to start blowing my load if I wanted to remain remotely professional around her. But then I started to spend more time with her and I decided that I didn't want to fuck around. You broke the seal, baby. Those condoms weren't open."

I yank him down hard so that he can reach my level and kiss me, and I part my lips immediately, begging him to come inside.

He moans as he laps his tongue against mine and then he murmurs into me, "You like that? You like that I've been saving this cock for you?"

"Yes," I whimper, my fingers desperately trying to rip open his pants. "Yes, I like that."

"And you?" he asks. "Since you got here, have you been saving this pussy for me?"

"Yes," I say, moaning and nodding as he slips his tongue around mine. "Only you," I whisper and he pulls away with a quick growl.

He yanks his chair back behind him and heaves himself down on it, kicking his legs out as he scrapes the seat forwards. I sit up slightly on my elbows, my feet dangling off the tabletop on either side of his thighs. He slowly leans forwards, tucking his fingers into the sides of my panties and tugging. We're both holding our breath as he pulls my panties away, exposing my heat as he rolls the cotton down my thighs. I raise my legs so that he can slip them fully off my ankles and then he repositions me so that I'm splayed right in front of him, his thighs spread wide, showcasing the large hard-on straining against his pants.

"Jesus," he mutters, leaning back in his seat. One hand scrapes down his stubble and the other rubs firmly at his solid erection. He looks into my eyes, catching me watching him, and he asks, "You like getting your pussy eaten?"

I blink fast, my legs shaking a little. It's not something that I've experienced much of and in all honesty I hadn't particularly enjoyed it. I'm about to say no when he rephrases.

"Want me to eat your pussy?"

"Um, oh, um…" I run one hand through my hair, leaning up on one elbow.

I mean, when he puts it like *that*…

"I think, perhaps, maybe, if you'd like to–"

And then his mouth is suddenly between my legs, lapping warm and gentle as his palms massage my thighs.

"You're sweet everywhere," he grunts, the sound reverberating through my belly.

He eases my calves over his shoulders and I naturally succumb to laying backwards, my fingers twining in his hair as he licks and kisses at me. His palms rub up and down my thighs as he rolls his tongue between my legs, and then one hand disappears and I hear him grunt as he grips at his erection.

I lift myself slightly upwards and whisper to him, "I want you, now."

He looks up at me from between my thighs, unsure

for a moment, and then he begins kissing his way up my belly. One of his hands goes to grab a condom and he tears it open before his mouth has reached my neck.

He stands upright and my eyes fall to the bulging muscle beneath his suit pants.

As he undoes his zipper I say to him, "Do you always carry a spare drill with you like that?"

He laughs and shakes his head, his eyes flashing to mine as he pushes his trousers down his thighs.

He doesn't mess around with one piece of clothing at a time – his boxers are shoved straight down with his pants, meaning that I'm immediately met with his long thick arousal, the hard muscle that he's had ready for me for almost two months.

It looks like he's been ready for me for almost two years. He's more erect than a barge pole, his length dark and straining. The sight of the large sac behind it has me dragging him down on top of me, wriggling into place as I kiss his mouth with mine.

"Condom," he mumbles, leaning up so that he can fit it at the head of his shaft and then use his fist to roll it down.

"I've never had a, uh, a *Magnum* sized… you know… before," I whisper up at him with a slightly teasing smile.

His eyes flash on mine and he kisses me hard again.

"I'll go slow," he murmurs, resting one palm flat beside my head and the other gripping around the thick base of himself, aligning the domed head with my heat.

"I thought you worked hard and fast," I remind him, stroking my fingers over his bulging shoulders.

His cheeks turn ruddy and he smiles as he pushes gently at my entrance.

"On the site," he murmurs. "Not the bedroom."

When he's in place he moves his hand to my hip and then rubs it around so that he's cupping my ass, squeezing slightly to make me laugh.

"We're still on the site," I whisper up to him. "And technically we're not in the bedroom."

He swallows hard and takes a deep inhalation, his pecs heaving above my mouth. "Hard and fast is for fucking," he says to me. "We're gonna make love, Harper."

My eyes widen in surprise. *Make love?* I involuntarily knock my thighs against him and he makes a gruff sound as he accidentally pushes the large head inside.

"Oh!" My eyes bulge and I take a deep gasp of air, Mitch's left bicep bulging around the side of my cheek as he lowers himself down on top of me.

"Sorry," he murmurs. "I didn't… that wasn't…" His leashes his fingers into my hair, panting as he keeps his body still. "Tell me when you're ready."

To *make love?* In my mind I'm not so sure, given the reason why I fled to Pine Hills in the first place. But if I wipe away my past and I root myself in this very second I know that I would be a thousand million trillion percent sure.

"I'm ready," I whisper up at him. With a deep groan of relief he thrusts the rest of his length inside.

"Harper," he rasps, the hand on my hip tightening firmly. He slides out until only the head is inside and then he pushes back in, long and deep. "This okay?" he asks me, looking down at me from above my head.

I wrap my calves tighter around his firm behind,

feeling the strength in his stance as he carefully fills me up and withdraws.

"Yes," I whimper, my nails biting into the back of his neck.

He nods and then looks down at my body as he slides in and out in a gruff steady rhythm. The hand on my hip rubs up to my breast and he grips at it appreciatively as he pumps me against the table.

"I'm gonna pay you back for dinner," he murmurs, as the table scrapes heavily against the floor.

"Y-you're already paying me back," I moan, and he grunts as he slides back inside harder.

"Not like this," he clarifies as the table shoves backwards another five inches. "I'm talking finance. I'm gonna take care of you."

"Trust me, you're taking care of me," I gasp. "Besides, y-you already paid for dinner when you slid four-hundred dollars inside my purse."

He groans and thrusts faster, lifting himself up so that he can watch me at a higher angle. He moves both hands to grip my hips and he holds me hard against his crotch, keeping me firmly in place for his relentless movements. My eyes trail over the thick muscles of his abdomen and the swollen peaks of his chest and I recline totally backwards, lifting my breasts a little higher and watching him lick his lips as he watches them shake.

He can't resist. He presses himself back down on top of me, one arm holding my wrists above my head and his other moving in on my chest, rubbing fast circles around my nipples as he pounds into me harder.

"Why'd you have to be so fucking sexy, Harper?"

I pant and moan and his hand moves back to my hip so that he can shove his thick length into me faster.

"Good job we're alone on the site tonight, baby. Can't have anyone walking in here and seeing what I'm doing to you. Seeing what the boss is doing to you."

I gasp and writhe but he keeps me in place, his sac smacking against me, fast and heavy.

"I'm not gonna be able to stop making love to you, Harper," he says quietly, his face set with pain as he slides in and out.

My back arches and I whimper at his words.

Making love. He's *making love* to me.

He notices my reaction. The sudden slickness, the clenching, and his eyes burn despite his composure. "You like hearing that," he states simply as he tilts my ass further upwards, allowing him to stroke deeper. "You like it when I say that, don't you? Because that's what we're doing here, Harper." He swallows and his jaw clenches, like he doesn't want to continue. "It makes me think that maybe no other man's done it to you like that before," he murmurs, and I bite hard into my bottom lip, trying to stop my soft anguished sounds.

"Is it true?" he asks gruffly. "Am I the first?"

I can't keep it in anymore. I grip at the hard swells of his chest, moaning and nodding.

"Yes," I whimper. "You're the first to do that. You're the only one."

He presses down onto me hard, pinning my back completely against the table, and he rolls his hips between mine with long rough strokes.

"You're beautiful," he says, looking down at me.

He allows barely a millimetre of light to penetrate the shield that his shoulders have formed above my face.

"You're gonna break the table," I whisper back at him as it scrapes another five inches across the floor.

He breathes a laugh and shakes his head. "I promise I made it real secure," he murmurs. Then he thinks about it and says, "I can make you another one."

I laugh too but suddenly he's hunching as far down as he can, kissing me in a frenzy and grunting with every thrust. Then I'm clenching and writhing, and he's pulling back to hold me in place whilst I climax, watching me with a jaw set harder than steel. His own strokes begin to turn sloppy and he makes gruff snarling sounds, his biceps bulging as he grips me against him, until he can't control it any longer and he growls as he finally unloads.

I cling onto him as he settles his heavy body down against my own, our breathing laboured as we recover from what just happened.

When he finally lifts himself up our eyes lock together. Then we both look backwards, sensing something amiss.

Laughter bursts out of both us.

The table has scraped all the way to the other side of the room.

CHAPTER 16

Mitch

Like clockwork I wake up at 5:29.

At first I keep my eyes closed and regulate my breathing back to its usual steady rhythm. The calendar in the back of my mind tells me that it's Sunday – no work today – so I'm off the hook unless I want to get ahead on next week's paperwork, which is what I'd usually do.

Then I feel what I've got my hands on, last night comes racing back to me, and I suddenly don't want to keep my eyes closed anymore.

Harper's lying on her back, her head turned to face me, with her hair poufed around her in a soft golden halo. Her cheeks are flushed with heat. Maybe from the warm sheets bunched around her, maybe from my right forearm lying heavy on her stomach, or maybe she's not recovered from last night, when we couldn't keep our hands off each other.

After dinner there was no stopping us – I wanted it, she wanted it, and once we had it there was no going back. The second that we got her perfect ass perched up on her new table we both knew what was going to happen. I got her out of her clothes, ripped a condom out of my wallet, and saw to the job I'd been meaning to see through since that first morning way back in October. She wrapped herself around me, lithe, golden, and gorgeous, and I took her right there on the table, so damn lost in it that when we finished we were on the other side of the room.

And I couldn't even bring myself to pull it out. I stayed on top of her and inside of her until I was ready to give her round two, only then dragging it slowly out and watching her as I rolled the condom off. Tossed it on the floor and stood there for a few seconds, letting her take it in without a rubber to shield it. She looked up at me, biting into her lower lip, and let me peruse her lying back on the table as brazenly as she was looking at me. Flushed cheeks, panting breaths, those soft sexy breasts. Then a little further down, over her smooth soft stomach, all the way until I got to that area at the apex of her thighs, blushing, and swollen, and ready for me.

I went to the other side of the room, yanked the chair back over to the table, then took a seat as I tore open a new condom, Harper's legs dangling on either side of my thighs and her body slightly raised as she watched me from her elbows.

As soon as the rubber snapped into place I reached forwards to grip her hips and eased her right onto my lap, her arms automatically wrapping around the back of my neck and her soft little tits pressed up against my pecs. I used one hand to keep her ass hovering just above my thighs and the other to grip the thick base of my shaft, rubbing the head against her pussy to get her writhing and ready to take it again. Then I got the tip in place, clutched both my hands over the sexy curves of her ass, and pushed her right down the length of me, all the way until her cheeks slapped off my thighs and her eyes rolled back in her head.

She was in the position to ride me but all she could do was cling on, her legs spread wide and her body limp as I held her hard against my lap and rutted deep thrusts into her belly. She was moaning from the feel of my muscles scraping her nipples alone, so by the time that she was on the verge of her climax she was the hottest mess that I'd ever seen. Her brow arched in desperation, and her tits bouncing like they were made to taunt me. I got a hand on them as I lifted her up, ready to take her to the bedroom to finish her off, but the movement before I stood got me shoving it in so deep that she was already coming, and all I could do was get us over to the bedroom doorway and pound her up against it until she slumped bonelessly against my chest.

I jerked it into her a couple more times so that I could come quickly, and then I laid her down on the sheets, subtly knocking that toy bear to the floor behind her because I wasn't going to have those beady little eyes on me.

I pulled out and then kissed her until those pained whimpers turned into sleepy moans. Tucked her in, then went to the dining area to grab my shirt and the rest of the condoms, chucking them onto the bedside table when I was back inside the bedroom.

I got myself under the quilt with Harper and wrapped her up in my arms, expecting her to already be in a sex coma, but the second that my rigid cock poked into her side she was kissing at me again, begging for just one more round. She wrapped her legs up around my waist as she rolled herself onto her back, and I reached over to the bedside table as she scratched her nails hard down my skin.

I dipped down to kiss her and filled her up with those slow deep strokes of tongue.

And then I gave it to her, just how she wanted it.

In my head a mental alarm clock beeps 5:30. I want to brush my thumb down Harper's belly and then roll her tightly against my chest but the need to let her rest prevails. She's wearing nothing but my shirt and I'm wearing nothing but the sheets, and the sight of her breasts gently poking through the fabric makes my bare cock grow heavy and thick. I steel my jaw to stop myself from groaning and I close my eyes.

I'm guessing she's going to need at least another hour or two of sleep. The memory of her beautiful body, soft yet strong, gripping at me whilst I buried deep inside of her, has my sac aching so hard that I have to reach down and clutch at it, disbelieving how badly I need her again after everything we did last night.

Jesus, this isn't normal. I move my fist up to my shaft and give it a couple of hard tugs, hoping that that'll sate it for now. Then I wrap my arm over Harper's chest, keeping her safely locked down whilst she rests.

I hear a small gasp and I immediately want to

suffocate myself with her pillow. It's the sound of Harper's breathing hitching because I just fucking woke her up. Goddamn it. I open my eyes and look down at her, her own fluttering open, then widening when she comes face to face with my pecs.

She instantly rolls onto her side and presses herself between them, and I wrap my biceps firmly around her head, swaddling her. My cock pokes ramrod straight into her belly and she jolts, moans, and then she's wrapping her fingers around it, trying to get me off not ten seconds after she's woken up.

"Good morning," I murmur to her, trying not to thrust into her pumping fists, but damn she's doing it just how I need it.

She releases a breathless sound which I take as her *good morning*. I slide an arm between us and reach down to her heat, pressing two fingers against her clit and then beginning to rub small firm circles. Two can play at this game.

She arches back and whimpers, draping a thigh over my hip to give me better access. The harder I rub her the faster she pumps.

"You sleep good?" I grunt, using my free hand to quickly knead her ass.

She looks up at me and nods, and then a thought crosses her face, a small cloud of doubt. "I think so," she says quietly, leaning up against me so that my pecs can stimulate her tits. "Did I... did I sleep weird at all?"

I almost frown, breathing out a laugh. "Why're you asking that? You slept like a princess."

She moans and pants when I hit the spot particularly good and then she gives herself a moment before she says, "I have this… sleep thing. Like, sleep paralysis. I have to sleep on my back, otherwise I wake up and it's like I'm... like I'm dying. So, if you're sleeping with me, just – just make sure I'm not on my sides, okay?"

Didn't expect that, but sure, okay.

I nod down at her, then take her lips with mine and press a hard kiss against her. She squirms and tosses me faster, my tip catching against her belly and making my balls tighten, getting ready.

When we pull apart I look deep into her eyes and say, "I'll keep you on your back all night."

She squeezes me hard and presses her thighs together, my fingers encased in her softness, caressing her with as much pressure as I can. Then she starts to move, rubbing my length against her thighs and trying to get me in her entrance, so I quickly release my hands from her, getting a condom from the dresser as fast as possible. I roll it down myself before her eager body can convince me to forget about protection and just have her bare.

"You want it?" I ask her as I throw the wrapper on the floor, probably right next to her damn teddy bear.

She reaches up to kiss me, parting her lips so that I have no choice but to dive right in and tongue-fuck her. I use one hand to slip between the open buttons of the shirt and rub at her tits, gently squeezing at them in that way that makes her spread her legs for me.

"What time is it?" she asks breathlessly, helping me pull the shirt off her shoulders. Freeing her beautiful breasts. I almost forget her damn question.

"Early," I reply quickly. "And it's Sunday, so we've

got all day."

"Good," she moans, and then she rolls over onto her side, putting her back to me.

Holy shit. She arches her ass right against my hard-on and I grab her hips instinctively, slipping my cock between her legs and letting her squeeze me with her soft thighs.

I slide back and forth beneath her pussy, teasing her.

"You're getting me off before I'm even inside of you," I say to her quietly, looking down over her body so I can get my eyes on the peaks of her breasts. I move one hand from her hip so that I can give them a shake, making her arch her back further and giving me an even better view of them.

I thrust a few times between her legs but then I can't deny us any longer. I get a fist around myself, nudge it against her heat, and then after waiting a few painstaking seconds I push it straight up inside, right to the hilt.

"*Mitchell,*" Harper whispers, squirming her ass against me whilst I hold her down against my groin.

"We have to give it a few seconds, Harper. We have to get you used to the size, then I'll start pumping, I promise."

I press my chest into her back as she wraps her arms backwards around my neck, but I keep her firmly in place until she stops writhing. Then my palms go up to her breasts, kneading her gently as I withdraw, wait, and then push back inside.

"There we go," I murmur when she moans and falls back against me. Her ass slaps loudly against my thighs as I refill her. Her head's resting against the tops of my pecs and I look down at her beautiful face, her eyes meeting mine. "You like that?" I ask her, keeping up a steady rhythm.

"Yeah," she whispers, her tits bouncing in my peripheral.

"Yeah?" I ask, squeezing them a little faster. "You like taking the boss between your thighs?"

She clenches hard around me as her body falls limp against the quilt.

I'll take that as a yes.

"You've got me working overtime, haven't you?" I rasp. "Laying down early morning pipe. It's off the books, Harper. It's our little secret."

She flutters her lashes up at me and runs her fingers over the stubble on my jaw. I feel like an animal, taking her from the back whilst she treats me so gentle, but she's so soft and so sexy that I have no intentions of stopping.

"I love that you're the boss," she whispers, teeth grazing into her swollen lower lip. "And..." She looks nervously up at me. "And I love that you're a daddy."

I thrust faster, my balls slapping non-stop against her. "Say that again and I'm gonna make you a mommy."

"Oh!"

She squeezes her eyes shut and clenches tight. She's there, I know she is from the way that she's drenching me.

"Do it," she whispers. "Please do it."

I'm almost growling. *She wants me to knock her up?* I move two fingers to press hard against her clit and then she's gasping for me, begging me not to stop.

"I'm not gonna stop, baby," I groan. "I'm gonna

finish you."

I take her like a wild man, my hands groping every curve whilst she comes apart in my arms. Even when she finishes she still isn't done, with aftershocks jolting through her making her brow pinch as quiet moans leave her throat. Her throat that I can't help but sink my teeth into as I begin to thrust rough and deep, finally chasing the release of my own.

"You got a taste for it now, don't you?" I ask, my voice deep and gravel-rough as I knead at her tits, pressing her back against my chest. "Thick blue collar cock."

She smushes her face into the pillow moaning *yes,* and I roll her onto her belly, beginning to pound into her hard from the back. One hand stays at her chest and the other grips nice and tight against her ass, settling my haunches between her thighs as I ride her into the mattress.

"Almost there," I grunt, thrusting as fast as I can. "Look at me, Harper. Look at me and you'll send me over."

She turns her cheek, flushed deep pink, and then she gives me that little ray of sunshine smile. Just a tiny one as she pants with exertion, and suddenly I'm done. I crowd a bicep above her head and begin to uncontrollably spill, my other palm kneading her ass cheeks and then giving her a couple of quick spanks when she taunts me with kisses that are just out of reach.

She's laughing and moaning and then whimpering again as I drop heavily on her back, groaning as I finish, and gently caressing her nipples. Then we're catching our breath in the silence and I sporadically reach down to kiss at her cheeks. She lets out a soft purring sound and arches her ass back against my lap, my cock still wedged inside.

"Baby," I grunt as she teases my shaft.

I glance back over to the dresser and see one last condom, waiting to be unwrapped.

It doesn't have long to wait at all.

CHAPTER 17

Harper

"He did *what?!*"

My mom's voice comes through the cell phone in my hand shrill and surprised.

I nod my head and the pom-pom on top of my winter hat wobbles.

"He's completed the reno with three weeks to spare," I repeat, watching his men down in the bowl of the valley as they load the equipment that they've been using for the past months back up into their trucks. "They're all done."

I'm getting the first taste of winter from my favourite spot on the bungalow's rooftop, the air frozen with the chill and a thick blanket of snow sparkling as it undulates over the curves of Pine Hills.

My mom ticks off all of the assignments that Mitch and his team have had out loud, highlighting the enormity of their feat. "Re-tiling, re-flooring, kitchen remodelling, making the new furniture, all of that pipe-work."

I don't comment on the last one.

"Shit, do we need to give them a bonus or something?" The whoosh of the phone being pulled away from her ear and a pen scratching at a paper pad sounds through the speaker. When she comes back she says, "I'm sending the details to Accounts so your father can see to a thank-you bonus." The pen taps and then she breathes out a disbelieving exhalation. "Jesus, they weren't messing around, were they? When my assisting manager told them that the Pine Hills job could lead to bigger ventures, he came back to me and said that the Team Lead had seemed no-nonsense as hell, totally determined to become our future go-to crew. He wasn't kidding."

I look down from the scene in the valley and rifle the fingers of my free hand through the pages in my notepad. I stop on the pencil sketch that I secretly did of Mitch when I first got here and I think about how neurotic I'd felt during that first week, still distressed from what had happened at home but with a spark of inspiration flickering to light as soon as I saw Mitch's icy blue eyes.

"So, now that they're finished, are you going to tell me?" my mom asks, snapping me out of my musing.

I close the notepad and blink blankly down at the cabins.

"Tell you what?" I ask, confused.

"Which of the men you were interested in," she says like it's obvious.

Oh jeez. I blow out an exasperated breath and look

warily down at Mitch's office. If I stare for long enough I can catch a glimpse of him walking past the side window, retrieving another finalisation document before he returns to his desk. He's spent pretty much the whole of the last two days in there, preparing for his departure.

I picture my mom's expectant expression, a youthful shimmer in her eyes as she waits for me to spill the juicy gossip, and I can't help but feel the need to indulge her.

"It was the Team Lead," I say, a hot sensation clutching at my heart when I see him walk absentmindedly past the window, unaware of my stalking. "Mitchell Coleson. The guy running the operation."

I hear chair springs creak as my mom reclines in her seat. "Fascinating," she says, and in my head she's twirling her finger between an invisible phone cord. "An outstanding choice, by the way," she adds on. "Not at all like the last one."

I narrow my eyes and concur, "Definitely not at all like the last one."

"Did anything come of it?" my mom continues, and this time I picture her villainously stroking a fluffy white cat.

She reads my silence like a billboard.

She changes the subject.

"Which night of the press tour are you going to? The whole crew have bitten their fingers raw waiting for information about your disappearance to get leaked. And, before you ask, I of course will not be sharing anything." She pauses and then mutters, "Holly on the other hand…"

I roll my eyes. I don't even want to hear her name. Her annoyingly lovely name.

"Probably the final night," I say. And then, just before I hang up, I decide to give a little fuel to my mom's fire. My eyes lock in on the portacabin and a sense of strength spreads through my chest. "And I'm bringing a date."

*

I wade through the snow all the way down to Mitch's office and then I huddle against the side of the open doorframe and knock on the panel.

He looks up from his stack of paperwork and as soon as he realises that it's me he shoves his chair backwards, jerking his chin at me to get inside, and he walks across the room to meet me.

"Hey," he murmurs when we reach each other, wrapping one hand around the back of my neck as he leans down to give me a kiss.

"Hey," I say, smiling up at him. I rub my hands up over his pecs and he briefly closes his eyes, savouring the feeling. "I know you already emailed the office your progress report but I just called my mom so that I could tell her direct about you completing the project so ahead of schedule. They're organising you a bonus."

He watches me intently as I speak, frowning, then raising his eyebrows. Then he sighs and gives me another kiss.

"You're too sweet," he says, rubbing his warm palms over my shoulders. "And that reminds me – I want you to know that when the cheque comes in… I'm gonna split it all between the guys. After what's been going on here between us, I'm not taking any money for this job. Wouldn't feel right."

Now I'm the one frowning, shaking my head adamantly up at him.

"Mitch, no, don't be silly. It's not like *I'm* the one giving you the money. It's Ray Corp's money. It's the money of a multi-million dollar property business, not the money of the woman you've been getting to know."

He shrugs like he's already decided. "I'm hoping that Jace and I are gonna be working with Ray Corp a lot in the coming years but on this specific project I just…" He shakes his head and then gently cups my cheek. "No part of this felt like work to me. This whole Fall has been a dream."

"But… but–" He kisses me again, and my body melts against him. I run my palms up his stubble and he makes a pleasured grumble in his chest.

"Don't worry about the money," he murmurs, pressing us forehead to forehead. "Trust me, I'm–" He almost chuckles, his mouth curling with amusement. He shakes his head and simply finishes with, "Money isn't a problem, baby."

I frown up at him and this time he pulls away laughing.

"Harper, I'm serious. In fact–" He turns slightly and pulls his whirring laptop closer to us. Leans down a little so that he can open up a new tab and then after hitting a few keys he jerks over to the screen with his thumb.

I squint down at it, blinking to try and make sense of the tables. Then I see the bank logo in the left hand corner and my eyes instinctively travel to the column on the far right. I frown trying to read the small font.

Then my eyes almost bulge out of my head.

I look up at him, startled and amazed. He has the good grace to look a little embarrassed.

"That's how much money you have in your bank account?" I ask him.

"That's how much money I have in *one* of my bank accounts," he clarifies quietly.

I came from money so it shouldn't surprise me, but in the context of one man's small-town business I'm so shocked that I almost keel over.

"Mitch–" I begin, but he shuts me up, snapping down the lid of his laptop and then turning his full attention to me, gripping my hips in his hands and pulling me up to meet his mouth. He slides his tongue slowly against mine and I lean backwards so that he can go as deep as he needs to. He grunts and suddenly wraps a hand around my pom-pom, pulling off my hat, and then tangling his fingers in my hair.

When we part for a moment I ask him, "So are you going out tonight with your guys? Like, celebrating or something?"

He shakes his head and then gives my bottom lip a little tug. "My guys would rather celebrate with their women, Harper. They're about to have their first morning of not having to wake up at 5:30 and they're gonna make the most of that. I know that I want to."

We share a smile, our hands relentless in their caressing, and then I lean up against him, wrapping my arms tighter around his neck.

"So what do you want to do tonight, boss?" I ask him coyly.

He groans and presses his forehead against my

shoulder. "First," he mumbles, "definitely never, ever call me that again. Especially not when we're standing in my office, and there's no-one around to stop me from... from..."

I can't help but giggle and I reach down to rub him through his cargos.

"To stop you from what?" I whisper. "From letting you have your woman over your desk?"

He makes a gruff sound as he lifts his head and he forces my hand off his erection as he stares down at me. "I wanna save the sex for later," he tells me quietly. "I wanna just spend some time with you tonight. Take you for dinner up in the town, then go see a movie. Just spend some time together, you and me."

I feel a warm glow in my chest as I smile up at him, nodding. "You're a softie," I tell him, and he grins down at me.

"Okay," he says, shaking his head with embarrassment. "So what d'you wanna see? They do reruns of the classics if you wanna see something old."

I give him an amused look. "Isn't that what I'm already doing?"

He smirks and gives me another firm kiss.

"You have the smartest mouth," he says as his hands travel down my back.

"Thanks," I say, shaking my hair away from my cheeks. "And I already know that we're definitely seeing whatever the latest car-action movie is. When I spent the weekend dying at your place I saw your DVD collection, Mitch. It looked like it was personally curated by Vin Diesel."

He drops his eyes, smiling and getting flushed.

"Yeah, okay," he murmurs. "If you don't mind," he adds on, looking up at me questioningly.

"I don't mind," I tell him. "I want to just spend some time together, you and me."

CHAPTER 18

Mitch

The high up canopy of dark rustling pine leaves has protected the Nature Trail's steep road from the beginnings of the winter snowfall, but it won't stay like that for long. Even now in the nightfall, heavy masses of snow are occasionally breaking away from the sheltering treetops, thudding down onto the roof, the windscreen, and the bed of my truck. I keep the wipers going as we head up the incline, the view already obscured from the surrounding blackness.

Harper takes a long pull on her slushie as I put the car in park outside of the bungalows. I look over to her as I unfasten my seatbelt and she smiles up at me with her eyes, her lips preoccupied with their work on the straw. I watch her suck for a couple of seconds, both of her hands wrapped around the base of the movie theatre cup, and I let myself succumb to the need throbbing through me. I feel my cock extend, pushing hard against my boxers, and I grip a hand over my groin so that I can suppress the growing ache.

She slips the straw from her lips and places her drink in the cup holder before settling back into her seat, snuggling further into the jacket that I gave her to wear. On the bottom half she's wearing a pair of her pale denim jeans fitted in all the right places, but on the top half she's wearing my work shirt, covered by my jumper, covered by one of my jackets. She looks so perfect that I have to reach over and gently cup her cheek, loving the way that she gets a soft flush when I stroke at her with my thumb.

"Was the movie okay?" I ask her, and she lets out a tinkling laugh.

"Mm-hm," she grins. "So many muscles."

I grin back at her and give her a quick kiss. Today was probably the best day of my year so far. The team and I finished our huge project ahead of schedule, I got an email confirming an upcoming boatload of renos on the horizon, and then I spent the evening having dinner and cosying up in front of an easy movie with the most beautiful woman that I've ever seen. It doesn't get better.

When Harper finally pulls away she tucks some hair behind her ear and says, "Hey, I just wanted to, um, remind you about the, uh…" She swallows and glances away from me, looking nervous. "Um, about my premier? The press week begins on Monday and I was thinking about flying back for the final night so, um, if you still think that maybe you'd be okay to come with me…?"

I stroke at her cheek again and give her a nod when

she glances back up at me.

"Of course I'll come," I tell her calmly, but beneath my shirt my abs are clenching tight. Like hell would I actually let her go on her own when her piece of shit ex-fiancé is going to be there, supposedly still wearing his goddamn engagement ring.

Which reminds me.

I hunch lower so that I can kiss her again and when she starts losing her strength, melting up against me, I ease my palms under her ass and scoop her over the stick-shift onto my lap.

She sucks in a breath when she lands splayed on my spread thighs, encouraging me to kiss her harder and rock upwards slightly, making sure that she's feeling me and making sure that she's getting ready.

When she presses her left hand against the swell of my pecs I seize the opportunity and grasp it with my right fist. I pull backwards and then hold her hand between us, rubbing pointedly at her ring finger as she blinks up at me in an over-stimulated daze.

"I wanna ask you something," I rasp, the heat from Harper's pussy on my lap making my voice more gruff than I mean for it to be. "About your engagement," I add on, my eyes boring hard into her own.

She's so breathless that for a moment she looks like she forgot that she was recently engaged. Fuck yeah.

"Uh, okay, yeah," she pants. "Anything – you can ask me anything."

I tap her slim finger and ask, "Did he give you a diamond?"

She stays silent for a couple of beats, wondering where I'm going with this, before she finally whispers, "A small one."

I grunt. "You keep it?"

"I…" She looks at her bare finger, frowns, and then looks back up at me with a sad arch to her brow. "I posted it back through his letterbox before I came here. But I… I don't like talking about this. I haven't really thought about him in a while. I prefer to think about you."

I graze my teeth over my bottom lip, liking that sentence way too much.

"Good," I tell her. "I'm glad you got rid of it. And we won't talk about it anymore, I promise. But I was thinking about when we go to see your movie and how maybe… maybe before we do that we should head to the jeweller's in town."

She looks up at me in surprise. "The jeweller's? Why?"

I move my hands to her hips so that I can grind her slowly over my shaft, and then I slide my palms up to her waist, clutching her tight against my chest.

"You need some new diamonds," I say simply.

Her eyes grow wide and I quickly dip down so that I can kiss her again. My tongue rubs firmly against hers and she moans gently into my mouth, processing the information that I just gave her.

"Diamonds, plural?" she whispers breathlessly against me as my fingers quickly tug down the zip on her jacket.

"Yeah, diamonds plural," I murmur back to her, shoving the jacket off her shoulders and then getting to work on her jumper. When she's left in nothing but her jeans and my work shirt I wrap a hand firmly around the side of her throat and say, "You're gonna wear them here."

Her long lashes flutter as my thumb strokes over her clavicle.

"A diamond necklace?" she whispers, entranced.

I can't help but smirk as I nod down at her.

"It's too much," she says, her brow creasing.

It's only the beginning, I think to myself as I gently rub away her frown. "Don't you think that you deserve some new diamonds?" I ask her quietly as I pull my phone and my wallet from the pocket of my jeans, tossing them onto the vacant passenger seat.

"Um... uh..." she pants, fast-blinking with contemplation.

I breathe a laugh and shake my head, flipping open my wallet so that I can slide out one of the two condoms that I shoved in there before we headed out this evening. She glances at the big black square and bites at her bottom lip.

"That was rhetorical," I tell her as I chuck the foil packet onto the dashboard behind her and ease open the button on her jeans. "But the answer's yes."

She flushes with pleasure and arches back, letting me get a good look at her as I drag down the zipper on her jeans. I push the denim down off her hips and then press two fingers firmly against the warm cotton hiding her pussy.

"Are we gonna do it in here?" she asks me, watching my fingers rub at her with dilated pupils.

"We can do it wherever you want," I murmur, slipping her gusset aside so that I can finally touch her soft heat. "Jesus, that's beautiful," I whisper, dropping my forehead to her shoulder as I rotate my fingers in gentle circles on her clit.

"Mitch, please," she whimpers, her nails biting into

240

the back of my neck and her hips grinding desperately against my hand. "I need you, right now."

I pull back and nod, preparing to shove down my jeans, roll down the condom, and then get her pants off so that I can take her on my lap in the driver's seat of my truck. But then her eyes flash down to my right, drawn to the light suddenly beaming up from the passenger seat.

I follow her gaze, staring down at my phone. Then my eyes go back up to hers, knowing what she's seeing.

"What–" she begins, before reaching down and grabbing it, hastily swallowing as she scrolls through an endless page of messages, unopened and unread.

Her eyes shoot up to mine, confused and frowning.

I couldn't care less about what's on the screen of my phone right now. In fact, I could continue ignoring those messages for the next three weeks. What I want is for Harper to put the cell down, wrap her arms back around my shoulders, and then let me give it to her the way that no-one else ever will.

"It's… it's your birthday?" she asks, her brow dropping lower by the second. "It's your birthday… today?"

I look at her for a long moment. I can already see that not telling her this information has put a big black cross next to my name.

I steel my jaw and give her a nod.

"Yeah," I admit, because that's the extent of it. But I can tell that to Harper, for whatever reason, this is a big deal.

She blinks rapid-fire at me, then looks back down at my phone as more messages silently come through.

"It's your... fortieth birthday. A significant birthday. And you didn't think that you should tell me that."

She stares at the screen for a few more seconds and then drops it down onto the seat beside us.

Honestly, right now nothing would make me happier than if she just shot-put the thing right out of the window.

I still have my hands on her waist as I try to think of how to describe my rationale behind this decision. She isn't shoving me away from her so I don't think that she hates me but it's becoming crystal clear that this has some sort of deeper meaning to Harper than I'm currently understanding.

I didn't tell her that it was my birthday because it's not significant to me. I didn't want it to alter her behaviour – which evidentially was a valid concern. I didn't want her to feel the need to alter the dynamic, to please me for the sake of it being the day that I was born on. Today went exactly how I wanted it to without her even knowing it.

The only other thought that I had to contemplate was the fact that I'm forty now. With Harper not even being thirty yet that realisation may make her want to end this where it's at. So I guess that I was being selfish, holding off on telling her so that I could spend just a little more time with her. But none of that was done with malicious intent.

I just want to keep things exactly as they are.

I move my fingers to redo her jeans and when I look at her face I can see that she's embarrassed. Which is probably the worst emotion that she could be feeling right now.

I cup her face in my palm, ducking down a little so

that I can catch her eyes.

"Hey, look at me, Harper," I say quietly, guilt settling in my gut like a tonne of bricks. "I didn't mean to upset you. Birthdays aren't a big deal to me. I just wanted to spend the day finishing up the Pine Hills project and then having my evening with you, and that's exactly what I did. It was perfect. Why're you looking so upset?"

"Because what if I wanted to get you something? What if I wanted to make the day more special?"

I try to find the most diplomatic way to say that that's exactly why I *didn't* tell her.

"You give me more than enough every day — the only thing that I want is you. I never want you spending cash on me, Harper. It's my job to take care of you, not the other way around."

She scrubs angrily at one of her eyes, and I narrow my gaze on her. If I catch sight of one single tear I'm going to be even more pissed that today's my birthday than I was twenty seconds ago.

"It doesn't make any sense," she says, shaking her head like she's got a whole argument going on in there. "Today's about you and you actually... you tried to make it about me." She looks up at me, bewildered. "You literally just told me that you wanted to buy me diamonds. On *your* birthday. Like it's some kind of treat for *you*."

I shrug a shoulder.

"It is," I say. "Using the money that I've earned to treat the woman that I—"

She shakes her head adamantly, cutting me off, but her hands are still on my shoulders, keeping us together. Showing me that she's not mad at me.

Just hurt.

"It's not the money," she says. "It's the fact that you hid it from me. If you don't want to celebrate, that's fine – I get it. It's kind of girly and you're, like, the most manly man that I've ever met. But I just… I hate it when people withhold the truth."

She winces, like she's said too much, and she clambers off of me before I can stop her, clicking open the passenger door and then jumping out, heading straight for her door.

I stare after her in confusion and I try to make sense of what just happened. I watch her unlock her door and close it quietly behind herself.

Maybe it was dumb for me to not mention it to her, but it sounded like she understood my indifference about celebrating. So what the hell is it?

I mull over her words, the frosty air coming off the snow pile drifting in through the still-open passenger door.

It's as I'm leaning over to click it shut that I realise.

I hate it when people withhold the truth.

I drop my head into my hands, groaning, and then I'm shoving my wallet and the stray condom back into my jeans, grabbing the jumper and jacket that I gave to her, and throwing myself out into the snow.

How could I be so fucking stupid? Of course she hates it when people withhold the truth. Because withholding the truth is the same thing as lying. Which is why she fled to Pine Hills in the first place.

Because that's exactly what her own sister and fiancé did to her during her literal engagement.

I've just given her a reason to maintain her trust issues over the dumbest thing of all freaking time.

Hell no. I slam my door shut, lock up, and then crunch my way through the icy blanketing, my boots sinking so deep that the bottoms of my jeans darken with water.

I'm at her door in under ten seconds, giving it a quick rap as I rest my forehead against the pane. I'm not about to let my blind ignorance ruin the best day that I've had in over a year.

"Harper," I call through the wood. "Harper, I'm an idiot. Please open the door."

She leaves me to sweat for another minute, my balls about freezing off as the winter chill penetrates the denim. Then I hear the sound of her undoing the bolt and the door opens up a millimetre.

A sparkly eye appears in the gap, her soft hair falling over her face as she whispers, "Go on."

If I wasn't so pissed at myself, that would've actually made me laugh.

"I'm an idiot," I repeat. "It was the dumbest thing to not tell you, and I'm sorry. I'm so sorry, Harper. Going forward I swear, even if something's not a big deal to me I'll tell you about it. I'll tell you every goddamn thing. I never want you to think that I'm hiding anything from you, good or bad. It's not in my nature, Harper – I would never. I swear, I would never–"

She opens the door fully and I immediately have her in my arms, her breasts soft and warm against my chest, her lips urgent but gentle against my own.

"I know," she murmurs, not pulling away even to talk. I keep kissing her as she continues, "And you don't have to do that. They're my issues and I'll deal with them." She smiles against my mouth and

245

whispers, "It's no biggie."

I pull back only so that she can take a look at the seriousness in my eyes.

"It is, Harper. Your trust is a big deal to me. And I'm going to earn it, so help me God."

She laughs and kisses the centre of my pecs, making my heart damn near burst out of my chest.

"You speak so small town-y," she whispers, smiling.

I run my hands down over her ass and then pick her up with an easy swoop.

"You got your key to lock up?" I ask her, and she shakes her head.

I pull the assortment of keys from my pocket and file through them until I find the one for her bungalow. Then I pull her door shut and work the metal in the lock.

"I love that you have a key to my bungalow," she whispers excitedly, her hands pawing at my chest.

I breathe out a laugh as I walk us next door to mine, because holy hell do I love that too. Then the second that I've got us inside I'm scraping her higher up my torso and she's clawing at my shoulders, both of us desperate to get as close to each other as physically possible.

"Shower," I murmur as I stride us towards the back of the bungalow. I flip a sconce on as we go and it illuminates the kitchen in a warm orange glow. When I get us in the bathroom I kick the door shut and then drop Harper to the floor, ripping my shirt over my head and quickly unsheathing the belt from my jeans.

She leans up against the sink to watch me, her eyes half-mast and stormy as they trail over my muscles, thick from four months of nonstop hauling, and rippling with energy that needs to be spent.

Once I'm fully naked I pull open the door to the shower and flick the handle so that the spray can start pouring. Then I'm back over to Harper, helping her pull off her jeans and gripping my hands around her hips so that she can jump up onto the sink, her thighs spread wide on either side of my abs.

I rub at the hem of the work shirt that she's wearing, half wanting to have her whilst she's wearing it. But then I realise that I need to see all of her, every inch of her, and I pull it off over her head, tossing it down on the floor and watching as her soft hair spills over her shoulders.

No bra, I think to myself, swiping my tongue over my bottom lip as I look at her wrapped around me in nothing but those white cotton panties. The perfect picture of the girl-next-door.

And that's what she has been whilst we've been staying in these bungalows. My boss's gorgeous twenty-eight-year-old daughter, that hot piece of ass that I'm not supposed to have. And now I'm rubbing the dark head of my shaft over the damp cotton of her underwear, teasing her heat as she arches back on the basin.

"C-condom," she pants when I reach down to suck her neck, my fingers pulling her panties aside so that I can rub and press at her clit. When I look back up her cheeks are flushed, her hair's sticking damply to her throat, and the mirror behind her has fully steamed up with the heat from the shower water that's now thrumming hard beside us.

"I know, baby," I rasp, and then I squat between

her legs so that I can grab the rubber from my jeans, placing it on the sink. But before I can stand upright again my eyes lock onto her heat.

I need it. Just one taste.

I grasp the sides of her panties and pull them down past her knees, leaving them to dangle off her ankle as I take in the sight of her sex. I lean forward, pressing my forehead against her belly, and she moans before I've even got my mouth on her, the feel of my heavy breathing and my rough palms behind her knees making her spread and writhe like I'm already inside of her.

I wrap a fist around my shaft and start tossing it, tight and fast.

"Can I?" I beg, my mouth hovering just over her heat.

When she whimpers but doesn't respond I look up at her from between her thighs and rub my thumb more firmly into her soft skin.

"Just for a minute, baby," I plead. "Just one minute and then I promise I'll take you how you want it."

She bites at her lip and nods her head, leashing her fingers in my hair and crying out the second that my mouth touches her sex.

I groan against her and instantly start stroking her with my tongue, long firm strokes that make her press my face against her harder. I release my cock so I can knead both of her thighs as I suck and lap, and then I let one palm slide up her waist until I can finally get a handful of her tits.

"Mitchell," she whimpers, grinding herself desperately against my face. I caress her breast, fingers playing with her soft nipple as my tongue laps relentlessly at her nub. My other hand moves around her hip so that it's gripped tight around her perfect ass and then I force her forwards, enabling me to lick her as firm and deep as possible.

"Mitchell, please," she moans. "If you don't stop I'm going to–"

"Do it," I growl, my hand moving from one breast to the other. I hunch down as I gorge deeper and the angle enables me to push my shoulders underneath her knees, get them steady, and then shove them backwards, fully exposing her to me.

"Mitch!" she whimpers, and then my hands are on both of her breasts, massaging them in my palms as she clenches tight and cries out with her climax. Her hands secured in my hair keep me pressed hard against her heat and I help her ride out the orgasm, her knees locked tight around my neck.

"Don't stop," I grunt as she squirms and jolts, my thumbs rubbing as fast as they can over her pointed nipples. "Keep coming for me, baby."

Her knees clench tighter as I suck at her clit and she moans desperately, her fingers too weak to hold on any longer. Her hands move to the sink behind her ass and she grinds against me with nothing but her hips, her breathing way too fast as the steam from the shower and her orgasmic exertion constrict and choke at her throat. When her body finally falls limp I give her one long last suck and then stand between her thighs, ripping into the condom as I watch her tits rise and fall.

"You have the sweetest pussy," I tell her as I get the rubber on my tip, grip it, and roll it down. Her lashes flutter as she looks down at my cock and I tease her with it by trailing it up her flushed thigh, its thickness and rigidity making her eyes roll back into her head.

I grasp my other hand behind her neck and kiss her, tilting her backwards so that my tongue can slide in deep. She takes it, too limp to return the strokes, and I grunt in her mouth as my tip finally nudges against her pussy.

I pull back and grip both of my hands around her hips, pulling her up off the sink and clutching her tight against my abs. I walk us into the streaming shower, the air so thick with mist that it's turned opaque, and I kiss her again when I've got her pinned to the back wall.

"I'm sorry about before," I murmur as I dip a hand underneath us so that I can align my cock with her entrance. "I'm gonna spend all night making it up to you."

She manages to open her eyes a little and I instantly duck down to kiss at her lips.

"Y-you don't need to be sorry," she whispers. "I forgive you, Mitch. It-it's your b-birthday, after all."

I grin down at her and then start pushing up, her teeth biting hard into her bottom lip as I try to breach her with my tip.

"This is what I wanted for my birthday," I grunt, my hands firmly wrapped around her waist as I try to fill her slowly. "My girl taking her pleasure all night."

I reach down for one more kiss before I finally thrust up, bringing us together as close as we can go.

I squeeze my eyes shut, my temples throbbing because of how tight she is. I press my forehead hard against the tiles above her and I slide out slowly, not wanting to be rough when she's at her most sensitive, post-climax. She shifts her legs slightly higher and wraps her arms more securely around my neck, and I stay still for a brief moment, revelling in the feeling of her beautiful body moving trustingly against mine. I wait until she settles, and then I bury my nose in her hair and thrust back inside.

She gasps and squirms, and I pull back a fraction so that I can look down at her gorgeous body. I keep my eyes on where we're joined and start pumping faster, the sight of her taking me damn near making me spill. I check her face to gauge how she's handling it, if it's too much or too fast, but the second that our eyes meet she's making those fuck-me whimpers and rubbing her sweet nipples up against my pecs, so I build up the tempo to a relentless in-and-out pounding, one hand kneading her ass and the other tilting her chin up to face me.

"I should tell you something," I pant, as I roll into her deeper, her thighs splaying backwards to give me better access. "If I'm gonna tell you everything, then there's something I need to get on the table right away."

Her eyes widen a little like she's scared, so I shake my head and rub my thumb up her jaw.

"It's not a bad thing," I clarify. "It's a... it's a really good thing. I think. But I'm... I'm not gonna lie, I'm kinda nervous, baby."

Her brow creases but she nods at me anyway. "You... you can tell me a-anything, Mitchell. Please."

Fuck. Why is it so goddamn sexy to hear her say "please"? I grit my teeth together and give her ass another rough squeeze just to help me calm the fuck down.

"First," I rasp out, "I love it when you call me that. When you call me Mitchell, instead of Mitch. No-one ever calls me that – it's only you, baby." I stop speaking before I get to my second point, immediately feeling the heavy weight of expectation settling in my abs. I try to stay focused, determined to tell her how I feel.

I try to use it to my advantage, using the surge of adrenaline to pump her faster and deeper, my hips smacking loud and wet against the hot centre of her thighs. My eyes drop down to her tits and my sac is suddenly aching with the need to release, the sight of them bouncing for me making me bite back a snarl.

"What I really wanted to say to you," I pant, cupping her cheek in my palm and trying to hold it together whilst I get these words out, "is that I… I don't know how this is for you, but for me this is it. The real thing. And I'm not talking about the sex," I add quickly, aware of how in this moment my words might get misconstrued. "Although the sex is fucking amazing, baby. I-I'm trying to say that this – you and me – us… it's the real thing for me. And I… I…" I swallow hard, looking deep into her eyes. And then I say it. "I'm in love with you, Harper. I've fallen in love with you."

Harper gasps, her eyes sparkling and wide. But then she's suddenly screwing them shut as she's overcome by a second climax, the combination of what she's heard and what she's feeling too much to contend with anymore.

I hold her tight against my chest as I finish her off.

"You don't have to say it back," I murmur quickly,

my hand moving to her clit and rubbing hard. "I just had to tell you. I had to tell you that, if this was all up to me, you'd be mine now. No going back. I know we haven't talked about the future, and that's okay. But I had to let you know where I stand." I press my forehead against the top of her head and she looks up at me from under her lashes. "And it's right here. Taking care of you. For as long as you'll let me."

"Oh my God," she whispers, her hands cupping either side of my jaw as she rides out the rest of her orgasm.

I move both of my palms to grip at her behind, lifting her slightly higher against the wall so that I can pound her deeper as I finish. The new position means that her lips are close enough to mine for me to be able to lean down and reach, so I give her a long firm kiss. I keep it chaste until she opens up for me, asking me to give her my tongue. I give her a couple deep strokes of it and then I'm the one who's on the edge, pulling back so that I don't completely over-stimulate her and picking up my thrusts again so that I can finally spill my load.

"Mitchell?" she whispers, and my eyes flash down to hers, full of heat. Maybe it was a bad idea to tell her how hot it gets me when she calls me that, knowing that she could sweet-talk me into doing anything she wanted with her husky voice alone.

"Yeah, baby?" I rasp as my hands grip into her, bouncing her up and down my shaft.

"Are you… are you sure?" she whispers, looking imploringly into my eyes. "I want to believe you so bad. I want you to love me. But I just want you to be sure before I let myself believe you."

I bounce her faster, steeling my jaw to stop myself from growling.

"How could I not love you, baby?" I whisper back to her, my voice low beneath the thrum of the water. "I've never been more sure about anything. I'm so in love with you that I want to skip past the diamond necklace section and go straight to the diamond rings."

Her hand grips at my jaw as her pleasure makes her lose control, but then it's running delicately down my abs, disappearing beneath us, and then—

"Harper," I growl, my head about to explode. She kisses innocently at my chest as she gently massages my sac. "Harper, you do that for one more second and I'm gonna come."

"They're so big," she whispers, not letting up.

"Baby, I mean it. Harper, please—" And then I'm groaning, my body locking her tight against the wall and pounding into her harder than I should.

"S-sorry, Harper, just one more minute. Just one more—"

"I love you, too."

I bite down hard on my cheek, holding back the expletives that want to rip out of my chest so that I don't ruin the moment. She lets me pump her exactly the way that I need to, my cock sliding in and out of her thick and fast, and then when I'm done I keep her up against the wall, grunting when she tries to climb down, needing to stay inside of her for just a minute longer.

Her fingers stroke up and down my back, more delicate than I've ever been touched before, and I press my face into her hair, listening to the beautiful sound of her panting combined with the relentless cascade of the spray.

"I love you," she whispers again, and this time I pull my head up so that I can look down at her as she says it.

I slide gently out of her and we're both instantly moaning, but then I pull her into my arms and hunch down so that I can kiss her, the water from the shower like a Phoenix Falls storm.

"I love you so much that I almost broke the condom," I murmur against her, my cheeks burning red.

She clings on tighter and whispers, "I love you so much that I wouldn't have minded."

CHAPTER 19

Harper

I knew something was up because he was all quiet in the morning. And by 'morning', I mean from eleven-forty-five, when Mitch had already been up for six hours and I had been watching him work the keys on his laptop from my blanket swaddle beside him.

"Your fingers are too big for the keys," I commented as I watched him aggressively backspace another typo.

His face had twitched with a half smirk and then he'd leant down to press stubbled kisses on my cheek.

"Go back to sleep, baby," he'd murmured against my ear, the low bass of his morning voice reverberating deep in my belly.

I stared up at him – up his tan forearms, and his thick biceps – and he looked down at me with that kind but confident assuredness that he radiates without even intending to. He moved one hand to my hair and let his fingers leash deeply, the warmth from his skin like heaven against me.

So I had gone back to sleep and then I woke an hour later to a brown paper bag and a takeout coffee cup on the bedside cabinet. I sat upright, snaffled the bag, and peeked inside.

Donut.

Yum.

As I ate my donut I read the note he'd penned on the label of the packaging. Just a simple *Meet me in the office when you're ready*, followed by a little *x*. I smiled at the kiss, picturing the crease on his brow as he deliberated whether or not to add it, and then the hard set of his jaw as he slashed the two tiny lines. I wondered if he knew that such a small thing was actually such a big thing. That it proved that his affection for me is bigger than his tough-guy ego.

I flip through the clothes that I brought to Pine Hills and never wore, pulling up a cream skirt and affixing my cream jumper over the top of it. Then I pull on my boots and open the door.

To four feet of snow.

I look back over to the paper bag and the coffee cup on my bedside cabinet with a new level of surprise and appreciation. Jesus Christ. Mitch risked life and limb just to get me a breakfast donut.

I lock up and walk down the path that Mitch has cleared, my eyes locked on his truck and the huge pile of snow next to it. Whilst I was blackout exhausted from everything that we did last night, Mitch must have been shovelling for at least an hour to get the area of gravel road between the bungalows and the gate to the Nature Trail clear enough for him to drive on so that he could take a quick trip to town.

I swallow hard and divert my eyes. Good Lord. How much stamina does he have?

When I reach Mitch's office the door is wide open, waiting for me, and Mitch is sat behind his desk, looking at his laptop on his right. He scribbles something down in a notebook with one hand and holds his cell to his ear with the other. He senses me before I even knock and he immediately stands, wrapping up his phone call and tossing it to his desk as he makes his way over to me. Just before he reaches me, his arms already out to grab and pull me against him, he pauses his movements, his eyes dropping to the hem of my skirt resting just below my hips. I think my thighs start to blush.

He rumbles quietly, "The hell's that?"

"It's a skirt," I say, almost laughing, but then I cross my ankles, suddenly feeling immature.

He closes the space between us, his eyes still down on my thighs.

"It's... it's cute," he rasps, two fingers tentatively lifting the hem.

Feeling shy I try to change the subject.

"Thank you for my donut," I say to him, wrapping my arms tight around his neck.

His eyes finally meet mine and I'm dazzled by his irises.

"You're welcome. You sleep okay last night?"

My cheeks turn pink and his pupils dial out.

"My sleep was a little interrupted," I admit in a whisper, but I clutch him tighter so that he knows that I liked it. Because Mitch's stamina *is* unmatched. Every time I roused slightly in the night Mitch would instantly wake up too, our eyes meeting in the darkness and then his body rolling on top of mine. Waiting for my approval and then rummaging for a condom, his free hand caressing firmly down my body, waking me up for what he was about to do.

"Next time I won't start my work beside you. I should've come straight to the office. I should've let you sleep in for longer," he murmurs, one hand dipping beneath the back of my skirt and sliding up over my ass. When his hand is full he squeezes my cheek tightly and grunts.

I shake my head and give him a reassuring smile. "I liked waking up next to you. It was sexy watching you work."

He gives me a headshake of his own, but his ruddy cheeks belie his true feelings.

"Spreadsheets aren't sexy, Harper."

"They are when you're doing them."

He ducks his head to hide his smile.

I press myself against him and he lifts back up, eyeing me questioningly.

"Why did you want me to meet you here?" I ask.

He gestures behind him to his laptop and I watch his jaw harden, like he's slightly unsure.

"Plane tickets," he states. "To go to your movie. I was gonna book them but I need, uh, I need you to tell me what you want."

"What do you mean?"

"What kind of ticket," he clarifies.

I'm still not totally sure what he's talking about.

He jerks his head in a *let's take a look* gesture and then walks us around the desk until we're at his chair.

He pulls it out for me and nods for me to sit down. I take my seat and then look at the laptop screen when he pulls it in front of me.

"I got the departure date and the airport details but…" He pauses for a moment and I look at him behind me from over my shoulder. His eyes penetrate into mine and I feel a jolt of lightning in my belly. "I need to know if you're staying, Harper. I need to know if you're staying here or there."

I blink at him, lost.

"Staying," I repeat.

Realising that I'm not following he lays it all out, crystal clear.

"I need to know if I'm booking you a one-way ticket out of my life, Harper, or if you're going to let me keep you. The ticket's either going to be a one-way or a return, and I don't know where your head's at because we haven't spoken about it. It's… it's your choice, Harper."

Oh.

Oh.

So that's what was on his mind this morning – the uncertainty about our future together.

I keep looking up at him, nervous to tell him what I want.

"Do you have a preference?" I ask him quietly, my fingers twiddling with the hem of my skirt.

His eyes track the movement for a brief moment and then they fly back to mine, his gaze so intense that I feel pinned against the seat.

"Yeah," he murmurs. "I do. I know exactly where I want this to be heading. But it's up to you, Harper. It's up to you where we go from here."

The weight of the responsibility combined with the heat in his eyes makes me arch and writhe on his seat with nervousness. He follows the motion and swipes his tongue over his lower lip.

"Tell me," I demand simply, frowning up at him like a child.

He ducks down and kisses me, slipping his tongue inside my mouth and gently rubbing it against mine. I move my arms so that I can reach up to him but he pulls away before they get there.

"You know what I want," he says quietly. "You know that I want you."

I watch him warily for a few moments and then I spin back to the screen, intending to look at the flights he pulled up, but as I turn my eyes catch on something else on his desk. From behind me I know that he won't be able to see exactly what I'm looking at so I study the page for a minute, heat climbing up my cheeks.

It's a brochure from the jeweller's in the town above Pine Hills. But it's not open on a page for necklaces – it's open on a page for rings.

He's spending his free time browsing for engagement rings.

Butterflies flutter in my belly and I quickly look away, pretending that I didn't see anything. But I did see. It shows me just how serious Mitch is and how sincere he's being. It shows me that his intentions are long-term and as pure as they get. He isn't reading from a script and telling me what I want to hear. In fact, he's working behind the scenes and putting in overtime. I didn't even ask him to buy our plane tickets – he simply remembered and decided to do it to save me the hassle.

I click on the ticket type and select the word 'Return'.

Suddenly my chair is being pulled back like a reverse husky-sled and I squeal as Mitch spins it around before dropping to his knees. He pulls my thighs apart so that he can position himself between them. He wraps his hands around both sides of my behind and shoves me forward so that my heat knocks against him, and then he's cupping my jaw and kissing me hard and firm.

I lock my arms around his neck and tangle my fingers in his hair, and he moans into my mouth, his hands kneading me eagerly. Warm contentment spreads deep in my belly, my body pulsing with pleasure because I've just pleased *him*.

"You're staying with me?" he murmurs, his hands roaming to the front of my thighs and sliding up the fabric of my skirt. His fingers leash in the sides of my underwear and he grips at them so roughly I hear a tear.

"Yeah," I whisper back. "I could stay in the bungalow for the weekdays and come to your place on the weekends–"

He shakes his head, his shoulders bunching with restraint as he stops himself from ripping my panties clean off. "You're staying at mine, all week and all weekend. We're gonna move your stuff into my room, and I'm gonna have you in my bed. You can do your writing remote, right?"

I nod. "Yeah, I can work from anywhere–"

"Good," he grunts. "So if I need to travel to a site in a different county you can come with me."

I blink fast with surprise. "Oh, well–"

I thought I knew what men were like. They like space and testosterone. Not too much oestrogen or they get kind of depressed. And lots of distance. Because distance makes the heart grow fonder, right?

But Mitch has me unravelling the theory. He leans back over to the desk and quickly works his fingers across the keyboard. In less than a minute he's booked us two return flights to LA, completely unfazed by the crazy total sum for such a short trip. Then he clicks on a separate tab showing luxury private hotels in the area.

"I still have a place in LA," I tell him, rubbing my thumb in gentle circles over his swollen shoulder muscles. "We don't need to book a hotel."

He glances up at me as if he'd forgotten about the fact that I still have a life that isn't here, but he quickly recovers, simply nodding and then shutting his laptop down.

He stands to his feet and walks around the room, shutting the front door to the office to stop the icy stillness drifting in. Then he bolts the lock for another reason entirely.

I cross one leg over the other and lean back, suddenly drowsy with lust as he turns to face me. His body is a broad dark mass against the doorway. He walks slowly over to me and I uncross my legs, his eyes automatically dropping down, making his chest heave and still.

"Are you gonna keep your place?" he asks me without looking up.

I shrug. "For now, yes. It's convenient for meetings and press things for when I'm down there. Plus, I already paid off my mortgage."

That makes him look up, surprised and impressed. He's probably working out how much money I've made in such a short space of time to be able to afford a property that's classified as prime real estate in Los Angeles.

"I'm a big girl," I murmur to him huskily.

I see a smile teasing the corners of his mouth, the creases in his cheeks dimpling with amusement.

"Yeah?" he asks, pulling me up from his seat once he reaches where I'm at, his handsome face towering a good foot above me.

I crane my neck to look at him and he wraps his hand gently around the side of my throat.

"Yes," I whisper, not feeling like such a big girl anymore.

"Hmm," he murmurs, smiling. "You look petite to me."

I frown and he laughs out loud.

"Everyone looks petite to you," I say obstinately.

He smiles again and rubs his nose against mine.

"I'm happy that you're staying, Harper," he says quietly. "I'm gonna show you how happy you make me."

"O-okay," I whisper as I cling to him, and my breathing hitches when he pushes me lightly against his desk, my ass hitting the edge and then his hands helping me up onto it.

He takes his stand between my thighs and looks down at me with his composed unwavering calm. The calm of a boss. The calm of a CEO. He's not in his uniform seeing as he's the only man now working on the site, but he's never looked so full of authority.

I swallow slightly as he pushes my skirt up, my

winter boots waggling nervously above the floor as he exposes my underwear.

"I feel like a naughty employee," I admit on a whisper, as he presses his thumb gently against the centre of my cotton panties.

As soon as the words leave my mouth he's scraping one hand down his jaw, his stubble making a rough scratching sound, and then he ducks his forehead to mine, pressing us together.

"I'm gonna put you on the books. I'm gonna put you on the books, just so that we can…" He swallows thickly and squeezes his eyes shut, a sordid fantasy that I'm the star of clearly taking place in his mind without an off switch. He grips his groin through his jeans and steels his jaw as he hardens.

"I can't take your money," I say quietly, wrapping my thighs around him tighter and massaging my palms over his pecs.

He breathes out a laugh, no smile on his face.

"You never heard the phrase 'what's mine is yours'?" he asks seriously. "Not only are you going to take my money, you're going to take my last name."

Then he's shaking his head, pulling back a little as he tugs a hand roughly through his hair.

"Sorry – fuck, I'm sorry. That was too much, I know it was. We… we don't need to talk about that kind of stuff yet. I'm getting too ahead of myself."

He doesn't seem to realise that I'm melting against him, my breathing getting laboured at how ready he is. To move me up here. To get me into his house. To make me his wife.

"Harper Coleson," I whisper, my body pounding as I say the words out loud.

Mitch's eyes burn into mine, his pupils blacking out his irises as we look at each other in silence.

"That... that sounds good," he says, dipping down so that his mouth is only a millimetre away from mine. "It... it makes it sound like you're mine."

I smile a little but then shove gently at his chest. He grunts and presses me against him tighter.

"I don't belong to you," I whisper against his lips.

He smiles and whispers back, "Tell that to the diamonds I'm about to put around your neck."

In the next second he's pulling a long box from underneath the stacks of paperwork and my breath is catching in my throat when I see what he's got. He holds it between us, his eyes on mine, and then gently clicks open the lid, exposing a delicate chain adorned with ten glittering diamonds.

My eyes fly up to his, my lips parted in shock, and the faceted refractions sparkle magically against his eyes.

"Mitchell, what–?"

"I couldn't wait," he says simply, as if he doesn't have thousands of dollars worth of diamonds resting in his palm. "I headed to the town this morning and as soon as I saw it I knew it was yours. If you like it, that is," he adds quickly. "We could, uh, probably do an exchange if you don't."

I blink up at him, too astounded to speak. I can only imagine what his accountant is going to think when they take a look at his upcoming bank statement.

Coffee. Donut. Diamond necklace.

"Mitchell, I love it. Of course I love it." I look down at it and it twinkles innocently up at me. "It's the most beautiful thing that I've ever seen."

After a long stretch of silence I hear Mitch swallow thickly and then quietly murmur, "Yeah. It is."

I look back up at him and find his eyes on mine.

"It's too much," I say to him, somehow keeping my voice level despite the heat swirling in my belly.

"It's not enough," he replies, not breaking our eye contact.

I try to stay strong, to keep my eyes burning into his as confidently as his are burning into mine, but after another ten seconds I look away, my breathing coming out in a hard wavering exhalation.

I see Mitch's chest swell with victory and then his attention is briefly returned to the necklace. He unfastens it from its padding, the fine chain pouring like silk across his fingers, and then he jerks his chin at me as he places the box beside his laptop.

"Lift your hair up," he commands.

"No," I say defiantly.

He stares deeply into my eyes.

I lift my hair up.

He delicately presses the tiny claw clasp with the large pad of his thumb and then he holds the chain in front of my throat before twining it around the back of my neck, leaning over me slightly so that he can carefully get the fastening into the loop.

I wait nervously, my breathing growing laboured as I breathe in the heat of him, the top of his abdomen pressing gently against my head. When he finally clicks the necklace into place he moves his fingers to encase the back of my neck, exposed totally as I hold my hair up, and we stay like that for a moment, almost panting in the silence.

After a cautious beat I slowly allow my hair to

cascade down, spilling over his hands and making him breathe in a deep inhalation. He leashes his fingers through it as I rub my hands around the sides of his abdomen.

"Let me look at you," he says.

I keep my face pressed against his middle, blocking out the world so that I see nothing but him.

"No," I murmur back.

He breathes a laugh above me. "I love how stubborn you are."

"Really?" I ask quietly, my head still bowed down.

He gently releases a hand from my hair and moves it so that it can grasp one of my own. Then he trails it down his abs and I suck in a breath when I feel what he's doing. He cups my hand over the crotch of his jeans and I squeeze my legs around his at the sensation of how hard he is.

"Really," he rasps in confirmation.

I tilt my head back and look up at him, exposing my neck and the diamonds draped across my décolletage.

The hand compressing mine against his groin instinctively grips tighter, but then he moves both of his hands to the sides of my neck, caressing me adoringly with the warm pads of his thumbs.

"Perfect," he murmurs captivated, his eyes soaking in the sight of his money wrapped around my throat. He takes it in for a while and I stay pliant, allowing him to peruse me. Then he lifts his eyes to mine and asks me, "You wanna have a look at it?"

I shake my head. "I'll look at it later. There are other things that I'd rather be doing right now."

His eyes darken.

"Are you gonna wear it for your premier?" he asks, his hands moving down to my thighs to lift them higher against his hips.

"Yes," I whisper, butterflies in my belly.

He grunts and then leans down to kiss me, my arms wrapping around his neck and my body pressing desperately up against his. The second that my chest reaches his he's ripping my top off my body, gripping and squeezing me everywhere.

"Good," he murmurs as I push down his jeans, a gasp leaving my throat as his engorged length knocks against me. "You're so good."

He pushes my skirt back to uncover my underwear and he makes a low pleased sound before tearing into a condom.

Then he gets himself into position, lays me back against his desk, and he shows me just how *good* he thinks that I am.

CHAPTER 20

Mitch

She didn't warn me about what we were getting ourselves into. Hell, even if she had I don't think I could have expected the scale of it.

I knew that Harper had made a lot of money writing manuscripts, so I knew that her movie was going to be big.

But I hadn't known that it was the movie of the whole damn *year.*

When we went to the cinema earlier in December she hadn't told me that the huge boards and cardboard cut-outs that they had in there were for the movie that she had written. She'd walked past them all with complete indifference, as if she'd never seen them before. But as the limo that had been arranged to bring her to the premier pulls up to a stop at the silver barricades, blockading the swarming crowd from the wide red carpet, I can see the posters clear as day.

I stare out of the window in horror, thanking God that these windows are tinted as thousands of cameras flash violently at Harper's unopened door.

"Harper," I say. My brow is furrowed. My eyes are wide with disbelief.

She lets out a little cough and then says, "Yeah?"

I look between her and the window, out of my comfort zone but determined to stay level, knowing that this is the moment that she's been feeling nervous about.

"You didn't tell me how big your movie was, Harper. You didn't tell me that you're…" I have to choke the next words out of my throat. "That you're famous."

Harper looks up at me innocently, her hands smoothing down the pale gold satin of her dress over her thighs.

Head to toe she looks like champagne. Her blonde hair is in a soft sexy pouf, her skin is glowing with the remnants of her summer tan, and her dress is wrapped around her body as tight as cling-film, the neckline draped low across her pushed-up breasts and the hem going all the way down to her ankles, her glittery little toes peeking shyly out.

A particularly bright flash explodes behind Harper's window and the diamonds around her neck glint dangerously. That sedates me a little. It's a reminder that she's mine, and that this kind of big city chaos is only temporary. I can stay calm, secure in the knowledge of that. But that doesn't mean that I have to like the way that thousands of people are screaming for her out there, clambering to get a look at her, to touch her.

Like hell are they going to touch her. I readjust my suit jacket, the fabric tighter around my shoulders than I'd like it to be, and I arch my neck, undoing a second button on my shirt, just to get a little air flow.

I look like I'm her bodyguard. I have every intention of acting like one too.

Harper's eyes drop to the small section of tan skin exposed between the white cotton of my shirt and she squirms on the seat, uncrossing and re-crossing her legs like she wants me to do something about that ache I know she's got between her thighs.

I lean down to kiss her and she melts against me, my hands roaming up to squeeze gently at her warm breasts. She falls back against the seat and pulls me down with her, arching against me like she doesn't want me to stop.

And I *definitely* don't want to stop. But we have a driver not ten feet away from us, plus a thousand cameras out there that, for all I know, have fucking x-ray lenses, so I pull myself up, panting as I lean over her.

"After," I rasp. "Do your red carpet, and then I'll do you."

She drops her arms to her sides and howls.

I stoop down to kiss her again and she clasps her hands around the back of my neck, digging her nails in hard.

"You're kinda spoiled, aren't you?" I murmur, hunching over so that I don't hit my head on the roof as I get to my feet, and then I grip at Harper's elbows and pull her up with me.

She scowls up at me but I can see the fear behind

her eyes. She doesn't want to be here. I stroke softly at her cheek.

"Yes," she snaps, getting defensive to hide her nerves. "I'm a spoiled princess. Take it or leave it."

I smirk down at her, kiss her hard, and then give her a couple deep strokes of my tongue.

"I'll take it," I murmur, pulling away so that I can look at her. "You're *my* spoiled princess."

She ducks down to hide her smile at the same moment that her driver opens his door.

I lean down the aisle to try and catch his eye and I jerk my chin at him when he looks at me questioningly.

"It's okay, man," I say to him, cocking my head over to the door beside Harper. "I've got it from here. But thank you."

He pauses briefly and then gives me a nod, getting back into his seat and closing his door, dulling the bright flashes.

I turn back to Harper, her teeth biting hard into her bottom lip, and I duck down to kiss between the centre of her breasts. She gasps and shoves her fingers into my hair, rubbing herself against me so that my stubble scrapes her sensitive skin.

"Mitch," she moans as I kiss and suck. "Mitch, please, don't make me go."

I grunt between her breasts, unable to stop my fingers from rubbing her nipples.

"Mitchell," she begs. My cock instantly grows heavier.

"Goddamn," I growl as I stand upright again. Her eyes have blacked out and her chest is heaving, making it look as though she *has* been getting pounded in the back of her limo. I pull her against my chest and give her a reassuring squeeze.

"You've got this," I tell her firmly. "I'm gonna be right behind you the whole time."

"Okay," she whispers nervously, her eyes darting to the door.

"I'm gonna get out, open the door for you, and then you're gonna walk down that red carpet like it's your fucking property. Because it is, Harper. None of this would be happening without you right now, and I want you to act like it. We show face and then we haul ass, okay?"

She tries to pull me down to kiss her again but I'm not having it. We'll save that for once this is over and done with.

"Okay?" I repeat, harder this time.

She narrows her eyes on me, then rolls them. "Fine," she mumbles.

I give her ass a rough squeeze and she presses her lips against my neck, moaning.

"Good," I say simply. Then I reluctantly release her from my arms and hunch over to the door, take a steeling breath, and shove it open.

I'm instantly blinded. The flashes are going off at a million-a-minute so I quickly turn back to the car and hold the door wide for Harper, my jaw clenching hard at the thought of all these people trying to get a look at her.

It's just one night, I remind myself, and my shoulders ease up a little. *Just one night and then you're taking her back to Phoenix Falls. Taking her and keeping her.*

One golden foot appears at the step and I instantly move forward, holding my hand out to help her down.

She takes it and dismounts, and then the flashes get even crazier.

Because she's perfect. She's smiling her perfect white smile and sashaying her perfect little ass, the lights flashing all over her making her glow in a thousand shades of gold. What I told her in the car is something that everyone here already knows – without Harper, none of this would exist, and they are beyond grateful for the escapism that she's given to them.

She walks confidently down the main stretch, her nerves from the limo seamlessly hidden, and I walk one millimetre behind her, my muscles tight and my eyes hard.

When we reach the next cordon saved solely for the press she turns and smiles up at me, her soft hair spilling over her shoulder. Her diamonds sparkle like crazy around her neck.

"You can put your hands on me," she whispers, stopping her walking so that I bump right against her ass.

My eyes flare and I glance quickly over to the paparazzi, their voices a high-pitched mass, asking her to look at them, to smile for them, to turn this way and that. And that would probably be unusual for a member of the behind the scenes crew, except for the fact that Harper looks like a fucking goddess. Of course they want to take five billion photos of her.

I resist the urge to scoop her up and steal her away.

I look back down at her and whisper, "Where?"

Her smile gets even wider. "My hips," she whispers back.

I swallow hard and tentatively wrap my hands around her hips. Then she's grinning at the cameras,

275

swishing her hair over her shoulders and posing confidently against my chest. And it makes me feel better about this whole thing. Knowing that my being here for her is making her have a better time. And that makes *me* have a better time. I mean, I'm not about to smile for anyone, but I ease up on the scowl and just wait the flashes out.

Only problem is that they don't freaking end. We're walking at nought-point-one miles per hour down the tiny press corridor and I'm slowly getting irreparable retina damage. I look down at Harper and she's still smiling, then looking serious, then smiling again but at a different camera. I breathe out a laugh, suddenly loving watching her enjoy all of this attention, and she looks quickly up at me, giving me her widest smile yet.

"Okay, I'm done," she whispers and I almost groan with relief. In less than three seconds I've marched her to the end of the carpet and bundled her into the adjoining enclosed room, leading to a further corridor and the movie theatre beyond.

She waves excitedly at a few of her colleagues before turning back to me, unaware that even when she isn't looking at them no-one else can look away.

"That wasn't so bad," she admits, wrapping her arms up around my neck.

I smile down at her and caress the small of her back.

"But I think as soon as I've said 'hey' to the crew over there we should go." She bites at her lip, checking that I understand what she's referring to. I do, but she adds on anyway, "I just don't want to bump into–"

"Harper?"

A voice comes from behind us and I feel my back

muscles lock and tighten. It's a guy's voice, and from the sudden loss of colour in Harper's cheeks I'm pretty certain that I know who it is.

It's her ex fiancé. Our eyes remain locked in on each other, Harper's hands suddenly trembling at the back of my neck and my body rigid and unmoving.

It doesn't matter. He takes a step closer and coughs to get Harper's attention.

That gets *my* attention. I grimace and glance down at him, wondering in what universe he thinks that he has the right to cough anywhere near my future fucking wife.

Harper takes a deep breath, lowers her arms from my neck, and turns to face him.

I don't move an inch, keeping my hands nice and secure around her hips.

"Evan," she says, and she gives him a begrudging half-smile, a cute dimple popping in her cheek. And I must have lost my mind because I feel protective about it. I don't want this guy looking at her damn dimple.

"How, uh, how's things?" he asks her, his eyes flickering between Harper's face and mine. I take a calm inhalation and stare blankly back at him.

"They're great," Harper says, her tone even. It's the kind of tone that says *I don't want to talk to you, asshole.*

I give her hip a gentle rub with my thumb. *Good girl.*

He stares back at her, his expression faltering and his eyebrows twitching with confusion as he reads Harper's emotions. He's probably never seen this side to her before.

It's the only side to her that he'll ever see again.

"Uh, aren't you going to ask me how I am?" he

asks, his arms folding defensively across his chest.

Harper doesn't blink. "No."

I look away to hide my smirk and Harper presses her body closer into mine.

"Didn't your mom tell you?" Her ex shifts on his feet in discomfort, glancing around like he's looking for back up. "Didn't she tell you that, you know…?"

Harper allows him to sweat before she finishes his sentence for him.

"That you broke up with my sister? Yes, she told me. I'm not sure what kind of response you're expecting for that one."

He takes a step closer and I'm instantly on high alert. He meets my eyes and I give him a look that reads *not one more step, buddy.*

He pauses on the spot but I can see that he's growing agitated. I glance down at his hand and a plain engagement band glints back at me.

Prick.

"I think we should have this conversation in private," he says sharply, and then he gives me what I assume he thinks to be a meaningful glare.

I watch him with vacant disinterest until he looks away.

"I don't think we need to have a conversation," Harper replies, shrugging a little. "You moved on, and now so have I."

His eyes fly back to Harper's, incredulousness blazing behind his irises. "You can't be serious," he says, his voice hysterical. "You blocked me on everything. We haven't even had a chance to talk about this."

Harper stares back at him in disbelief, her

expression almost amused.

"Evan, you literally cheated on me. Whilst we were engaged. With my *sister.*"

"Everyone makes mistakes, Harper!" Then he slides his eyes up to me and adds on, "Evidently."

I breathe out a laugh and give him a tight smile.

"You know what else would be a mistake?" I say quietly. "Continuing this conversation."

"You think I wouldn't be able to take you?" he sneers, the reality of the situation making his neck turn red. "I gym, like, every day."

I almost smile. He's leaner than a French fry and a short guy at around five-ten. It would be borderline unethical for me to fight him.

But if push came to shove I know that his skull would split like a walnut with one crunch of my bicep.

I say nothing, hoping that it'll encourage him to handle this situation like a man, apologise to Harper, and then get the fuck away from us.

He eases up a little but then refocuses his attention on Harper.

"You really want some sort of small town nobody?" he asks her, and this time I actually do laugh out loud.

Harper looks up at me, worried that I'll be angry, but I give her a reassuring smile.

I transmit her a message: *it's no biggie.*

She smiles up at me and then turns back to her ex.

"I forgive you for what you did to me, but you can't talk about my loved ones like that. He's not a nobody."

Evan narrows his eyes on Harper and smirks. "Without me, *you're* a nobody."

Suddenly I feel completely fine about breaking this

guy's neck, my fingers flexing and tightening around Harper's hips. But she saves me the prison sentence with the best comeback that I've ever heard.

She flashes a smirk of her own and whispers back to him, "I'm the nobody who made you a somebody."

When I hear the gasps around us I finally realise that we've gathered an audience. I'm pretty sure that the entire cast and crew is here, clutching champagne flutes in front of their dropped jaws.

Harper notices the crowd a second after I do and she looks up at me, silently telling me that she wants to go now.

I nod down at her, determined to wrap this up, but her ex is putting on the performance of his life, desperate to get the last word.

"Harper, don't be stupid. What use to you is a fucking six-foot-two gorilla?"

Harper narrows her eyes on him and clutches at me tighter.

"He's six-foot-three," she snarls.

I decide not to tell them that I'm actually six-four.

"I know you aren't going to throw away two whole years together, Harper. And he can't be that special because your finger's still bare."

That's the final straw.

"Listen up," I say to him, done with this conversation.

He looks up at me expectantly and I try not to smirk down at him, Harper's soft hair brushing beneath my chin as she turns slightly, placing her hands over mine.

"You may have put one diamond on her finger but I've already put ten around her neck. She's had it better from me in two months than she had from you in two *years*. Ever heard the phrase 'put your money where your mouth is'? Where I'm from you either put up or shut up. It's time for you to do the latter."

Suddenly everyone's looking at Harper's neck, the noise from the red carpet behind us mixing in with the loud whispers in the small room until it's just a whir of sound. Harper glances around us and tries to hold back a laugh.

I don't look at the crowd. I only have eyes for Harper.

"We done now?" I ask her quietly, and she looks up at me with her big playful eyes.

"So done," she whispers back.

Then I'm grinning down at her and hauling her up, my forearms tight around her ass as I start walking us out of the circle. The audience parts like the Red Sea and I glance over her to try and find an exit.

"You didn't want to stay for the movie did you?" I ask, my mind already back on that limo and all of the things that we could do in there before we arrive back at Harper's house.

"And watch my ex for another two hours? I'd rather take another bout of food poisoning."

I smirk and kick open the first exit door that I see, hitching her further up my torso as we enter the back alley and moving one hand to rub her ass. She makes an innocent humming sound and when I look over at her I get an eyeful of her tits, squeezed together right in front of me.

I swallow hard, determined to get us back to the car before I start ravaging them.

"Hot damn," I grunt, looking at them spilling out

of her dress. "You're so beautiful, baby."

She strokes a hand up my stubble, making warmth spread painfully through my chest.

"Just a few more seconds, baby. Just let me get you back to the limo—"

I half-jog around the corner, desperate to get her back in that car, and then I instantly halt, stopping dead in my tracks. Harper glances over her shoulder and bursts out into a fit of laughter.

We're staring at twenty identical parked-up limousines.

I run a hand through my hair and then wrap it back around Harper's thighs. She snuggles her face into my neck and smiles against my skin.

"Which, uh, which one is it?" I ask her, trying to recall the licence plate as if I paid that a single second of attention.

"I don't know," she whispers back to me, her fingers slipping beneath the collar of my shirt. "Maybe we should forget about the limo. Don't you have a monster truck rental dude on hand or something?"

I snicker and start walking down the middle of the road, Harper securely in my arms and white limousines glistening on either side of us. All of the windows are tinted but I'm guessing that if the drivers are still inside our guy is going to make an appearance when he sees us.

Sure enough I haven't walked ten paces when a driver's door clicks open and Harper's chauffeur from earlier steps out, his expression stoically professional but a confused curiosity playing behind his eyes.

"Did you forget something?" he asks, already opening the door to the main stretch just in case.

"Yeah," I say, giving him a nod as I settle Harper on her feet and guide her by her hips into the back of the car. Whilst Harper climbs back inside I mouth the word *airport* to the driver.

Forget going back to Harper's place. We're getting a flight straight back to mine.

"No problem," he says, and then he ducks back behind the wheel.

I hunch down, following Harper inside, and when I close the door I see that she's sitting in the space where I was holding her just before she hit the red carpet, giving me a smile that's so innocent it's naughty.

I lower myself next to her and drag her up onto my lap, her arms wrapping around my neck as I rub a thumb over her diamonds.

"What did we forget?" she asks me curiously as the driver kicks the engine to life and pulls the car off the curb.

"That we have somewhere better to be," I murmur, one hand tucked in her hair and the other helping her pull off her heels. When her feet are bare I start gently rubbing them.

She sighs dreamily, her fingers suddenly exploring the buttons of my shirt. I smirk as she starts toying with them, unfastening and then refastening them, unsure about whether or not we should get naked whilst there's a driver present.

There's not a chance in hell that she's getting naked whilst there's a driver present, but I let her play around with my shirt because I can tell that she's turning herself on. I lean down and press a kiss to her cheek, and I feel her shiver as my stubble grazes her skin.

"Somewhere better to be," she whispers back to me, locking her eyes in with mine and dazzling me so hard that my brain goes blank.

On instinct I reach down to kiss her, the hand that was in her hair moving to grip at the side of her neck. She instantly grows slack and falls against my chest, her head lifted upwards and her fingers pawing at my pecs.

She's perfect. The whole moment is perfect. And it's so perfect that I can't help but smile against her lips, the hand that was around her ankles climbing up her dress so that I can caress her thighs.

She smiles back against me and murmurs, "So where are we going now?"

I pull the thick set of keys from my pocket and select the one for my house in Phoenix Falls.

The second that she sees it she beams up at me, her cheeks dimpled and glowing, and I lean down to give her another deep kiss.

"Home, baby," I tell her. "We're going home."

EPILOGUE

Mitch

Once I've got the last stake wedging the tent securely into the snow I turn back to face my truck and smile at Harper.

"What do you think?" I ask her.

She's sat in the back of the bed with her booted-feet dangling above the snow. She has a shy smile on her face and her cheeks are the prettiest shade of pink. I'm sure that she's just blushing because of the cold but I could almost swear that there's something nervous about the way she's looking at me, like she's chewing herself up on the inside, bursting with a secret.

I trudge over to her from the tent and position myself between her thighs, gripping my hands around her hips as she leans up to kiss at my mouth.

"I've always wanted to go camping," she whispers up to me with a smile, pulling back so we can look at each other.

"I know, baby," I murmur back to her, glancing back over my shoulder to look at the tent I purchased from the store in Phoenix Falls before we drove back up to Pine Hills so that we could camp out in the forest for New Years.

It's a big khaki one that I've managed to shove a blow-up mattress and three million quilts inside. Through the pulled back door I see Harper's toy bear, snuggled up against a pillow.

"Do you like it?" I ask, locking my eyes in with hers.

She bites her lip and nods, "Uh-huh. I love it."

I smile back at her and duck low to take her lips.

"I love you," I tell her, suddenly heaving her up from her position on the bed of the truck and carrying her over to the open tent. She lets out an excited squeal and clings to me tighter as I hunch beneath the threshold of the tent. I lower us onto the quilts and then lay her down on her back. She arches up and lifts her arms behind her head, laying for me patiently whilst I take her in.

She's wearing head-to-toe thermals, plus ear-muffs and furry boots, and I don't think that I could have fantasised a hotter outfit if I'd tried. I run my hands up her waist, loving the sight of her wrapped up in navy, and knowing that she does it just to taunt me, to turn me on. To make me think of her wearing my uniform. To make me think of her teasing me on my site.

I pull off the muffs and reach down to remove her boots, and then all that's left is her skin-tight winter one-piece. My eyes rake over it for a moment and then I'm zipping our door shut and stuffing her bear underneath a pillow.

Harper makes a whine in protest but then I'm filling her mouth with my tongue and suddenly she's moaning in pleasure. I shove off my jacket whilst I slide in and out and then I pull back so that I can rip my shirt over my head.

Harper lifts herself onto one elbow, her pupils dialled out, and she grips hard at one of my pecs, her fingers icy cool.

I grunt, slip off my belt, and then settle back down on top of her.

I cup one palm around her jaw, rubbing her soft cheek with my thumb, and I look into her eyes as I murmur, "What's on your mind, Harper?"

Her eyes widen for a brief moment and then she looks down, her cheeks flushing harder and her nails clawing anxiously at the back of my neck.

"Tell me," I say to her, rubbing her nose with mine. "Don't be nervous, baby. Not with me."

"Um, uh…" She keeps her eyes away from mine, biting hard at her bottom lip, and her body squirms beneath me, almost distracting me from our conversation. I try to still her hips with mine but all that does is make her moan harder, the pressure of my groin making her gasp and writhe.

"Harper." I say her name firmly, trying to refocus her.

"Mitchell," she whispers back, and I have to look away from her, clenching my jaw. "I… I want to tell you. But I'm scared," she says quietly, her fingers rubbing at my abs.

I look back down at her, confused about why she'd ever be feeling like that.

"Scared?" I ask, my brow furrowing low. "I don't want you to be scared, baby. Why would you be scared? Is it because the tent's outside in the open? We don't have to sleep in it tonight if you don't want to."

She shakes her head adamantly, her nails now gripping into my lower back. I'm trying not to get too hard because I can't tell if she's horny or anxious or a combination of both, but it's damn well easier said than done.

"It's not the tent," she says quickly, pulling me against her harder. "I love the tent, it was so thoughtful of you. It's that… that…"

Then she's not talking anymore and suddenly we're kissing, one of her hands leashed through my hair so that she can press me hard against her. My mind goes blank, thinking of nothing but her – the feel of her body underneath me, pliant and supple, and her mouth as she takes me, submitting to my tongue.

I give her those long firm strokes that make her go limp against the mattress, and her brow arches high, in a pleasure-pain purgatory.

"I – I – I have to tell you," she whimpers, her beautiful legs wrapped tight around me and locking me against her sex.

"Tell me, baby," I say back to her, positioning one forearm above her head so that I can crowd her with my bicep, and dropping my other hand between us so that I can start rubbing between her thighs.

She moans and arches backwards, panting as I caress her over her thermals.

"Mitch," she whispers. "I – I –"

I rub her faster. "Say it, baby."

She presses her face into my bicep. "Mitch, I missed my period."

My heart stops in my chest and my eyes drop straight to her belly.

Then every muscle in my body is swelling.

"What did you just say?" I rasp.

She peeks up at me and then whimpers, squeezing her eyes shut and squishing herself back against my bicep.

"I missed my period," she mumbles.

"Say it again."

"I missed my–" She stops herself short and turns to look at me. This time her cheeks heat up for a different reason. She reads my expression, surprised and a little unsure. "I missed my period," she whispers.

"We used protection," I say, my voice deep and even.

"I know," she whispers back to me. "You wore a condom every time."

I tighten the fist above her head, trying to suppress my growing satisfaction.

"Did you take a test?" I ask, shifting slightly so that I can undo my zip, grunting when my shaft is free and unleashed.

She shakes her head, her eyes still twinkling with nerves. "Not yet."

"How many periods have you missed?"

She stares up at me silently with those big wide eyes and I bore down on her, my body rippling with tension. Pleasure. I try not to smirk but all I can think is *fuck yeah*.

I know her answer before she even says it.

She swallows hard. "Two."

I inhale deeply, closing my eyes for a brief moment.

She's pregnant. She got pregnant the second that we started having sex, and she's now carrying my baby.

I move my hand gently from her heat so that I can press it firmly against her belly and she gasps, her fingers flying up to my hair.

"Are you gonna keep it?" I ask, my eyes on hers.

"I–" She pauses before she can reveal what she wants, and says instead, "It's not just up to me."

I suppress a growl.

"It's your choice," I grit out, trying to hold it together. "But I want to know if you're gonna... if we're gonna–"

"If it was just up to me," she begins, and my eyes burn into hers. I am very fucking interested to hear the end of this sentence. "I would... I would make you your baby. Our baby."

Right answer. It's the right answer. I groan and press my full weight on top of her, slipping my tongue into her mouth and rubbing her until her thighs are struggling around my abs.

She tries to mumble something against my mouth so I pull back, letting her speak.

"If it was just up to you, what would you want me to do?" she asks, her eyes wide and still uncertain, making sure that we're on the same page.

I press my hand into her belly again and her eyes almost roll into the back of her head.

I lift up slightly so that I can shove my jeans down my legs, only keeping my boxers on so that I can draw out the foreplay for her, and then I start undoing the poppers on the top half of her one-piece. When they're all unfastened I push the top apart and my breath catches in my throat as I take in what she's wearing.

She avoids my eyes, flushing crimson.

I practically rip the bottoms off of her, throwing the suit behind me towards the door so that I can get an unobstructed view of Harper laying on her back and wearing nothing but her diamond necklace and that godforsaken red lingerie set that I got my fingers tangled up in all those months ago.

"Finally," I growl, hovering over her. I keep one hand firmly against her shoulder, pinning her down on her back. "I've been waiting to see you wearing this since the dawn of fucking time."

She chews at her lip, her hands gripping nervously at my shoulders.

"Do you like it?" she asks me shyly.

I push my groin hard against her inner thigh, and she moans in understanding.

Then my eyes are back on her stomach, my mind thrumming with need.

"I did this, didn't I?" I ask her, rubbing one of my palms firmly over her belly.

Her lashes flutter drowsily and she nods at me, boneless. I slide my other hand beneath her, easily unfastening the clasp of her bra and then pulling it off, exposing her.

I free myself of my boxers and lower myself on top of her.

"You're gonna make me a baby, aren't you Harper?" I ask, slipping two digits up the side of her panties and then hooking them tight so that I can drag the lace down her legs.

She doesn't know how to handle all of the new sensations – the excitement, the fear, the arousal – so all she does is swallow and nod, letting me fully take the lead.

"That's good, Harper. I want you to make me lots of babies."

"Oh *God*," she whispers, squeezing her eyes shut. I pull her panties from her ankles and I keep them leashed around my fingers.

"I want to marry you before you're full term," I tell her, and she writhes beneath me as the full length of my shaft presses hard against her bare heat. "Think you can take a few more diamonds?"

"You're so annoying," she moans, breathing hard and digging her nails into me.

"How many babies are you gonna let me put inside of you?" I ask, grasping my fist around the base of my shaft and starting to rub the head up and down over her pussy.

"I – I can't have this conversation right now," she chokes out, wrapping her legs tighter around me. "I c-can't think straight."

"I want you to do at least four."

"*Mitchell*," she whimpers, throwing her head back against the pillows. Then she looks at me with a new concern in her eyes and asks, "Condom?"

I give her a long look, knowing what I want, but at the same time only wanting to give her what she wants.

"Do you still want to use one?" I ask her.

She pauses before whispering, "I haven't done it bare before."

Jesus Christ.

I hold myself motionlessly above her and ask through clenched teeth, "Do you want to try it?"

She gives me an embarrassed look and says a quiet, "Yeah."

I drop my face into her neck and take a deep inhale. God, she smells good.

"You sure?" I mumble against her, my stubble scraping up her neck.

She nods and says breathlessly, "I'm sure."

I groan with relief and move one hand between us to align myself with her entrance. "I want that, too. I want to make sure."

"Make sure of what?" she whispers, gasping when the head starts pushing in.

I rub my free hand over her belly, not yet showing, and I murmur back, "Of this."

I thrust upwards hard, and Harper gasps as I fill her.

"That's it," I rasp, my biceps crowding around her face. I withdraw slowly and then slide it back inside. "That's good, baby. Tell me if it's okay. Tell me if you like it raw."

She can't speak. She just nods, moaning and panting, as I give it to her in the middle of the forest.

"You're so good, Harper." I wrap both of my hands around her waist, my thumbs rubbing her belly as I pump her slow and deep. "I can't wait until you're showing."

She scrunches her eyes shut, her nails biting into my shoulders. Our bodies slap together loud and wet in the confined silence of the dark tent.

"Mitch – *ah* – Mitchell, are you sure? D-don't you need to think about this a little more?"

God, she's cute. She really has no idea.

"Harper," I murmur, "this is *all* that I think about. From the moment that I laid my eyes on you all that I've been fantasising about is this. My sole purpose in life is to make kids, to have a family."

Having my son was the best thing that ever happened to me. And now he's almost ready to have kids of his own. So the thought of being able to experience that again, only this time being with a woman who wants us to stay together, as one big family?

It's almost too good to bear.

She blinks up at me, her lashes fluttering. "Y-you fantasise about... about getting me...?" She swallows and mouths the word *pregnant*.

I smirk down at her, flattening both of my palms over her belly so that I can press into it with every thrust.

"Say the word, Harper," I command, my voice low and deep.

She mumbles it, embarrassed, her cheeks glowing pink.

I remove my hands from her belly and her eyes flash immediately to mine.

"*Pregnant-pregnant-pregnant,*" she says quickly, gripping at my wrists so that she can get my hands back on her stomach.

I breathe out a laugh and she lets my palms roam upwards, a whimper leaving her throat as I start massaging her breasts.

"I've been wanting to fill you up since I first saw you in your bungalow, Harper. Since I first saw this beautiful body of yours, naked and dripping wet. I wanted to take you on my lap. Show you who's the boss."

I start pumping faster and Harper arches her neck, moaning quietly.

"I wanted you too," she whispers nervously up at me, the innocence in her eyes making my abs clench and my chest tighten.

"Yeah?" I ask her, beginning to rub at her nipples. "Fuck, Harper. Now you've got me for life. Got me inside of you for another seven months, and after that I'm gonna do it to you all over again. Gonna get you in my bed, roll on a condom, and show you just how strong your man's load is."

She clutches her arms around my neck, bringing me closer, and my eyes drop to her tits, bouncing in a frenzy.

"And these," I grunt, squeezing them roughly. She gasps and writhes at the gruff sensation. "They're gonna get so full, Harper. They're gonna ache so good, all because of what I've done to you. What I'm gonna keep on doing to you, for as long as you want me to."

"I love you so much," she whispers desperately, her lips brushing warm and soft against my neck.

"I love you too," I rasp back, and I move my hands from her breasts to the quilt around her, because I'm starting to lose control. Gripping too tight. Shoving it too deep. Overwhelmed with the pleasure of knowing that I've got the woman that I love for life.

"Mitch – Mitchell – I c-can't wait to watch you be a daddy," she whispers, and suddenly I'm growling, flipping us over so that she's riding me, her breasts and her beautiful belly right there for me to look at. I flatten a palm between her shoulder blades and shove her roughly on top of me, grunting when her tits plump up against my pecs.

I hold her hips in place as I thrust up into her.

"Say that again, Harper," I demand.

She moans softly against my throat. "I can't – *oh* – I can't wait to see you being a – a – a daddy."

"Yeah?" I pant. "Again."

She whimpers into the crook of my neck. I grip and squeeze at her ass.

"I want to watch you being a daddy, Mitchell, you're going to be such a good – a good–"

Her orgasm finally breaks, and she clenches and squirms. I keep up the intensity whilst begging my own body to hold on for just a few more seconds. The heavy ache in my sac warns me that I'm about to spill.

I roll back on top of her, wanting to be inside as deeply as possible, and I leash my fingers in the back of her hair, holding her face against my neck as I start jerking hard.

"It – oh shit – it won't be too much, Harper, I swear. Just a, *ugh*, just a couple more strokes–"

And then I'm spilling, hot and deep, my body pressed hard against hers as I fill her up on the mattress. From the way that she's gasping I can tell that she's never experienced this before. It makes me want to give her more, to pump it deeper.

My jaw clenches tight, my brow creases with pain, and I hunch further down so that I can press my forehead against hers. She's slick with sweat and totally limp for me. I move a hand back down to her belly and try to finish as quickly as possible.

I grunt low and tight when I finally collapse on top of her and I keep our bodies locked together, fulfilled by what we've just done. I kiss gently at her forehead, thinking about how lucky I am. How beautiful and funny Harper is. How much she must trust me to want to make a family together.

Her pussy's still quivering around the thickness of my shaft so I lift up slightly and rub tenderly at her waist.

"Can we stay like this for a few minutes?" I ask quietly, not wanting to leave her perfect heat.

She swallows and nods, smiling shyly at me as she pulls my hand up to caress one of her breasts.

"That's beautiful, Harper," I murmur, squeezing her gently.

She trails her toes up the back of my thigh and whispers up at me, "I… I'm really happy. And scared. But mainly happy. And I meant what I said by the way, about wanting to see you be a daddy. Looking after our–" She pats softly at her belly and my jaw instantly hardens.

I grunt and press my hand on top of hers.

Then she smiles bashfully and adds on, "And looking after me."

It takes me a few moments to calm down but then I rub my nose against hers and give her a tender kiss.

"I love you, Harper. And I'm always going to look after you."

She gives me a sparkly smile. "Forever?"

I grin back at her. "Forever."

ABOUT THE AUTHOR

Sapphire is a romance writer, specializing in contemporary love stories. She has a First Class Honors degree in English Literature and Education Studies from Durham University, and she graduated from Cambridge University as a Master of Philosophy.

Where We Go From Here is an interconnected standalone book, and it is the third book in the Phoenix Falls Series. The first book in the series is *Where We Left Off*, which is an enemies to lovers romance. The second book in the series is *Where It All Began*, which is a brother's best friend romance.

If you are looking for books that will give you butterflies, you have come to the right place.

Author website: www.sapphireauthor.com
TikTok: @sapphiresbookshelf
Instagram: @sapphiresbookshelf
Pinterest: @sapphireauthor